SWEET AS SIN

'Are you *mad*?'

'Perhaps I am, with desire for you, Rolf.'

'I'm your mother's husband, your stepfather.'

She drawled, 'Yes. Forbidden fruit, right, Rolf? You know what they say about that. Am *I* forbidden fruit, to you? Does that make me more desirable? I hope it does.'

'This is crazy.'

'Am I bad, Rolf, really bad? If I am, I should be punished. Will you punish me, Rolf?'

She stood. For the first time since her perverted caresses had woken him, Rolf realised that she'd discarded the pants to her pyjamas. Her legs, her incredible long legs, were bare. They were within his reach. Rolf knew, and the knowledge terrified him, that if he reached out and stroked her thigh, she'd welcome the caress.

By the same author:

DOMINANT

SWEET AS SIN

Felix Baron

This book is a work of fiction.
In real life, make sure you practise safe, sane and
consensual sex.

First published in 2007 by
Nexus
Thames Wharf Studios
Rainville Rd
London W6 9HA

A catalogue record for this book is available from the
British Library.

www.nexus-books.com

Typeset by TW Typesetting, Plymouth, Devon
Printed in the UK by CPI Bookmarque, Croydon, CR0 4TD

The paper used in this book is a natural, recyclable product made
from wood grown in sustainable forests. The manufacturing
process conforms to the regulations of the country of origin.

ISBN 978 0 352 34134 1

Distributed in the USA by Holtzbrinck Publishers, LLC, 175
Fifth Avenue, New York, NY 10010, USA

One

Trixie Sanders's oversized sunglasses matched the lavender-pink of her lipstick, the gloss on her eyelids, the enamel on her fingers and toenails, and her two chiffon scarves – one knotted around the crown of her big black straw hat and the other tied loosely at her hip. Her one-piece swimsuit was also black, with legs that were French-cut to her waist. A net 'V' plunged between her breasts, down as far as her navel. At forty, her body was no longer as toned as it had once been. It was still very shapely and deliciously 'ripe'.

Penny, her daughter, was nineteen, tanned, lean and lovely. Tropical sun beat down on her perfect young body. Hints of her bikini showed in the pale blue strip barely visible between the taut ovals of her bottom and the thin line of her bra's strap across her back. She was stretched face-down on a beach towel at Trixie's feet, with one hand in the inky shade of her mother's beach umbrella. Her fingers were wrapped companionably around Trixie's slender ankle.

'You're going to get a tan line,' Trixie's liquid contralto warned.

'Mm?' Penny made a half-hearted attempt to reach behind herself, to the bow of her bikini's top. 'Please?'

Trixie gave a motherly sigh, leaned forward out of her lounge chair, and tugged the bow loose. 'Be careful when you sit up,' she warned.

'Lotion?'

Indulgently, Trixie spritzed her daughter's back from a spray-bottle. 'There ought to be a nice young man around to rub that in for you,' she observed.

1

Penny snorted and flicked her long platinum ponytail. 'Fat chance! There's only two kinds of people staying here, divorced men and divorced women. The men in their fifties; women in their forties – the women wiggling their bait and the men trying to nibble on it without getting hooked.'

Trixie sank back into deep shadow. 'My bait could do with some serious nibbling on, if the right man should come along.'

'*Mother!*'

'*Daughter!*' Trixie pushed her hat back on her honey-blond curls and her sunglasses up to her brow, so she could get her miniature binoculars to her Saxon-blue eyes. She scanned the beach. 'Right man – rich man – handsome man – sexy man – where are you hiding? Come out, come out, wherever you are,' she mused.

Penny sighed as if giving up on her incorrigible mother.

'Aha!' Trixie exclaimed.

'Spotted the man of your dreams?'

'Unfortunately, no, but an interesting male none the less. I spy Juan, the water-boy, the one with the muscles.'

'They *all* have muscles, Mother. The resort picks them like that, to keep you horny widows and divorcees amused.'

'Juan's special, or so I'm told.'

'Special? How? Who told you?'

'Magda, the masseuse, told me. All the boys on staff have muscles, but apparently Juan has one muscle in particular that's quite spectacular.'

'You shouldn't gossip with the hired help, Mother.'

'No, I should swap tuna casserole recipes with old frumps like the pair we were forced to endure at dinner last night.' Trixie craned her neck and called out, 'Water-boy! Juan!'

'You've never drunk plain water in your entire life.'

'No, but this Zombie could do with some ice.'

Juan padded over, his canvas bag of ice swaying on his hip. 'Bottle of water, lady?'

'Spare me a couple of cubes of ice, would you?' Trixie held her half-empty Zombie glass above her head.

Juan ducked under the umbrella and into the deep shade. 'Sure thing.' The way Trixie held her glass, the lad had no choice but to stand close to her chair. His fingers sorted a lump from the mush and melt in his bag.

Trixie's free fingers brushed his muscular thigh just above his knee and stroked up under the baggy leg of his shorts. 'Take your time,' she told him.

He grunted and froze. His Adam's apple bobbed.

Trixie said, 'What Magda told me, Penny – it's absolutely true.'

Her daughter pretended to be asleep.

Juan, an ice cube melting between his nervous fingers, swallowed hard. His face went crimson under its tan. He started to make little noises in his throat.

The ice dropped into Trixie's glass.

'Good boy,' Trixie said. 'In future, when I need ice . . .'

'Lady?'

'You come, and you come fast, you hear?'

'You bet, lady.'

After he'd retreated, Trixie asked Penny, 'Pass me one of those nice cool wet-wipes, would you, darling?'

'Sticky fingers?'

'No dear, but for some reason I'm feeling quite flushed.' She dabbed her brow and returned to scanning the beach. 'Penny, you have a gentleman admirer.'

'I do?'

'There's a handsome young man watching you.'

'Oh?' Penny pushed up as if she'd forgotten her bra was loose but grabbed it to herself just before the tips of her breasts lifted off her towel. 'Who? Where?'

'Twenty feet closer to the ocean, at two o'clock.'

Penny squinted. 'He's a bit young for me. You know I prefer older men.'

'He's three years your senior – Andrew Carmichael, only son and heir to Rolf Carmichael, widower.'

'You've checked him out.'

'That's why God gave us Google, dear.'

'His Daddy's rich, I presume?'

'Comfortable. He's an extremely successful engineer,

3

now semi-retired, whose lawyer wife left him a considerable fortune. He's worth close to twenty mil.'

'So why aren't you going after the Dad instead of siccing me on the son?'

'The big bull spends all his time in their suite, doing business by phone. The moon-calf is right there, in our sights. Give the boy a chance, Penny. He's good looking. Maybe he's charming as well.'

'Maybe.'

'Go take a swim, dear.'

'What?'

'Do as Mother says. Mother knows best.' Trixie leaned down to retie her daughter's bra.

'I hope you're doing that properly,' Penny said.

'I know how to tie a bow, daughter. There, you're done.'

'Well, I could do with cooling off after your outrageous behaviour.' Penny writhed to her feet and did a hot-foot dance across the beach. By the time she was walking on cool wet sand, Andrew Carmichael had stretched, yawned, and was casually strolling towards the waves. Trixie grinned and lay back with her binoculars to her eyes.

Penny waded into backwash waves and braced herself. A waist-high breaker rocked her.

Andrew called, 'Look out, Miss,' as an incoming ten-foot swell began to curl and break. A wall of green and white water washed over Penny and crashed on the beach. When it receded, sucking at the sand, she was nowhere in sight.

Andrew shouted, 'Hey.' He loped awkwardly for a few strides before throwing himself through the next wave. When he stood up in waist-deep water, there Penny was, standing with her back to him, not ten feet away. 'You OK, Miss?'

She turned to face him, her hands inefficiently shielding lovely young breasts that were now naked. 'I'm fine, thanks, except . . .' Her shrug came perilously close to exposing areas that weren't tanned. 'Oh – there it is!' One hand darted out to point at her bikini's floating bra and was snatched back so quickly that Andrew couldn't be sure if he'd glimpsed a rose-pink bud or not.

4

'I'll get it,' he volunteered. He returned with the scrap of fabric and held it out to Penny. She raised a brow and shrugged again. There was no way for her to take it without uncovering a breast. 'Oh – sorry,' he said. Andrew turned his back and flopped her bra back over his shoulder for her to tug from his fingers.

A few minutes later, Penny told him, 'Thanks. I'm decent now. You're a real gentleman.'

He turned. 'You OK now?'

'I'm fine, but if you wouldn't mind walking me back, just in case another savage wave attacks me?' She rocked to one side, as if moved by an underwater current.

Andrew offered his hand but she moved past it, close in, so that his arm went around her waist by reflex.

'I think I'm a little shaken,' Penny explained.

'I'll get you back safely.'

Penny's head lolled onto his shoulder. 'My knight in shining armour.'

As they waded back towards the beach, Penny's hip was brushing his thigh. Andrew cleared his throat. His mouth was suddenly dry.

'Oh, it must be cocktail hour already,' Penny said when they got back to the beach. 'My Mom's gone in.'

'Do you have to follow her?'

'I don't like to be out here all alone.'

'I could keep you company, if you like.'

Penny looked down at the sand and whispered, 'I'd like that.'

Two

The cha-cha ended. The Golden O Orchestra struck a chord. A trumpeter and a guitarist laid their instruments aside and picked up a violin and an accordion. The main lights dimmed. Three spotlights, red, green and white, hit the mirror-ball that was suspended far above. Penny moved in close to Andrew's chest and said, 'I think that means the next number's a tango. It's my favourite dance.'

'Sorry, Penny. I always thought the tango was for old people. My Dad does it but it's beyond me.'

Penny pouted. 'Maybe I should dance with your Dad, then. Is he here?'

Andrew's face turned to stone. 'Sure, if you like. Come on, then.' He forged ahead of Penny, not so quickly as to be rude but not at a companionable speed. The orchestra began to play *Jealousy*.

Andrew blurted, 'Dad, this is Penny, the girl I told you about. She loves to tango and I know you do and I don't so I thought . . .'

Rolf Carmichael stood, beaming. 'I'd be delighted!'

Penny looked the older man up and down. His silvery hair was slightly long and shaggy. Rolf had to be in his fifties by the interesting creases in his craggy face. He had the body of a very fit man of forty, broad across the chest but with narrow hips. He might have been an inch or two taller than his son. Rolf took Penny's hand and bowed over it briefly before whisking her onto the floor.

'Did Andrew tell you he saved me from a watery grave this morning?' Penny asked.

6

'He mentioned something about protecting your modesty.'

'He's very gallant.'

As Rolf swung Penny round, her thighs parted to accommodate his right one, which was inevitable with that step. The press of her pubes on his leg wasn't, but it might have been accidental. Rolf moved her a few inches further back. The next turn brought her close again. The tango is a dance of love and lust. It simulates male domination, female defiance and eventual surrender. With lovers or potential lovers as partners, it's formalised foreplay. When the man is in his fifties and his partner is a teenage girl, he can feel awkward, especially when the close contact, her scent, and the deep 'sweetheart' cleavage he gazes down into all conspire to give him a raging erection.

'I should introduce you to my mother, Mr Carmichael, but I don't know if I'm going to.'

'Please call me "Rolf". Why wouldn't you introduce me to your mother?'

'If she finds out what a good dancer you are I won't get another chance at you.'

'You'll be too busy dancing with younger men; my son for instance.'

Penny looked up at him from under sweeping lashes. 'Mature men have their own appeal, Rolf.' Her satin-sheathed tummy brushed across the fly of Rolf's pants. Was that a secret little smile that twitched the corners of her mouth? Was she aware of his physical reaction to her closeness? Rolf was almost glad when the dance ended.

'My Mom's over there,' Penny told him. 'Come and say "hi".'

With one hand deep in his pocket and a finger controlling the jut of his erection, Rolf followed. He found Trixie just as attractive as her daughter, but in a very different way. She was petite but voluptuous, with the sort of full-bosomed, pinch-waisted, flaring-hipped figure that isn't fashionable any more but that men will always admire. Her clinging black jersey dress came to her wrists and throat but it was backless so deeply that Rolf could

7

see that the narrowness of her waist wasn't the result of corsetry. Nor was the pout of her plump breasts augmented by a bra.

He had a sudden urgent need to see her naked and felt an instant stab of guilt. It had only been two years since his Rachel died. Was feeling lust for another woman so soon a betrayal?

Trixie extended a hand. Rolf bowed over it.

'I'll go find Andrew, shall I?' Penny suggested.

Rolf nodded. Trixie flicked her fingers, dismissing her daughter. Penny swished off to leave the newly-met couple gazing into each other's eyes.

'Dance?' Rolf asked.

If Penny had danced flirtatiously, her mother's moves were blatant invitations. The tango is a 'full-contact' dance but neither the quickstep not the foxtrot are, except as danced by Trixie. By the end of the second number, Rolf had given up trying to keep an inch of air between their bodies. By the end of the third, his splayed hand was on the base of her spine, encouraging her torso's undulations. He had no doubt she was aware of his erection. It was the focus of her writhing.

'Dad!' Andrew reprimanded, when the couple returned to the table.

'Get a room,' Penny added.

Rolf averted his eyes. 'Sorry.'

'Nonsense!' Trixie said. 'We're mature adults. Consenting adults, come to that.'

Rolf beckoned a waiter. 'Ladies?'

'Martinis. A pitcher's best, Rolf,' Trixie told him. 'It saves time.'

'White wine spritzer?' from Penny.

He ordered a Tuborg lager for Andrew and told Trixie he'd share her pitcher. By the time he'd poured his second glass, Trixie was halfway through her third. The youngsters were on the dance floor.

'I think I'd like some fresh air,' Trixie told Rolf.

He walked her, holding her elbow, out onto the raised patio. The night air was creamy with the scents of hibiscus, rhododendron and frangipani. Trixie led him diagonally across the flagstones, away from the French windows to the ballroom and behind a group of potted bushes. Taking the hint, Rolf turned her into his arms and bent to kiss her. Their lips brushed. He savoured the soft yielding texture of her full lower lip for a heartbeat before the seductive invitation of her open mouth drew his tongue into its liquid depths. She tasted of gin. He wasn't averse to that but he couldn't help wondering about her natural flavour. He fancied it would be fresh and floral, with a trace of lemon, perhaps.

Trixie broke the kiss and turned to lean on the stone balustrade, holding his arms around her. Rolf nuzzled her nape. She arched against him and sighed.

'Are you planning to take advantage of me?' she asked. Her hand guided his over the gentle swell of her belly.

'Yes, but not tonight.'

'Not tonight? Why not?' Trixie's hips rotated against him.

'The first time – we should both be sober, stone cold sober. When I seduce a woman, I don't want it to be with any help from Mister Beefeater or Gospodin Smirnov.' If he'd been honest he'd have confessed he needed time to think. Rachel had been his first and only real love. How would it be, making love to another woman?

'Ah! You're a gentleman, I see, and a patient one.'

'Not too patient.' Rolf moved so that his erection, although confined, prodded into the valley between the yielding cheeks of Trixie's lush bottom.

'So I see! Are we going to see each other tomorrow?'

'I'd like that. Trixie, do you play bridge?'

'Bridge? Why yes, some. I'm not brilliant at the game. My Penny's much better.'

'Then why don't the four of us get together tomorrow afternoon, say about four? We could play till dinner and then I'm sure the kids would find some way to amuse themselves for the evening, leaving us to – to get to know each other better.'

'I'd like that – the getting to know you.' She swivelled in his arms and gave him a peck on his cheek. 'So, if I asked you to see me up to my suite, you wouldn't take it as an invitation to follow me in?'

'Even if it were, I wouldn't.'

She pushed him far enough back to look into his face. 'I love it that you're a gentleman, Rolf, but moderation in all things, especially virtue.'

'I understand. Before I lose my resolve, shall we go?'

'Just a second.' She pulled a tissue from her purse, wet it with her tongue and dabbed at the corner of his mouth. 'We mustn't make it too obvious what we've been up to, Rolf, must we.'

'Right. Thanks.'

Three

The bandleader announced that the Golden O was taking five. Andrew escorted Penny back to their empty table. 'I wonder where they went?'

Penny pointed to the French doors. 'I saw them go outside, about ten minutes ago.'

'Maybe we should go look for them.'

Penny grinned. 'They're adults. Could be they don't want to be looked for. Maybe they're busy "getting to know" each other.'

Andrew raised a brow. 'My Dad? No way! He's past that kinda thing.'

'You think?'

'Anyway, he's way too old for your Mom.'

'There's lots of women my Mom's age, and some even younger, who'd find your Dad very attractive.'

'Well, if my Dad and your Mom *are* . . .'

'Making out?'

'Whatever – I don't want to know.'

She grinned. 'I suppose you were an immaculate conception.'

Andrew frowned. 'You're teasing me.'

'Sorry.' She nibbled her lower lip. 'Andrew?'

'Yes?'

'Your Dad said you were at university. He seems very proud of you. What's it like? What are you studying?'

Half an hour later, Penny allowed that they ought to check up on their parents. On their way out onto the patio,

11

Andrew took her hand. Penny cuddled his arm. She called, 'Mom?' and released Andrew's hand to run towards the area that was hidden by plants.

Andrew followed with a querulous 'Dad?' When he caught up with Penny she was posed by the balustrade. The light from a three-quarter moon, high overhead, silvered her hair, her cheekbones and the upper slopes of her young breasts. Andrew froze, his willpower drained. His mouth dried. The background had become two-dimensional and unreal. Only Penny had depth and substance.

She pointed to the rhododendrons that grew just beyond the buzz-cut lawn. 'I thought I saw a firefly.'

Andrew was released from his paralysis. 'It was likely a cigarette. Some of the staff here, the young ones, hang out in those bushes at night. You know – hang out and make out?'

'Can they see us?'

'I don't think so. It's too far.'

'So we can't see them making out, and they couldn't see us if we were, right?'

'Right.' He strode to her, as masterfully as he could, and took her in his arms.

Penny's head was back, eyes closed and lips parted. Pretty sure she wouldn't object, he bent over her and put his lips to hers. Andrew hadn't meant to be so bold but somehow her tongue was in his mouth and then his was in hers and she was supple and yielding and their bodies were pressed together from chest to knees and something primitive woke in him, telling him he was a *man*.

Pressing his advantage, Andrew worked a hand between their bodies to cup the fluttering dove of her left breast.

'Oh Andrew!' she gasped. She twisted against him and he realised that the movement had partially bared the breast he held. When his thumb stroked, it felt her *nipple*. By instinct, his forefinger joined the ball of his thumb and rolled the tiny, tender, incredibly intimate nub.

Penny melted in his arms. Her thighs parted to bracket his left leg. He had to brace it and push up against her, just to keep her from falling.

12

'Andrew,' she gasped. 'When you touch me like that – it feels so good I can barely stand it.'

'You like this?' He rolled a bit harder and wondered if a slight tug would please her. He'd touched other girls' breasts, and even fingered between the legs of two of them. They'd just been girls, though, at high school. If he'd made any wrong moves, well, they'd have expected him to be unpractised. Penny was different. She was older, more sophisticated. She'd expect him to be expert. Penny was . . . She wasn't just more mature than the other girls he'd made out with. They'd been pretty. Penny was beautiful. In fact, if there was a word that went beyond 'beautiful', Penny was it.

Her tongue was sinuous and wet in his mouth again. Her pubes were moving on his thigh. Did this mean she wanted to . . .?

'Andrew,' she sobbed, 'please, can you do both, like this?' She took and held his hands as she twisted round in his arms to face away from him. Somehow, in turning, she managed to pull the top of her dress down or her breasts up, because when she put his hands back on her warm flesh, both of her breasts were bare, lifted up to nestle in her low-cut neckline. He was a foot taller than Penny. With her head rested back on his shoulder, looking down, he saw her breasts for the first time. He could watch what his fingers were doing. Penny's aureoles were puffy mounds, like miniatures of the sweet breasts they adorned. Their nipples were beads. He couldn't be sure of the tints because the moonlight washed the colours out but they seemed to be all about the same, breasts, aureoles and nipples.

'Tease me, Andrew, please? Be merciless.'

Andrew let the pads of his forefingers drift around the circumferences of her haloes. A fraction at a time, they spiralled in until they rested softly on her peaks. He tapped their tips. She shuddered. He gripped and tugged gently. Penny arched and groaned. Andrew almost groaned himself. His erection had become so hard it felt ready to snap off.

A spark arced behind the distant rhododendrons. Someone had flicked a cigarette butt away.

As if sensing Andrew's discomfort – of course she could, as it was pressed against her lower back – Penny reached behind herself and gripped the thick throbbing base of his penis through his pants. 'Oh! I didn't know that men were so big there!'

Did that mean she'd never touched a man intimately before?

'Andrew?'

'Yes?' he croaked.

'I want to . . .'

'You want to?'

'You know, *do it*.'

'Are you sure?'

'I'm sure I *want* to, but . . .'

Andrew felt a cold chill in his stomach. 'But?'

'My Dad. Before he died, I made him a promise. I swore I wouldn't – not until . . .'

'I understand,' Andrew lied.

Her hand felt its way up his shaft, through the serge of his pants. 'It must be painful.'

'Some,' he admitted.

'I can't leave you like this. It wouldn't be fair.' She moved to his right a little, so that he was only half behind her but could still fondle her breasts. Her fingers reached back to find the tab on his fly's zipper. Andrew froze in case a movement would break the spell. He felt the tab rasp down. He felt her fingers squirm into his fly. They fumbled, searching for the slit his bikini briefs didn't have, before moving up to tug his waistband down.

His cock was suddenly in her hand.

'What?' he asked.

'Just a minute.' She manoeuvred, hampered by his shaft's stiffness, but managed to draw his cock free to jut into the night air, below the balustrade's cap, between two stone columns. 'I've never done this before,' she told him. 'You must tell me if I do it right.' Her fingers trailed delicately from the base of his shaft to its head before releasing it. 'Is that right, or is this better?' She took a firm grip and slid up, tightening her grasp as it went, then

14

pushed down, dragging his foreskin back firmly but not too hard.

'Mm!' Andrew managed. 'Like that.'

Penny's hand pumped, much too slowly but Andrew dared not ask her to move faster in case it offended her. He started to pant and arch. His fingers squeezed her nipples with more force. Just when he thought he'd *never* get relief at the pace she was going, his scrotum tightened and he felt the long liquid rush as his semen jetted out into the darkness.

Reflexively, his fingers clamped. Penny groaned and jerked.

'I'm sorry, Penny. Did I hurt you?'

'I'm fine, Andrew. That was the best part, when you pinched me.'

'Oh?' He filed the information for future use.

'Do you feel better now?' she asked. 'Did I do it right?'

'You were wonderful.'

She started to tuck his less-stiff but not yet limp cock back into his fly but he took over before her handling made him as needy as he'd been before.

'Shall we go in, now?' Penny asked.

'Of course. Penny, want to go for a swim in the morning?'

'I'd like that. Did you like that bikini I was wearing today?'

'You looked so hot!'

'Well, I've got one that's even tinier. I'll wear it for you tomorrow if you like.'

15

Four

As soon as she closed the door behind Rolf, Trixie shrugged and peeled out of her clinging evening gown. It was one of her favourites and she didn't want to spoil it. Five minutes later, in an old dark-blue sundress that she didn't care about any more and with canvas flats on her feet, she let herself out again. It was only one floor down and the emergency stairs led to a crash-bar exit. Leaving her shoes wedged beneath the steel door, she padded off into the night, barefoot. Next time, if there was a next time, she'd devise a better wedge.

Unseen and unheard, she made a circuit of the ballroom's exterior. There were clumps of hibiscus and frangipani dotted about the broad lawn, all the way over to the grove of rhododendrons. Trixie crept from one to another, always in shadow, always sure to keep bushes between herself and the raised patio.

There were voices and the sounds of movement. She skirted a couple who were on the ground, the girl on top of the boy, as far as Trixie could tell. Further on, she dropped to all fours and crawled through deep shadows. She'd recognised Juan the water-boy's voice.

The handsome lad was standing with a bush between him and the patio, with binoculars pressed to his eyes. Another youth, shorter and broader, was beside him.

Juan was saying, '. . . hand up the leg o' my shorts an' felt me up.'

'Yeah, sure, an' Magda the masseuse is beggin' me to let her suck my dick.'

'Carlos, I swear on my mother's grave.'

'OK. See anything?' the shorter one asked.

'Guy makin' out with some chick.'

'For real? Gimme the glasses.'

'Wait.'

'What's he doin'?'

'He's got her tits out an' he's playin' with 'em.'

'Gimme.'

As Juan turned to pass the binoculars to Carlos, his wagging cock was caught in a beam of moonlight. Trixie licked her lips. The poor boys had to be *desperate* if they got their kicks from jerking off while they spied on the rich guests.

Carlos flicked a cigarette end away in a fiery arc. With one hand holding the glasses to his eyes, he reached across and took hold of Juan's shaft. Juan returned the favour. They slow-fisted each other as they passed the binoculars back and forth.

'She ain't got much tit, has she,' Carlos remarked.

'Bet she fucks like a bitch, though.'

'She would if it was *my* meat she was ridin'.'

'After me, bro.'

Their strokes were becoming more urgent. Trixie stood up and pushed between the two bushes that had been hiding her. Petals fluttered to the grass. She brushed a twig from her hair and announced, 'We've got unfinished business, Juan.'

Both lads whirled, their cocks waving. Carlos gaped. Juan tried to hide his cock.

'Leave them out where I can see them, boys.'

Grinning foolishly, they spread their hands and thrust their hips forward. Juan said, 'It's her, bro, the lady I tol' you about.' To Trixie, he said, 'You liked what you felt, huh, lady?'

For reply, Trixie took two steps closer and dropped back down to her knees. With one hand wrapped around Juan's impressive shaft, she unbuttoned his shorts with the other and yanked them down to his calves. 'See this?' she asked, tapping the head of his cock on her lower lip. 'It's not a

17

mouth. It's a *cunt*. Do you know what you do with cunts, Juan?'

Carlos answered for him. 'Y' fuck 'em.'

'Right.' She moved Juan's hands to the back of her head and parted her jaws as wide apart as they would stretch. The boy shuffled forward an inch. The great round dome of his cock nudged her lips. He paused as if unsure how to continue. Trixie wrapped her arms around his narrow hips and flattened her hands on the lean cheeks of his muscular rump. Dragging him closer and working her face from side to side, she forced her lips to stretch around the massive head of his young cock. He filled her mouth. Trixie sucked air through her nostrils. She paused to savour the sensations; the ache in the hinges of her jaws, the smooth heat of his cock, pressing her tongue down, the first taste of his seeping juices, like burnt spices, but liquid.

Juan was mumbling something in Spanish. It sounded like a prayer but she couldn't make it out even though she knew a little gutter slang in the language. Perhaps he was giving thanks.

Carlos said, 'Fuck her face, man! That's what she wants!'

Trixie managed to grunt and hoped they'd understand it meant she agreed. Juan still didn't move. Either he was awestruck or else nervous he'd hurt her. Trixie pried his clenched buttocks apart and felt for the tight knot of his sphincter. Merciless, she rammed the stiff index finger of her right hand deep into his rectum. Juan jerked. His cock impaled her mouth, all the way to the back, forcing an obscene wet sound from her throat, 'Golk!'

Trixie fought her gag-reflex. Her mouth flooded with saliva. She could feel it flow from the corners of her mouth to saturate the boy's dangling balls.

Juan made a whimpering sound and reached behind himself to grab her wrist. Perhaps hers was the first finger to ever violate his young bottom. It felt tight and hot enough that it could be virgin. When he tried to pull her finger out, Trixie simply hooked it. He released her wrist but she kept her finger bent and dragged him back, moving his cock in her mouth until only its head was between her lips, when she thrust again.

At last, the lad learned. Guided by her push and pull, he slow-fucked her mouth at a rhythm *she* set, which wasn't what she wanted. Hell, she'd put herself totally at the mercy of these crude youngsters. Didn't they have the balls to give her a thorough ravishing? A line from a Victorian novel came back to her, 'He bent her to his will.' *That's* what she craved – to be bent to their wills.

Carlos was fumbling with the buttons of her dress. It'd have been better if he'd just ripped it off her, but, she had to admit, that'd have made her return to her suite a bit awkward. That was her last coherent thought for a while. Carlos's broad peasant hands closed on her breasts, mauling them, milking at them, heedless of the pain he inflicted. That was enough to send Trixie into what she thought of as her animal state. From there on, she was aware of everything the youngsters did to her but she didn't *process* any of it. She felt Carlos's one hand scoop under her bottom and lift her to her feet, bent at her hips to still take Juan's thrusts into her mouth. His thick fingers dug into her sex.

'*Muy caliente! Tener furor uterino!*'

Even in her erotic daze, Trixie understood the first phrase, 'Very hot!'

His fingers worked her soft wet flesh mercilessly. His thumb – it was at the pucker of her anus – forced a brutal entry. Trixie's insides churned. When a man gripped her that way, his fingers in her sex and his thumb jammed into her rectum, it was devastating. It was like he was holding her internal organs at his mercy.

She was helpless! Her belly convulsed, squeezing out a long liquid orgasm that peaked and held for an eternity but didn't bring her true release. Rather, it stoked her ravenous need.

Juan screeched, '*Oy, estoy por acabar!*' His cock gushed, filling her mouth and flowing down her throat.

Trixie clawed at his bum, *insisting* that he keep pumping. He held her face to his pubes, his softening cock still filling her mouth, and made little throat noises. She tongue-lashed his glans, desperate to restore the boy's lust. His hips twitched. Trixie redoubled her efforts but was distracted by Carlos, who now had both of his thumbs digging into her, spreading the cheeks of her bottom. She'd have protested, just by reflex, but her mouth was full. The hardness of his cock pressed against her knot. She forced herself to relax. She'd only glimpsed his shaft but remembered that although it lacked the length of his friend's, it was, if anything, thicker.

The invasion was deliciously painful. Trixie let out a gurgling yelp as she felt the monstrous *thing* surge into her. The bastard laughed, and thrust harder, pushing her bodily, so that his friend's recovering cock was forced into the back of Trixie's throat again. Juan pushed back, spiking her poor bottom harder onto Carlos's cock. Carlos's drive pushed Juan's shaft deep again.

It was like their cocks became one, a spit of hard flesh that transfixed her body, from rectum to lips, and she was nothing but an *object*, shuttled backwards and forwards from impalement to impalement. Trixie grew delirious with lust. At some point, they turned her around bodily. Her legs no longer functioned to hold her up. One held her hips, the other her breasts, both with hands that dug deeply into her flesh.

They climaxed several times each, as young men can. Her lips drooled their seed, as did her anus. For some reason, neither used her cunt. She wondered about that, but not then. She was beyond wondering about anything until she found herself alone and discarded like the trash she knew herself to be, sprawled half-naked on damp grass.

At three in the morning, Trixie let herself back into her suite. There were leaves in her hair, a white crust in one corner of her mouth, and the buttons of her little blue dress were in the wrong holes.

Penny put the book she'd been reading in bed aside. 'What have you been up to, Mother?' she snapped.

Trixie looked at the floor and muttered, 'Just a tiny little stroll on the wild side, Penny. Nothing much, really.'

20

'*Mother!* Things are going very well between Andrew and me. Do you want to spoil it all?'

'No, Penny, of course not. I won't do it again, I promise.'

'You're a mess. I can smell you from here. Go take a long hot shower, for goodness sake! And don't forget to brush your teeth and gargle.'

Meekly, Trixie headed for the bathroom.

Five

At ten, Penny and Andrew 'accidentally' bumped into each other at the gate to the beach, where he'd been hovering for just over forty minutes. He smiled and looked past her, searching. 'Your Mom not with you?'

'She's never up before noon. Your Dad?'

'He's been up since five, on the Net with London, England. His morning's booked solid.'

'So is his afternoon.'

'Huh?'

'Didn't he tell you? He's having lunch with my Mom and then they're playing tennis.'

Andrew grinned. 'Then we're orphans for the day.'

'Until four, when we meet up with them for bridge, we're stuck with just each other for company,' Penny agreed. 'Do you think we'll be terribly lonely?'

'I'll try to amuse you.'

'I bet you will!'

Andrew took Penny's raffia bag and beach umbrella and let her precede him onto the hot sand. 'I like your wrap.'

'Liar. You're wondering what I'm wearing beneath it.'

'Well, you did mention something about a special bikini.'

'I promised you that it'd be even tinier than the one I had on yesterday.'

'That's hard to imagine.'

'But you've been trying to, I bet.'

Andrew made an embarrassed noise. Penny pointed to a

spot on the sand just a few feet from the receding ocean. 'Umbrella there, please, Andrew.'

As he set it up, Penny continued, 'It has to be a secret, OK?'

'What does?'

'My bikini. My Mom hasn't seen this one, and she mustn't.'

'She seems pretty liberal to me.'

'She is, but even *she* has limits.'

'Oh.'

'Would you fetch me a lounge chair, please, Andrew?'

Andrew hurried as quickly as was seemly. Although he was ready to slay dragons for Penny, anything that delayed the unveiling of her bikini was a bummer. When he returned with the intricately folding chair Penny had him set it up, then move it, then adjust the umbrella, then move it again, so that the chair was in deep shadow. A lesser man would have been cursing by the time she was content with the arrangements.

Perhaps she sensed his impatience because she said, 'I want the umbrella just so, 'cause I don't want everyone on the beach to be able to see me when I take my wrap off.'

'Oh.'

'I'm wearing this bikini just for you, Andrew.'

'Oh.'

'Could you step back a bit and tell me if I'm visible from out there, in the sunshine?'

'Of course.' From fifteen feet away, Penny and the chair were concealed in inky shadow. 'You're invisible.'

'Thanks.' A shape moved inside the shadow. Andrew returned in what seemed like two strides. Penny was posed in the chair with her wrap hanging behind her. Andrew blinked to adjust his eyes.

He hadn't known that bikinis were made that small.

'It's called a "tear-drop",' she told him. 'Do you like it?'

Her bikini was lemon, three ovals of fabric, each about three inches long and two inches wide, even the one at her pubic mound. The scraps were held in place by tapes. Penny's nipples were covered, just, as was most but not all of the intoxicatingly tender bulge of her sex.

Andrew looked around, in case there was anyone close by.

'Do you like it?' Penny repeated.

'It's, um . . .'

'I could put my wrap back on.'

'No. Please don't. It's just that . . .'

'No one but you can see me, Andrew.'

'I suppose.'

'Am I embarrassing you?'

'I'm no prude,' he defended himself.

'If someone else was to see me like this, would you be jealous?'

'Maybe.'

'That's so sweet. May I have an ice cream? Chocolate if they've got it?'

The vendor was a hundred and fifty yards along the beach. Andrew rushed there and fidgeted while the slow-moving idiot behind the counter built a triple cone. What if someone came by and started to talk to Penny, or made a pass at her, or . . .? What if it was a big guy, a really big guy?

Andrew was sweating by the time he got back to Penny. She thanked him and took a long lick of her treat, with her eyes on his, seeming to send him some sort of message that he couldn't decipher. Between laps, her lips nibbled tiny portions and then had to be licked clean. A dribble of chocolate ran down her chin. She caught it with her little finger and sucked on it so hard her cheeks hollowed.

She wasn't doing anything that was actually sexual, and yet his cock was reacting as much to the way she ate as it had in response to his view of her fabulous body. Andrew dropped onto his belly to conceal his erection. Penny grinned. Melted ice cream was trickling over the backs of her fingers. She changed hands and extended the messy ones to him.

'Want a taste?'

Andrew's lust slammed into his gut. Speechless, he reared up and captured Penny's precious fingers between his lips. Desire gave him courage. One by one, he licked and then sucked on each finger, discovering the points of her nails with the tip of his tongue.

Penny plucked her hand away. Before disappointment struck him, she switched the cone back and offered him her other hand. Eyes closed, he devoured her fingers, fancying that he was becoming quite expert at that exotic form of lovemaking.

She said, 'Oh!'

Andrew blinked. Penny pointed. Somehow, a small chocolate blob had fallen to splash onto her incredible kneecap. He looked into her eyes for permission. She nodded. Andrew's heart stopped beating as his lips pressed around the offending bead of ice cream and his tongue was granted the exquisite joy of laving it off her golden skin.

'I think it's gone,' she told him after about five minutes.

He looked up. The cone was finished. Penny was licking her fingers. Before he could protest that it was *his* job, she writhed to her feet.

'Suddenly, I'm very hot. Race you to the raft!'

By the time he'd scrambled up, Penny was fifty feet into the ocean and swimming strongly. Andrew ran into the water and plunged, determined to get to the raft at least as soon as she did. He was a man, after all. Perhaps he was a better swimmer than he knew, because he passed Penny halfway out to the platform.

'No you don't!' she shouted across the waves. Her arms and legs thrashed water in her efforts to catch him but Andrew had heaved himself up to stand on the bobbing surface by the time she reached it.

'Here,' he said, bending and reaching down.

Her two hands took his wrist. Andrew heaved. Penny sprawled flat on her back on the raft, looking up at him.

'You're so strong!' she gasped.

Andrew felt his chest expand and his shoulders broaden. It felt so right, standing with his legs astride, looking down on the supine body of a girl who obviously admired him.

'Oh,' she said.

Andrew followed her eyes. Despite having been

25

immersed, his cock was fighting the restriction of his Speedo. He said, 'I'm sorry,' and dropped a hand to cover himself.

She grinned. 'No need to apologise. I take it as a compliment.'

Andrew made himself plant his fists on his hips, just as if he wasn't ashamed of the betraying bulge he was displaying. 'You seem to have that effect on me.'

She gave him a coy look. 'Me? Little old me?'

'Yes, you.'

'Follow me,' she challenged, and rolled across the raft to flop into the water on the far side.

Andrew took two strides and dived in over her head. When he came up she was holding onto the raft with one hand and beckoning him with the other. 'We can't be seen, here,' she observed. 'No one else swims out to the raft. They're all old folks, like my Mom and your Dad.'

It didn't seem the right time to defend his father, who was an excellent swimmer. Andrew executed a showy crawl back to Penny, who turned as he approached and held her free arm wide, inviting him into her embrace. He caught hold of the raft with his left hand and let their bodies come together. The skin-on-skin sensations, her smooth thighs pressed against his, her sinuous torso undulating against his, combined with the cool saltiness of her mouth and the warm sweetness of her tongue, overwhelmed Andrew.

Through his fog, he was vaguely aware that as they kissed, Penny was moving purposefully in the crook of his arm. Her legs wrapped around his thighs, giving her leverage to thrust her barely-covered mound against the base of his rigid Speedo-covered cock. From her waist up, she writhed, dragging her breasts from side to side across his chest. For a moment he thought her movements were simply passionate caresses but then he realised that she was deliberately scuffing the thin strips of her bra aside, freeing the delicate beauty of her breasts.

Andrew broke the kiss and held Penny away from himself, one-handed. The water was calm and clear. Bracketed by two strips of fabric, her dear sweet breasts

26

were squeezed together, pouting at him. She arched her back to lie on the water from her waist up. Andrew put his free hand into the small of her back and curled over her, lifting her breasts halfway out of the water, so that he could get his lips to their pale nipples.

His gentle kisses made her pant and push up at him. Andrew tried suckling, first at the left, then the right. Penny moaned. Encouraged, he nibbled.

'Yes, yes!'

His teeth gripped her right nipple, indenting its rubbery flesh. His tongue flickered on its tip. Penny made 'uh, uh' noises. Her mound ground and then beat at him. Andrew wondered if he dared touch her between her legs but one of his hands was holding them both up by its grip on the raft and the other supported Penny's back. He was still trying to work out some way to free a hand when Penny flipped upright, plucking her nipple from his mouth, squealed, and thrust her lashing tongue into his startled mouth.

Had she climaxed? He thought maybe she had, but he'd never made a girl come before, so he couldn't be sure. If she *had*, what sort of super-stud did that make him? Just the way he sucked on her nipples had driven her so mad with lust that she'd rubbed her pussy against him till she'd got off on it. He felt so proud of himself that his own raging need took second place, almost.

Penny pushed herself away from him and clung to the raft with both hands, panting. 'That was incredible, Andrew.' Her eyes travelled down his body. He followed them. She was staring at the aching bulge that his cock made in his swimsuit. She took on a sly look. 'Andrew?' she whispered.

He managed to croak, 'Yes, Penny?'

'I've never actually seen one.'

'One what?' he asked, knowing the answer but wanting to hear it from her kiss-swollen lips.

'A man's – a man's . . .'

'Do you want to?'

She reached a tentative hand towards Andrew's crotch.

27

'Yes, I really do. Not any old one, though. It's *yours* that I want to see.'

Made bold by her admission, Andrew told her, 'Help yourself,' and pushed his hips forward.

'You know I don't want to break my promise to my father, don't you?'

'I respect that.'

'I know I'm safe with you, Andrew, and I'll take care of you, I promise, just like I did last night.'

Andrew grunted. The thought of what she'd done on the patio and the anticipation of her doing it again had robbed him of the power of speech.

Treading water, Penny hooked her thumbs into Andrew's waistband. She pulled the Spandex towards herself and eased it slowly down until his bikini was around his thighs and his cock reared up. 'It's, it's magnificent,' she said.

Her right hand wrapped his cock's base. 'May I take a closer look?'

Andrew nodded. Penny pulled herself underwater by her grip on his cock. Wide-eyed, she inspected it from a foot away, then from six inches. Andrew could hardly contain himself. His cock had *never* been so close to a girl's face, to her mouth. The thrill of it knotted his sphincter.

And then she kissed it!

Andrew almost screamed with joy, but managed to contain it. He held himself rigid, just in case ... She did it again, with softly parted lips. Andrew thought for a moment that she was actually going to take him into her mouth, but she bobbed up out of the water, grinning.

'You didn't mind?'

He shook his head.

'Put your back against the raft. Hold onto it with both hands, above your head, OK?'

He nodded and obeyed, taut with anticipation. Bent over so that she could watch what she was doing, Penny took his cock in both hands and stroked it, pumping gently a few times, then with growing urgency. Andrew would have liked her to have made it last all day but his balls tightened and then nothing mattered but shooting his load and he thrust into her hands – and came.

Still holding his softening flesh, Penny said, 'It's like a miracle, isn't it. I've made you . . . . And I've seen your stuff come out. It's incredible. I don't think I'd ever get tired of watching it happen.'

Andrew opened his mouth to tell her that if she'd like to make out some more, he'd soon be ready to show her how he came again, but she dived under the raft and swam back towards the shore.

When they got to the beach it was filling up with sun worshippers and vendors. Andrew asked Penny to put her wrap back on. At noon, he fetched burritos from a vendor and pina coladas in coconut shells from the hotel's portable bar. After lunch, Penny dozed with Andrew sprawled at her feet, admiring her pretty toes and occasionally daring to gently kiss them.

She sat up with a start and ferreted in her bag for her watch. 'Two o'clock, gone. I have to get back, Andrew.'

'Already?'

'Bridge at four, remember. I have to get up to our suite and out of this bikini before my Mom goes up to change and catches me in it.'

Penny and Andrew made it into the lobby just in time to meet Trixie and Rolf, she limping and leaning heavily on his arm.

Penny pulled her wrap tighter. 'What happened?' she demanded.

'My fault,' Rolf confessed. 'I played too hard. Your poor mother twisted her ankle.'

Trixie grinned ruefully. 'He plays like a man Andrew's age. I'm surprised he never turned pro.'

Andrew frowned at being compared to his Dad for fitness. 'Are we still on for bridge? Penny and I won't mind if you cancel, will we, Penny?'

Trixie lifted her foot and pointed her toes. Although she winced, she declared, 'I'll be just fine. I only turned it. If you gentlemen wouldn't mind seeing us girls up to our suite?'

Six

Rolf tapped impatiently on the baize table. Trixie, in a clinging floor-length black velvet gown, limped into the card room leaning on Penny, who wore a scoop-neck crocheted top and a circular felt skirt. Rolf stood to greet them. Andrew followed him to his feet.

'How's your ankle?' Rolf asked.

'I saw the hotel's doctor. He says it'll be fine but I should stay off it as much as possible for the next couple of days and try to keep it elevated.' Trixie sank onto the chair that Rolf was holding for her. 'I'd hate to miss our game.'

'I could organise something, a footstool perhaps?'

'No, I'll be fine.' She grimaced and looked down at her ankle. 'Would it be all right if I rested my foot on your knee, Rolf?' She kicked her left shoe off.

'It'd be my pleasure.' He took his seat and stooped under the table to take Trixie's stockinged calf in a cupped hand and raise it to rest her heel on his knee. As her foot came up, a slit in her dress opened from its hem to her thigh. 'How's that?' he asked.

'Much better. I guess we're playing girls against boys, then.'

A waiter came in bearing a frosty flask and four martini glasses.

'I ordered the drinkies,' Trixie explained. 'It'll help me with the pain.'

Rolf signed for the drinks and cut the cards for first deal. Penny's queen of hearts won. She dealt and opened the bidding with a spade. Andrew passed.

Trixie bid, 'Two spades. Or should I bid clubs?'

Rolf passed and very quickly, so did Penny. Somehow her elbow nudged the second deck and it cascaded to the floor. 'I'll get it.'

To collect the spilled cards, Penny was leaning way down from her chair, to Rolf's left. Her top's neckline was deep and wide, and it was a little loose on her slender frame. As she stooped, the fabric sagged away from her. From the corner of his eye, Rolf could see one young breast quiver in the shadows and caught a glimpse of a delicate pink nipple. It occurred to him that her breast would fit into a martini glass, perfectly.

He snatched his eyes back to his cards, feeling guilty.

Trixie asked, 'So, where do you and your son live, Rolf?'

'New York – Manhattan.'

Trixie clapped her hands with glee. 'Lovely, us too, or will be. We're in the process of buying into a co-op a few blocks off Park Avenue.'

'That can be complicated, buying a co-op,' Rolf said.

'I hope not. My heart is set on it.'

Andrew led a small heart. Trixie fumbled dummy down. She had six clubs to the ace, queen, jack, but only two spades, the ten and the trey. If they'd bid it, they'd have had a sure game in clubs. By taking two risky finesses, Penny kept their losses down to a single trick.

Somehow, Trixie's heel had moved to midway up Rolf's thigh. As if absently, he caressed the nylon-sheathed sole of her foot.

'You're not trying to lose, are you, Mom?' Penny accused.

'Of course not. Why would you think such a thing?'

'You often used to, when you played against Dad. We aren't playing for a kiss a point, like you and he used to.'

Rolf grinned. 'Sounds like an idea to me. What do you say, son?'

'Dad!'

'My Mom's been known to lose by tens of thousands of points,' Penny told him.

'That sounds like a lot of slams, to me.'

31

'Oh no,' Trixie said matter-of-factly. 'We had special forfeits for slams. If he made a small slam against me, I had to . . .'

Penny growled, 'Mother!'

Rolf gently squeezed Trixie's foot, which had made its way up his leg until her toes just touched the seam of his pants at the base of his fly.

She licked her lips and stage-whispered, 'Maybe I'll tell you later, Rolf, when there are no children around.'

Rolf jerked his chair closer to the card-table to conceal the progress of Trixie's foot, the ball of which was now pressing rhythmically just above his scrotum.

Penny said, 'Mom, you're incorrigible!'

Trixie gave a solemn nod. 'True. So don't try to correct me, my darling daughter.'

Andrew, red faced, perhaps because the toes of Penny's left foot were probing up under the cuff of his pants, finished dealing. Rolf picked up his cards, distracted by the way Trixie's foot was moving on the base of his shaft. He put his hand on her ankle, thinking to move her foot to a more decorous position before either of the youngsters noticed what was going on.

Trixie stopped him with, 'Thank you, Rolf. A nice gentle massage would help the swelling go down.'

'I don't see any swelling. Your ankle looks absolutely perfect, to me.'

'Why thank you, kind Sir. Massage it anyway, please?'

Even though the ladies were making it difficult for them to concentrate, Rolf and Andrew were up by over eighteen thousand points by six p.m. 'That's a lot of kisses you owe us,' Rolf joked, half hoping he'd be taken seriously.

'And three slams that you bid and made,' Trixie added. 'Two small, one grand.'

'Don't start that again, Mother,' Penny warned.

'She's only teasing,' Rolf said.

Trixie grinned wickedly at her daughter. 'Am I, Penny?'

Penny stood abruptly. 'I'm going up to get changed,' she announced.

Trixie sighed. 'Then it's game over. You only need two to tango but it takes four to play bridge.' She gingerly lifted her foot from Rolf's lap. 'I don't think I should come down for dinner with this ankle.' She looked pointedly at Rolf, as if waiting for him to say something.

'I'll have room service bring something to your suite.'

'I hate to eat alone, Rolf.'

'I'll order *us* something,' he corrected himself. 'The kids won't mind dining and dancing without us, I'm sure.'

'That's very generous of you, Rolf. Eight o'clock? Oh, and Rolf, in case you were thinking of plying me with champagne, I'm more susceptible to martinis.'

Seven

An hour and a half later, Penny was pushing the final few self-covered buttons through the loops that fastened her scarlet silk cheongsam from its hem to her throat. She toed into clear slides that had five-inch heels and one-inch platforms.

From her languid pose on the chaise, Trixie looked her daughter up and down. 'It'd take Andrew forever to get you out of that dress.'

'I don't intend to let him get me out of it.'

'And those shoes – you'll be as tall as him, maybe taller.'

'Taller. He can look up to me for a change.'

'Going for the "untouchable" look?'

'You should try it some time.'

'Meow!'

'Mom, seriously, are you planning to "give your all" to Rolf tonight?'

Trixie arched an eyebrow and lifted her foot. 'With my poor wounded ankle? Of course not.'

'I see. We each have our methods, don't we, Mom.'

'Speaking of which, how do I look?'

'I'm sure he'll find you totally edible. Most men like black satin, but isn't a peignoir over a slip, stockings and pom-pom boudoir slippers, all in black, overdoing the *femme fatale* stereotype just a tad?'

'For men, there's no such thing as a woman looking too seductive. Don't worry, I'm trying to pique his appetite but I don't mean to give him more than the tiniest nibble at the goodies tonight. I haven't allowed him anything more than a kiss, so far.'

'You're cruel, Mom.'

'And devious.'

Penny leaned over her mother to tweak at her neckline and adjust the way her peignoir lay on her legs. 'That's better.' She paused. 'Mom, are you wearing panties?'

A voice outside announced, 'Room service!'

Penny, her question unanswered, opened the door to Rolf, who was pushing a chrome cart. Andrew hovered in the background. When he got a good look at Penny, he gawked as if he'd never seen a vision so beautiful. Penny allowed herself a satisfied smile and swept out to join him.

Rolf back-heeled the door shut behind her. 'Trixie, you look absolutely gorgeous!'

Trixie stretched like a cat in the warmth of Rolf's praise. Her legs moved together, dislodging the skirt of her peignoir to expose her legs to the tops of her stockings.

Rolf averted his eyes and pushed the cart to the table. With a flourish, he lifted a dish's lid. 'Olympia oysters on the half shell, drizzled with Pernod and lime juice. Here we have truffle-dressed medallions of Maine lobster, on a bed of Fiddlehead greens. For dessert, a confection the chef calls Chocolate Depravity – alternate layers of dark and milk chocolate, separated and topped by thick cream that has been blended with Bailey's Irish Cream and Kahlua. There are also some cheeses and crackers, should they suit Madame's palate better.'

'No caviar?'

Rolf's face dropped for a second, before he realised she was joking. 'I thought I'd save that for our breakfast, someday, when, I mean . . .' His voice trailed off in confusion.

Trixie rescued him. 'I'd prefer to eat at the table, Rolf, but I don't think I could walk there, not in these heels.' She wagged a foot that had a satin boudoir slipper with a three-inch heel dangling from its toes. When he was slow to react, she added, 'Would you mind carrying me?'

'Of course not. It'd be my pleasure.' Rolf scooped Trixie

up into his arms. Her peignoir parted from its waist-tie down, displaying her shapely legs to the lacy hem of her slip. Once more, Rolf looked aside so as not to take advantage. With her arms wrapped around his neck and her breath warm in its crook, he whisked her to the dining table, hastening because his erection was growing and he really wanted to sit down before it became too obvious.

Trixie didn't adjust her peignoir when she was seated. Rolf was considering how to advise her that her lovely pale thighs were exposed when she lifted her left foot.

'I should keep it elevated, Rolf, remember?'

'Of course.' He turned a knee out and guided her ankle to his thigh. 'How's that?'

'Much better.'

Oysters are easy to eat one-handed, if they've been prepared well. Rolf's free hand caressed Trixie's ankle, and calf, and he couldn't help but think about her leg being extended straight in front of her and that if one of his strokes just kept on going it would inevitably end up in the shadowy place under the flimsy fabric of her slip, which was an exceptionally short slip, from what little he knew of women's underthings.

'This meal,' Trixie asked, 'did you choose the menu?'

Rolf cleared his throat. 'Yes, is it all right?'

She gave him a melting look. 'You're a naughty man, Rolf.'

'I am?'

Trixie tilted her head back, showing off the beauty of her slender throat, and poured an oyster into her mouth. 'Everything you selected – reputed to be aphrodisiacs. Are you trying to seduce me?'

'I warned you, when we were on the patio, that I would.'

'So you did! How very honest of you.'

'You didn't seem averse to the idea, then.'

Trixie leaned forward over her plate. She looked directly into Rolf's eyes and told him, 'Nor am I now. I don't usually jump into men's beds, Rolf, but there's something very special about you, and a vacation doesn't give us a lot of time, does it. I have to confess, if it weren't for the pain in my ankle, I'd – well – I wouldn't exactly be fighting you off.'

'I understand,' he said, trying to keep the disappointment out of his voice.

Trixie dropped the last oyster shell into its silver dish and picked up the servers for the lobster. 'That doesn't mean we can't have a nice evening, does it?'

'Of course not.'

'Kisses and – and – you know – wouldn't hurt my ankle, if you were very gentle. Could you be gentle with me, Rolf?'

'I'll try.'

'Just so we don't get carried away.'

'I understand.'

There wasn't much more conversation. Rolf hadn't dated for over twenty-five years. Now he was alone with a lovely and very sexy woman who'd told him flat out that she was ready to 'make-out' as the kids say, but not 'go all the way'. His erection was a throbbing embarrassment. Rolf hadn't felt so awkward for as far back as he could remember.

Trixie asked, 'Shall we save the dessert for – after?'

Rolf nodded, unable to speak.

'Would you take the drinks and the phone to the chaise, please? I'm expecting an important call from Seattle, from my broker.' She lowered her foot from his thigh to the floor.

Rolf was able to keep his back to Trixie as he took the things to the table beside the chaise. He delayed there by pouring them two drinks but he still had to face her on his return. Her eyes were frankly on the bulge in his dress pants.

Rolf reddened. 'I'm sorry . . .' he began.

'Don't be. You've nothing to be ashamed of, from what I've seen so far.'

Her words helped but Rolf still felt awkward as he picked her up from her chair and her hip rubbed against him and then although he tried to carry her high, the cloth-covered head of his cock prodded one rounded cheek of her lovely bottom.

Trixie didn't seem the least embarrassed. She giggled and wiggled her rump in a way that inspired his raging lust, that he was honour-bound not to give in to. When he sat down, with her stretched out on his lap, Rolf was trembling with desire.

Trixie took his face between her hands and gazed into his eyes. 'Kisses, please, Rolf. Lots of slow gentle kisses. Let's make the most of the time we have alone together.'

Rolf hadn't made love since his wife had died, two years before. His pent-up needs had been stoked by yesterday's passionate kisses and Trixie's unspoken promise that today their lust would be consummated. What he craved was wild sex, him the ravisher, her the eager victim, but now she wanted 'slow gentle kisses', and a gentleman always defers to a lady's wishes.

So taut that his tendons ached, Rolf bent his mouth to Trixie's and closed his lips on her lower one. She sighed and relaxed in his arms. He turned his attention to her upper lip. Her lower one moved under his and then, very tenderly, sucked on it. Not sure if he was rushing her, Rolf touched her lip with the tip of his tongue. Her mouth opened to him. Their tongues touched, tentative little flicks. He wanted to crush her lips with his and thrust his tongue into the yielding sweet wetness of her mouth but he restrained himself. Tongues licked lips and tongues licked tongues. Trixie began to pant.

She had to be ready to surrender her mouth fully! Rolf took a deep breath.

Trixie squirmed under him, reaching up and back for her glass. With a grin, she said, 'I promise you, whatever we do tonight, it won't be because of the influence of alcohol.'

Her stretching had ground her bottom on him and tugged the top of her slip so low on the fullness of her breasts that he thought he could detect an arc of areola peeping through the satin's lace trimming. Speechless, he reached towards his own glass.

'No,' she said. 'We'll share.'

He took her glass and sipped.

'No, silly. You aren't supposed to swallow it. That's no way to share.'

Understanding, he tilted the cocktail into his mouth, leaned over Trixie, pressed his lips to her lips and let the drink trickle from his mouth into hers. God, she was uninhibited – and creative! Damn that ankle! Damn him, for making her hurt it!

'My turn,' she said. Her lips parted expectantly.

'What?'

'Pour it into my mouth, silly.'

Rolf obeyed, emptying half the glass. She pulled his head down and pursed her lips between his. He was still puzzled when he felt the jet of liquid gush up into his mouth. He held it for a moment before letting it dribble back between her lips. They exchanged the potent liquid, made more powerful by being diluted with their saliva, half a dozen times before the last drop disappeared.

Rolf said, 'I usually like my martinis very dry but that one was the best ever, and it was incredibly sweet.'

'As sweet as sin, Rolf. The flavour is still in my mouth,' she told him. Her lips parted wide in invitation.

Rolf sensed that the restraints had been lifted, insofar as kissing was concerned. He let his mouth ravish hers, stabbing and lashing with his tongue and sucking the dew from beneath her tongue with unabashed relish. He was so enraptured with her mouth that he wasn't immediately aware that her hand had taken his and moved it to the nakedness of a breast her slip had somehow fallen away from.

Rolf flattered himself he had the measure of Trixie, erotically. Without abating his assault on her mouth, he very tenderly smoothed his fingertips over her alabaster skin. Before long, she shifted under his touch. Rolf congratulated himself. It was worthwhile, restraining himself so strictly, if it made her impatient for more intense caresses. To prolong her agony, and his, he allowed one finger to brush over the hard peak of her nipple.

She pulled her mouth from his. With yearning in her eyes, Trixie begged, 'Please?'

'Please?'

'Please!'

'Like this?' he asked, revelling in his new-found mastery. Three of his fingers flickered across her breast's tip.

'More?'

He rolled her nub, hardly squeezing at all.

'You bastard! Do it, damn you!'

Her vehemence shocked him but he complied, pinching and tugging, elongating the flesh of her breast.

'Yes! Oh, that feels so good!'

Unprompted, feeling totally in charge again, Rolf jerked the satin down off Trixie's other breast and took its nipple in a vice-like grip.

'I can't stand it! Don't stop!' She arched and bounced in his lap. Every wriggle rubbed against his imprisoned cock.

Trixie grabbed his right wrist in both hands, pushed it down the length of her body and yanked it up under her slip. His fingers met soft wet folds. It'd been so long since he'd touched a woman there that he'd almost forgotten the intensity of the emotions generated when delicate flesh parts to eagerly welcome hard strong fingers. She was hot inside, and so wet her flesh felt slick. His two fingers squirmed, discovering Trixie's labyrinthine internal convolutions. There were smooth places, and folds, and soft subtle pockets. Intensely aware of how delicate and sensitive the inside of a woman's sex is, he explored slowly and cautiously. The thought of damaging her, the mere possibility of his bruising her internally, terrified him.

Trixie still had hold of his wrist. Her legs veed up. Her fists jerked his hand down. She drove his fingers into herself. 'Harder!' she demanded, her eyes blazing. 'Deeper!'

When he obeyed, she took one hand from his wrist and left the other to urge it. Her free hand insinuated itself between their bodies. Fumbling fingers found the tab of his fly's zipper. It hissed down. Her hand worked into the front of his pants, into the fly of his boxers, and pulled his burning flesh out into the open.

'We'll manage,' she hissed. 'Ankle or no damned ankle, if we're careful, there has to be a way.'

'Are you sure?'

'We'll try . . .' She swung around in his lap to face away from him and lifted herself. Perhaps it was to get purchase, but her feet flattened on the floor in front of the chaise. Trixie yelped, winced and sobbed. 'Damn, damn, damn, damn, damn!'

Rolf patted her shoulder. 'It's OK, Trixie. We don't have to.'

'Let me lie down, please.'

Gingerly, they both manoeuvred until she was flat on her back and he was perched on the edge of the chaise, half turned towards her, his cock drooping as it deflated.

'It's OK,' he told her again.

She gave him a wry grin. 'Tell your poor cock that.' Her hand snaked over to wrap around his shaft.

'That doesn't help,' he said.

'It will.'

'What?' His shaft was lifting and stiffening again.

'I can't leave you in this condition. Stand up.'

'Why?'

'Just do it.'

Rolf stood.

'Lean over me. Rest your hands on the back of the chaise.'

He obeyed, quivering with anticipation. Looming over Trixie like that, his cock was bobbing less than a foot from her luscious lips.

'You have a magnificent cock,' she told him.

He husked, 'Thanks.'

'Someday I'll take full advantage of it, but for now . . .' Her eyes fixed on his rigid flesh, Trixie started to slowly pump.

He managed, 'Do you have a tissue or something?'

'What for?'

'For when – you know.'

Her eyes hooded as she looked up at him. 'Rolf, let me explain in words you can't misunderstand. I'm going to jerk your gorgeous cock off. When you come, I intend your cock to be in my mouth. I'm not going to spill a single

41

drop of your cream. I'm going to swallow it all. Do you understand?'

Rolf nodded, speechless. His dear wife, the only woman he'd ever made love to, had never talked like that. Come to that, although she'd occasionally taken him into her mouth for special treats, on his birthday or at Christmas, she'd always been sure to pull his cock out well before his climax. She'd never even wanted to sleep on the wet spot.

Trixie pumped harder, licking her lips as if in anticipation. Rolf was in a delirium of happiness. How lucky he was to have met this incredibly beautiful and sexy woman! Pressure built.

'I'm close,' he gasped.

Trixie pulled herself up, mouth open wide, flattened tongue protruding.

The phone rang.

Trixie said, 'Damn!' With one hand still caressing him, but slowly, she reached for the phone with the other. 'Yes, Penny. Of course it's OK. Come on up.' She hung up with a sigh. Her hand stilled.

'It's the kids. Penny doesn't feel well. I suspect she's had a drink or two too many.'

Rolf felt numb. It'd been so close – the erotic event of his life – and now it had been snatched away from him. He considered asking Trixie to continue, though faster, but he knew he wouldn't be able to climax with the arrival of Penny and Andrew imminent. With a sigh, he staggered back.

Trixie quickly adjusted her clothing. 'You'd better sit at the table,' she told him. 'We don't want to shock our children with *that*.' She nodded in the general direction of his cock.

Rolf tucked in, zipped up and sat. There was a knock at the door. He growled, 'Come in.'

In a stage whisper, Trixie told him, 'I owe you one.'

Rolf didn't scowl at his son when he came in. Instead, he told the young couple, 'There's some chocolate dessert left, if either of you are up for it.'

Penny peered at the chocolate confection, mumbled something about needing to lie down and left, presumably

42

to her bedroom. There was an awkward pause. Andrew looked embarrassed. Rolf considered sending Andrew away, hanging in long enough for Penny to fall asleep and then resuming where he and Trixie had left off. He decided it was neither right nor feasible. Instead, he poured two martinis and handed one to Andrew. 'Pass this to Trixie, son.'

She toasted Rolf over her glass, with a wink and a blown kiss. The phone rang. She picked it up. 'Hello?' Trixie nodded, said, 'Yes,' and 'No,' and 'I'll get back to you.' When she hung up she looked ready to cry.

'What's the matter, Trixie?' Rolf asked, his erection forgotten in his concern.

'That was my broker. There's a problem with the co-op. They need two local New York references, one personal and one business. I don't know anyone in New York.'

Andrew said, 'Yes you do. You know us, right, Dad? You can take care of it, can't you?'

Rolf nodded. 'No promises, but I'll see what I can do. Who's your broker? How do I get in touch with him?'

It happened that Trixie had left her broker's card on the credenza, beside her open purse. She directed Rolf to it. He didn't mean to pry but there was a crumpled tissue with lipstick stains on it in her purse. He remembered her wiping his mouth after their passionate kisses. Could she be keeping the tissue as a souvenir? His heart melted.

'Come on, son. The lady needs her rest.'

Eight

Andrew had called Penny to check that she was OK and had been told that she'd be looking after her Mom for the morning but that they'd both be happy to meet him and his Dad on the beach, after lunch. His father had skipped the sumptuous buffet breakfast that was served in the dining room. He'd settled for coffee and an apple Danish from room service while he worked the phone.

Andrew was on the beach by ten, corralling the best spot and setting up two lounge chairs, two beach towels and the three biggest umbrellas he could find. He lunched in the private nest he'd built, on tacos and cola and a pack of breath mints.

He was rewarded at two, when his Penny arrived, supporting Trixie from one side while his Dad helped her on the other.

Rolf eyed the patch of seclusion that Andrew had contrived and told him, 'Well done, my son.'

'Were you able to help Trixie with her real estate problem?'

'It's all taken care of. My banker has agreed to be the business reference, on my say-so, and I'll be the personal one.'

Penny said, 'So we'll all be able to get together, for bridge and – and so on, very soon.'

Andrew pouted. 'I'll be away in another few weeks, back at university.'

'But there'll be vacations,' Rolf said.

'I guess.'

Trixie laid a hand on Andrew's arm. 'Penny and I owe you and your Dad, big time, Andrew. Anything we can do to repay you, anything at all, don't hesitate to ask, please.'

Andrew could think of a number of things Penny could do to repay him but he wasn't about to tell Trixie what they were. 'Ready for a swim, Penny?'

She stood and dropped her wrap. Her bikini was brief, but of course it wasn't the secret one that she'd worn for him the day before. 'OK, Mom?'

'Of course, but please don't go too far.'

'Just out to the raft,' Andrew said. Mentally, he added, 'And round to the other side, where you can't see us.'

Trixie frowned. 'Oh, that's such a long way. Please don't. Can't you have just as much fun closer to the shore, where I can see you?'

Penny said, 'Of course. Don't worry, Mom.'

Andrew bit his lip, took Penny's hand and tugged her towards the ocean. When they were in the shallows, out of earshot of the beach, he turned to her but she spoke first.

'I'm sorry, Andrew. My Mom has a thing about me and the water. It's the way my Dad died, you see. We were at the lake, just him and me, and he got tangled in the weeds, or something. He never was a strong swimmer.'

Andrew wanted to hug her but her mother was watching. 'I'm so sorry, Penny. Certainly we can stay close to the shore.'

'We can go out a little way,' she said, and dived.

Andrew swam after her. When he came up, chest deep, she wasn't in sight. Before he had a chance to start worrying, he saw her swimming under water. Penny gave him a wicked grin and accelerated straight at him. Her hands caught his knees. Using them for leverage, she sat on the bottom, her legs wrapped around his ankles. Her left hand yanked his Speedo down. Her right gave his cock three quick strokes before she eeled off, to surface a decorous ten feet away from him.

'Two can play at that game,' he warned her. He was underwater and heading her way before he realised that he

45

couldn't very well do to her as she'd just done to him. Yanking her bikini down and giving her sex a quick grope just wasn't on. He settled for taking hold of her leg and daring to lick her thigh.

When he came up, Penny scolded, 'Andrew!'

'I thought . . .'

'I'm teasing. Let's see what kissing underwater is like, huh?'

Trixie didn't see that the youngsters were disappearing underwater for minutes at a time and emerging flushed and breathless. Her eyes were closed. Her head was lolling back, rubbing sensuously against the bulge in the front of Rolf's swimsuit. He was standing behind her, massaging sun-block into her neck and shoulders, although the umbrellas they were under cast deep shadows. From time to time, he arched over her and they'd touch tongues. Once in a while, his caressing fingertips slid into the neckline of her swimsuit and brushed her nipples.

'Your ankle,' he asked, 'do you think it'll be better soon?'

'By tomorrow, I think. It'd better be, for travelling.'

Rolf felt a cold chill. 'Travelling?'

'Didn't you know? Didn't I tell you? This is our last day. Tomorrow, Penny and I are on the noon flight back to Seattle.'

Nine

Rolf had their new address. He drove to the high-rise complex. It wasn't exactly 'a few blocks off Park Avenue,' but then Trixie didn't know Manhattan. A hundred dollars secured the concierge's promise that he'd make sure the women's move went smoothly. Another hundred guaranteed that when they arrived, Rolf would be called immediately.

A week later, Rolf got the call. Andrew was on a day-trip upstate with some buddies. He'd have wanted to be with his Dad on their first visit but Rolf couldn't bring himself to wait. There was Cristal champagne in the fridge and a cooler-pack under the kitchen counter but Trixie liked her martinis so he'd take both. He filled a thermos with icy gin and added a splash of vermouth. He ought to have flowers but stopping would take time. Rolf called a florist and ordered delivery of two arrangements of orchids, one for Trixie and one for Penny. That wasn't inappropriate, was it? It wouldn't betray his lust for Penny – a lesser desire than the one he felt for Trixie – but a perverse passion that was strong enough to be undeniable?

What next? Another pass of the razor over his chin. Another gargle with mouthwash. Another spritz of cologne. Tan cashmere pants, beige silk shirt, parchment suede jacket, no tie, to keep it casual. He was as ready as he could be. The traffic was damnable. He jumped lights and cut cabs off to make it in just under an hour. The concierge saluted him. Rolf dropped a fifty on the man's desk and touched a finger to his lips, to be answered with a nod and a wink. The elevator crawled. Rolf found the door to eleven-sixty-eight. With the thermos under his left arm and the cool-pack of champagne in his left hand, Rolf rapped on the door and tried it, and it opened for about eighteen inches before knocking against something that wobbled.

Penny said, 'Whoops! Careful!'

Through the gap, Rolf saw a plank at the height of his groin and Penny's pretty bare feet, ankles and knees. His eyes travelled up her slender legs. Her cut-off denim shorts covered no more than bikini panties would have, and fitted just as closely. Her midriff was stretched, elongating the round dimple of her navel into an oval. Her ribcage was arched. The paint-splattered cut-off cotton top she wore was lifted enough to expose new-moon slivers of her delicate little breasts' undersides. Belatedly, Rolf croaked, 'Sorry!'

From somewhere inside the hallway, Trixie said, 'What a lovely surprise!'

Penny said, 'Minute.' She squatted to set the roller she'd been using on the ceiling into a paint tray on the plank, and dropped lithely to the floor.

Rolf handed his packages in to her and squeezed through the gap. Trixie was sitting cross-legged on the floor opposite, painting a baseboard. Her white shorts were neither as short nor as tight as her daughter's but their legs were wider and the way she sat, Rolf's eyes could follow the curve of one thigh into the shadows. Her floral shirt was unbuttoned, just knotted below her breasts, cradling them.

The women couldn't have looked more alluring if they'd expected him and posed carefully, awaiting his arrival. Trixie writhed to her feet. 'You've caught us looking our worst, Rolf. You might have called ahead.'

'Your phone isn't on yet. Besides, you both look lovely.'

'You're forgiven.' Trixie spread her arms.

Penny said, 'Mother, you'll ruin his clothes,' before Rolf could hug Trixie.

48

'Silly me! Sorry, Rolf.'

'I'll take the hug and damn my clothes.'

Penny wiped her hands on her shorts and moved in close. Trixie came at him from the other side, so that he had to hold one in the crook of each arm, which was nice but a little disturbing. He broke the silence with, 'I brought champagne and martinis. Glasses?'

Penny said, 'It's a bit early, isn't it?'

Trixie's childish pout made Rolf feel weak and strong at the same time – weak because he was vulnerable to her, strong because he felt he was her protector.

She said, 'It's never too early for champagne. Some people have it for breakfast.'

'*With* breakfast, Mother. Only *you* have it *for* breakfast.'

Trixie took Rolf's hand. 'Come into the kitchen and help me find something to put it in.'

The kitchen was littered with half-unpacked cartons. Trixie opened one of the cabinets over the counter and turned to lean her back on it. 'All we've unpacked is mugs, so far. Top shelf, Rolf. I can't reach that high.' She didn't move aside.

When Rolf pressed against her to reach above her head, her arms went around his waist and her head tilted up, lips parted. Fumbling mugs down with one hand, he held her close with the other and stooped to meet her kiss. Her bottom flexed beneath his fingers. Her hips rotated against him. Somehow, he got three mugs to the counter by touch, freeing his other hand. It squeezed her breast through her shirt. She sighed into his mouth. Encouraged, he let his fingers slide onto the smooth soft skin of a half-bared breast.

Trixie pushed him back. 'Penny might come in.'

He said, 'She knows better,' but he turned aside to take the champagne from its pack.

Using the plank in the living room as a table, Rolf popped the cork and poured.

Penny giggled. 'Champagne from mugs? How decadent!'

Rolf toasted, 'To your new lives, in New York!'

Trixie asked, 'Andrew couldn't come?'

'He's out of town today. I should have brought him. We could use an extra pair of hands around here.' He downed his mug and refilled all three. 'You should have got someone in to do this work, Trixie.'

'I don't throw money around, Rolf,' she scolded.

'I'd have picked up the tab as a "welcome" gift.'

'I pay my own way, Rolf.'

'Of course. I didn't mean . . .' Embarrassed, he took his jacket off and reached for a paintbrush.

Trixie put a hand over his. 'Thanks, but you aren't dressed for this kind of work. You'd ruin your lovely clothes.'

He dipped a finger into the paint and smeared it down his shirt and pants. 'Too late! Where do I start?'

An hour later, Rolf and Penny were side-by-side on the plank, putting the finishing touches to the ceiling, with Trixie standing below, where Rolf could look down into her cleavage, pointing out the spots they'd missed.

Trixie observed, 'I think that's it. Well done.'

Rolf dropped to the floor. 'Lunch?' He fished his cell from his jacket. 'We'll get something delivered. Your choice, ladies?'

Trixie handed a phone book up to Penny, who opened it to restaurants, scanned it and set it down on the plank. She squeezed in between it and Rolf, close enough that her knee touched his hip, and took his phone from him.

'You like Thai, Rolf?' she asked, nudging him with her leg.

Rolf cleared his throat. 'Very much.'

Trixie tapped his wrist. 'I can read your mind, you naughty man. Maybe it should be me sitting up there instead of Penny.'

Rolf went red. 'I . . .'

Trixie giggled. 'I'm only teasing, silly. Penny understands me.'

He looked from mother to daughter. 'You two are very close, aren't you.'

Trixie squeezed Penny's knee. 'I suppose we are. Since my Barney . . . All we've had is each other.'

Penny's hand covered Trixie's.

Rolf cleared his throat. 'Penny?'

'Yes, Rolf?'

'Me seeing your mother. It isn't a problem for you, is it? I mean . . .'

'Are you looking for my blessing? Well, you have it. Nothing – no man – could come between my Mom and me, but a woman needs a man in her life.'

'There are those who'd disagree with you.'

Before Penny could respond, her mother interrupted. 'Are we going to order something before we're reduced to eating each other?'

Penny smothered her laugh with her hand.

'*I* know what you're thinking, Penny! And *you* accuse *me* of having a dirty mind!'

Penny gave her mother a wide-eyed look. 'They have chicken, Rolf. Breast or thigh? Which do you fancy?'

Trixie said, 'Ignore her, Rolf. Don't be fooled by her looks. She's mainly innocent enough, but there's a streak of depravity in that girl, just waiting to emerge.'

Penny giggled. 'Isn't that what men want from us women, Mom? Depraved innocence?'

Rolf grinned at Trixie. 'I'll settle for the "depraved" and leave the "innocence" for younger men to enjoy.'

Penny dialled.

Trixie looked up at the ceiling and squinted. 'Oops! I see a spot you missed.' She picked up the roller and lifted a foot onto the steps.

Rolf reached out. 'No, Trixie. Not in those heels, not after the champagne.'

'I'm fine.' Three steps up, Trixie's foot slipped from under her. She tumbled, into Rolf's waiting arms. She grinned at him. 'It looks like I've fallen for you, Rolf.'

'Your ankle OK?'

'It's fine, but I could fake that it's injured if it'd mean you'd carry me.'

'Any time, injured or not.'

Penny said, 'I'll see if I can find plates,' and went to the kitchen.

Trixie nibbled on Rolf's earlobe. She whispered, 'We've got unfinished business, Rolf.'

He whispered back, 'I remember.'

'I wish . . .'

Speaking loudly enough for Penny to hear in the kitchen, Rolf said, 'Do you think you could spare Penny for the day, tomorrow, Trixie?'

'I guess. Why?'

'I know that Andrew is keen to show her the sights of New York. There's a lot to see. Even a small start would take them all day. I could likely arrange seats for a show and dinner reservations, so they could be out from say, nine in the morning, right through till midnight.'

She smiled up at him. 'I'd hate to be alone for so long, Rolf, not knowing anyone in the City.'

'You know me. I could come here with Andrew, at nine. You and I could find somewhere to go.'

'I'll be tired from today's painting, Rolf. I'd love you to come and visit, but don't expect me to be up to going out. We'd have to find some other way to amuse ourselves right here. Any ideas?'

Rolf grinned. 'I'll think about that. Anything I should bring?'

'I haven't had time to shop yet, so if you'd like a drink tomorrow, you'd better bring the fixings.'

Ten

Rolf had a quart of Tanqueray Number Ten in his left hand and one of Beefeater in his right. Andrew carried half a pint of dry vermouth, a hamper and a corsage of white orchids.

Penny opened the door in a clinging grey cashmere turtleneck sweater and a matching fully circular flirty little skirt. The orchids that Rolf had ordered, *Bordeaux Cattleyas*, covered the credenza behind her. She squealed and clapped her hands. '*More* orchids! For *me*, Andrew?'

He put down the hamper and took her into his arms. As the youngsters embraced, Rolf elbowed into the kitchen. 'Trixie?'

'She's sleeping in,' Penny called from behind him.

'Oh.'

'She said for you to wake her when you got here. If you don't mind a suggestion, wake her with coffee.'

'I can do that.'

'Dad,' Andrew said, 'the limo driver's waiting. Mind if we go?'

'Go ahead. Have a good time.'

Penny gave him a squeeze, picked up an overnight case, and left with Andrew. Rolf searched the kitchen and found a grinder and a French Press. He'd brought Blue Mountain beans. As the water heated, he put both bottles of gin in the freezer and unpacked a cold lunch from the hamper. Trixie's toaster accommodated two bagels, which he smeared with cream cheese and chopped chives. Guessing,

53

he put cream and raw brown sugar into Trixie's coffee. A spray of orchids stolen from the hallway display completed the tray that he carried into the sanctum of her bedroom. The heavy drapes were drawn, leaving the room almost dark. Rolf's fumbling found a sideboard to set the tray down on. He parted the drapes just enough to see by.

Trixie gasped from her bed, 'Coffee! You must be an angel. Please?'

Rolf expected tousled hair and a sleep-creased face. Trixie, though blinking as if just woken, was bright-eyed and subtly made up, with gleaming and neat honey-coloured curls. He suppressed a grin. She was entitled to her artifice, especially if it lured him into her bedroom. Even the perfume in the air smelled fresh.

'Sorry to wake you,' he said, playing to her game.

She looked at him over her coffee. 'You'll forgive me for greeting you like this?'

'Forgive you for?'

'I sleep in the nude.'

'You'll have to prove that.'

'You're bad, Rolf.'

'Then I'm in good company.'

Her eyes narrowed. 'I really should put something on.'

'Should I leave the room?'

'No. Will you help me?'

'With great pleasure.'

'There should be a pair of stockings hanging over the foot of the bed.'

'I see them.'

She twisted to put her mug down on a nightstand but managed to do so without quite revealing a breast, to Rolf's disappointment. He was mollified when she pulled her bedclothes to one side, baring one long lovely leg all the way up to her shapely hip.

'Please?' she said.

'Please what?'

'My stocking. Could you put it on for me?'

Rolf's mouth dried. He felt numb and thrilled at the same time. He'd never known a woman be so blatantly a

54

temptress before. Trixie was so intensely *female*. She made him feel more manly than he had ever felt before, even on his wedding night with Rachel. Rachel had been sweet and lovely. Trixie was what the kids called 'hot'. He'd never really understood that expression before.

His fevered fingers rolled translucent black nylon into a little nest, the way he'd seen a woman do, once, somewhere. It'd likely been in a movie. Trixie pointed scarlet-tipped pink toes. He fitted them into the frothy stocking and unrolled it slowly, savouring every sensation – the slither of nylon between his fingers – the delicate structure of the bones in her foot – the complementary curves of her arch and instep.

Her ankle was a miracle, sculpted by nature for fragile strength. The subtle flare of her calf felt so sensuous under his palms that it made his cock twitch.

'You've done this before,' Trixie accused.

Rolf didn't answer. He never had, but he couldn't admit that, in sensuality, he was a neophyte compared to her. Her knee was smooth and dimpled. Its cap moved under the pressure of his fingertips, exposing her vulnerability.

And then he came to her thigh.

Smoothing nylon over that intimate loveliness was almost more than Rolf could bear. Her skin was soft and yielding but beneath it the long muscle was very strong and almost hard. When Trixie walked, it was *this* muscle that propelled her. If – when – they made love, it would be *this* muscle that lifted her hips to meet him. The strength that he held between his palms belied her weak vulnerability. In the throes of passion, Trixie would give thrust for thrust.

Rolf adjusted the lacy top of Trixie's stocking. Her thigh was quivering under his hands.

'Are you OK?' he asked.

Her voice was husky. 'The way you did that – it was so sensuous. I've never . . . Rolf, you are an incredible lover.'

He grinned at her. 'I haven't made love to you yet.'

'Yes you have. You just did.'

Rolf leaned up the bed, to kiss her, but she stopped him with gentle fingers to his lips.

'The other stocking, please?'

'I don't know if I can bear doing it again.'

'Me neither. That's what makes it so good, it being unbearably exciting. I'm desperate for you, Rolf. Make me writhe with lust and then deny me and make it worse and worse and then – and then . . .'

'And then what?'

She gurgled deep in her throat. 'And then fuck me, silly!'

Rolf decided not to be offended by her crudity. It wasn't as if she'd sworn in casual conversation. She'd used the word in context, not as an expletive. To show that he wasn't offended, he said, ' "Fuck you silly", or "fuck *you*, silly"?'

'Either or both, just so you tease me till I beg for it, first.'

'You think I have that much self-control?'

'I'll give it to you.'

'How?'

'Put that other stocking on me and then I'll show you.' She pulled her nylon-sheathed leg back under the covers, rolled onto her tummy and thrust her other leg out for him to attend to.

This time her leg was knee-down. The delights were different. Instead of a dimpled knee to play with, he had the back of one, soft and very vulnerable, which he kissed and licked before covering with nylon. Trixie seemed to like that. His lick made her quiver and brought a soft moan to her lips. Caressing the back of her thigh was different from caressing its front, but equally exciting. Rolf thought of letting his fingers keep travelling up her leg, to the intimate places he'd been fondling and kissing in his imagination ever since that evening in the ballroom when he'd first met her.

Before he decided, Trixie whispered, 'Remember where we were, when we were interrupted? Come stand up here. Make a bridge over me the way you did then. Hold onto the head of my bed with one hand.'

Rolf wasn't the least ashamed to present the long bulge in his pants for Trixie's inspection. He would have been, he thought, with any other woman. She'd taught him something about candid lust.

Trixie's fingertips traced his cock's length through the cloth that restrained it, from his balls to its crown. Her hand reversed. Her nails trailed back down his column, scratching him gently through the cloth.

'How much of *that* treatment do you think I'll be able to take?' he asked, proud of his own boldness.

'Trust me. I know *exactly* what I'm doing.' She pulled on the tab of his zipper. Trixie had to lift herself on one elbow to slide her hand into his fly. The bedclothes fell back from one lush breast. He reached down to touch it.

'No!' Trixie said. 'Sorry. I didn't mean to be sharp. I *do* want your fingers there, but not yet, not now.' She looked up into his face with pleading eyes. 'Can you just do as I ask and no more, for a while, just a little while?'

'Of course.'

'Then take hold of my hair. Don't worry about hurting me. I like to have my hair pulled.' Her eyes twinkled at him. 'Is that kinky?'

'Kinky?'

'*I* think it is. I'm a bad girl, Rolf. Do you like bad girls?'

'I like *this* one.'

'Tell me if I ever do anything to really shock you, so I'll know to do it again.' Her fingers found his naked shaft and manoeuvred it into the open before they worked back into his pants to lift his balls out and let them hang. 'You have very big balls,' she said.

'Is that good?'

'Oh yes.' Her palm cupped his scrotum and lifted. 'So *heavy*! Are they full of hot cream, Rolf? Have you been saving it? Is it all for *me*?'

Rolf cleared his throat. It was the only sound he was capable of making. He'd never *dreamt* a woman could talk like that, nor realised how much it would excite him.

'Hair,' she reminded him.

Rolf took a strong grip.

'It's so you can steer me. You'll know better than me when your climax is coming. When it is, I want you to control my head to make sure you come in my mouth, right on my tongue, please.'

Rolf's sphincter tightened. A tingle ran up his spine. Trixie *asked* flat-out, for things most women he'd known couldn't be persuaded to do. He felt he was teetering on the edge of a bottomless pit of depraved desires. He had a choice. He could flee, right then, or he could let himself tumble and be lost, wallowing in oozing depravity, forever.

Mentally, he shrugged. If the options were cold virtue or hot debauchery, he'd had his fill of the former. It was past time he tried the latter. His fist tightened in Trixie's hair.

'Yes, like that!' She planted a kiss on the eye of his cock's head. 'I *adore* your cock, Rolf!'

The fingers that supported his balls stroked and tickled his scrotum. The fingers of Trixie's other hand ran lightly up his shaft with a touch so delicate that Rolf wasn't sure he felt it. He *was* sure that he could feel her warm breath on his cock's head.

Trixie adjusted her position, rising a little. The bed-clothes fell to her narrow waist. Rolf gazed down, his eyes feasting on this enchanting woman's lovely body and the deliciously obscene spectacle of her sweet face, in rapt adoration of *his* cock.

An incredible rush of *power* filled him.

Her stroking fingers applied more pressure. Even as she caressed him, Trixie inspected him. She moved his shaft from side to side, lifted it and depressed it, examining it from every angle as if she was memorising each ridge, each vein, every nuance of skin tone.

A bead of clear fluid emerged from his cock's eye. Trixie glanced up into his eyes. Her tongue flicked out, scooping the droplet into her mouth. She gave him a gleeful grin and announced, 'Hors d'oeuvres.'

Her fingers stopped stroking. They tightened into a fist around his shaft. Trixie jerked *down* towards his balls, then *up* towards his cock's head. Her face became fierce. 'I want your cream,' she demanded as she yanked on him. 'I want it hot, thick, filling my mouth. I want to swallow your seed, Rolf. Fuck, I want it all over me, inside me and out. I want you to come on my breasts, on my face, on my belly, in my hands, everywhere. Cover me with your come, coat me with it, Rolf, please?'

She was so powerfully passionate it was almost frightening. Rolf managed, 'I don't know that I can do all that in one go, Trixie.'

She laughed from deep in her throat. 'Then you must come often, and keep coming and coming until there isn't a single inch of my skin that hasn't been bathed in "essence of Rolf".'

She was so much fun, and that didn't distract from his lust at all. If anything, it increased it. Making love to her was gleeful but incredibly intense.

Her slow jerking on his cock was stoking his lust to unbearable heights. Something cruel rose up in him. Deliberately letting it hurt her, he dragged her head by her hair, tugging her mouth to his cock's head.

Trixie gasped, 'Yes,' before her lips touched his glistening dome and opened wide to take it into her warm wet mouth.

His pull on her hair forced his cock only just deep enough that its head passed her lips, but they continued on, to slither down the length of his shaft. Her tongue pushed up, pressing his glans against the roof of her mouth. And she *still* descended. He felt his bulb lodge at the very back of her mouth, at her throat, and wondered that she didn't gag on it.

And she nodded, hard, driving him *into* her throat with a gulping, clicking, wet sound like none he'd ever heard before but knew he'd remember for the rest of his life.

Rolf froze. Trixie's throat worked on him and then she slowly withdrew, sucking on his cock as she pulled back and off it.

'Trixie . . .' he began.

Her fingers clamped around his shaft. 'Don't talk. *Feel!*' She pumped in earnest, no longer teasing, just urging him. Her other hand stroked and tugged on his balls, almost milking. Her mouth was close enough that as her hand moved his cock, its head slapped on the flat of her tongue. Trixie glared up into his eyes, her look *insisting* that he climax.

And he did. And it was glorious.

The release gushed up through his shaft, so forcefully that he felt as if its passing thickened him. It flooded out from him in a spurt that jetted clean into the depths of her mouth. The second gush was less powerful and flopped onto her waiting tongue. Trixie grinned and swallowed. Her fist kept working as she reared up and directed his cock at her breast, which received his third and final squirt. The flat of her tongue smoothed over his cock's head. Rolf shuddered.

'That's a start,' she said. Trixie massaged his jism into the alabaster skin of her breast. 'That's my right tit done. Maybe you'll come on my left, next.'

Rolf panted, 'Not right now.'

'Of course not. Well, I promised you I'd make you capable of teasing me without getting carried away, didn't I?'

Rolf was drained of all lust, but a gentleman never left a lady wanting. 'I'm ready,' he said.

'Not yet, silly. We have all day. You get undressed and take a nice nap. I'm going to shower and be all fresh for you when you wake up. *Then* you can take your time driving me slowly out of my mind with desire, OK?'

'Perfect,' Rolf agreed.

Eleven

When Penny saw the white stretch Cadillac limousine she squealed in glee and pirouetted, knowing full well that doing so lifted her skirt to the tops of her thighs. When a boy does something right, like picking a girl up for a date in a luxurious limo, he should be suitably rewarded.

Andrew popped the trunk and put her case into it. 'What's the luggage for?'

'Your Dad said we'd be going to dinner and to the theatre later? I'll have to change for those.'

'Oh.' He opened the car's rear door for her.

Penny climbed in, giving him another quick flash of her thighs, and squealed again. 'Oh my God! It's enormous in here! It's like a travelling room or something!' She sat and stretched her legs straight out but her toes didn't quite reach the seat opposite.

He followed her in, grinning. 'You've been in a limo before, haven't you?'

'Honestly, no, not a stretch one, anyway. You don't see a lot of them, back in Ridge River.'

Andrew clunked the door closed and turned to help Penny with her seat-belt. *That* put his arm across her and *that* brought their faces close and *that* led to him kissing her, tentatively at first but with growing passion.

Penny broke the clinch, gently.

'I'd forgotten how good you taste,' he said.

'Thank you.'

He moved to kiss her again.

'Aren't we going somewhere?' Penny reminded him.

'Your choice. The Empire State Building? Staten Island? The Statue of Liberty? Central Park?'

'Isn't there a famous museum?'

'The Guggenheim? Sure. You into museums, art, architecture and all that?'

'You're an engineer, aren't you?'

'The Guggenheim it is!' He unhooked a phone from the wall. 'The Guggenheim, please, driver.'

'He can't hear us?' she asked.

'Only on the phone, and he can't see us. No one can.' He rapped a knuckle on a dark window.

'We can see out but no one can see in?'

'Exactly!' He grinned and took her back into his arms.

The kisses were nice but his fingers started to work up under her sweater. At that rate, he'd be out of control long before their day out was done. Penny knew how to slow him down. She eased out of his embrace gradually, making it seem like a mutual decision.

'Thank you, Andrew,' she said in her most earnest voice.

'Thank me? What for?'

'For making me feel so safe. I haven't been comfortable to be all alone with a man for a very long time.'

He preened a little at her calling him a man. 'Something happened? Something bad?'

'I had just turned fifteen,' she said. 'Back home, the river, Ridge River, is gorgeous in the summer. It's got wide beaches. That's where the kids hang out. There's swimming and picnics and stuff by day. After sunset there's bonfires and weenie-roasts, sometimes a little beer, and the kids make out, just kissing and petting, nothing too heavy.'

'Sounds like fun.'

'It was, till that awful Sunday.'

'What happened?'

'You can pretty well guess, I expect. An older boy, a football star, Billy Blair, took me into the bushes. I was eager enough to go. I didn't know he'd had a few too many drinks. We kissed and fooled around some and it was fine by me, until he put his hand up my skirt. I told him "No!"

He didn't stop so I slapped his face. It got ugly. He was on top of me and my clothes were all ripped when some other guys heard my screams and came to rescue me.'

'Thank goodness!'

'They roughed him up some and I should have let it go at that but we went to the same school and he scared me. I told my folks. They pressed charges – attempted rape.'

'Well, it was, wasn't it?'

'Yes, but he didn't actually rape me. He didn't succeed. I mean, he didn't get his . . .' Penny's voice broke.

Andrew patted her shoulder. 'You don't have to tell me if it's hard.'

'There's not much more to tell. I wasn't the first girl he'd attacked. He was still on probation from the last time, so he went to jail and he never did graduate. His folks blamed me. We moved to Seattle. We thought it was all over until a few months ago, when he was released, "a ruined man", as he claimed. We started getting phone calls. Sometimes he shouts obscenities. Sometimes it's just heavy breathing. That's when Mom decided we had to move again.' Her face brightened. 'And here we are, thanks to you and your Dad!'

Andrew frowned. 'That's terrible, what happened to you, but at least it brought us together.'

'And now I'm safe, with you.'

His chest expanded. 'Absolutely!' Andrew sat back with a smug look on his face, just because, Penny imagined, he wasn't at all like Billy Blair.

At the Guggenheim, Penny listened dutifully as Andrew lectured her on Frank Lloyd Wright and his struggle to get his revolutionary design accepted and about the genius of his 'nautilus-inspired' construction. She got no more than a glance at any of the art but there'd be other days, now that she lived in New York.

The Guggenheim is close to Central Park. The day was fine enough for a picnic. Penny felt as if transported back to the nineteenth century, sitting on a rug, under a tree, with a wicker hamper full of expensive treats and sharing a split of champagne with a handsome boy. She closed her eyes and imagined herself in a flowing white dress, twirling a frilly parasol, and Andrew in a striped blazer and straw boater, reading Tennyson to her and getting a raging erection from a glimpse of her ankle.

She sometimes drifted into fantasy like that, if the man or boy she was with proved boring. Andrew's newly deferential attitude, his care not to touch her unless it was absolutely necessary, his lack of flirtation, was all her doing, of course. Her Mom called it 'man-guilt'. If a decent man is told about another man doing something evil to a woman, the decent one feels guilty, just because the brutish one was male. Men are silly.

Penny decided that although she didn't want Andrew climbing all over her again, not just yet, she'd had enough of him treating her as if she were his older and very plain sister.

She knew how to take care of that.

Back at the limo, she asked, 'May we keep the hamper in the back with us, Andrew? There's lots left and I might fancy a nibble later.'

'Sure.' Andrew asked her, 'What next? Broadway? Times Square?'

'I want to see *everything*, Andrew. Can't we just drive around New York with you pointing out the landmarks to me?'

Andrew grinned. 'Welcome to Andrew's Personal, Customised tour of New York City, Miss. On your right . . .'

For ten minutes Penny darted from side to side of the limo, peering out left, then right, then left again.

'Could we have the sunshine roof open, please Andrew?'

'Of course.' He pressed a button. The roof purred open.

Penny stood up, in the middle, facing the front, and rested her arms on the limo's roof. The car swayed around a corner. She let the sway move her and faked being about to tumble. Andrew, of course, grabbed her legs just above her knees to save her.

'Oops! Sorry!' he blurted.

'No. Thanks, Andrew. I could have fallen. I'd feel much safer with you holding me, just like that.'

His fresh grip was a fraction higher, just under her skirt. Penny wondered if he could see up it at all. He must have been tempted to slide his fingers higher but he resisted the lure of her skin, even if the balls of his thumbs did caress the backs of her thighs, subtly. Penny made sure to flex the muscles in her legs with each sway the limo made. Good boys should be rewarded.

She thought hard but there was no reasonable way to tempt him further without it being obvious. He was being very restrained. She couldn't even feel his breath on the backs of her legs, which she'd expected. It wasn't until well after five, when they'd driven through most of Manhattan, that a car in front braked hard, making their driver do the same. Penny used the lurch as an excuse to topple back on top of Andrew and to roll from his lap to the floor with her skirt twisted up high around her thighs.

He pulled her up, both laughing. She sat back on his lap and kissed him and even let him get a hand on her breast under her sweater. Andrew had educated fingers, considering his age. At first he touched her nipple as if in awe of it, which is always nice. When she allowed her excitement to show, his fondling became firmer, more urgent. Andrew, she decided, had the makings of an excellent lover. A girl could do a lot worse.

She wriggled more, bearing down, enjoying the rolling of his erection under her thigh and deliberately stoking both his lust and her own. His, she would take care of before the day was done. She'd have to endure her own until she was alone, or would she? Penny considered letting Andrew touch her between her legs but decided against it. It was too soon in their relationship and she doubted he had the skills to bring her to climax with just his fingers. Anyway, for now, orgasms were for her to give and for him to enjoy. The 'giver' of orgasms always has more power than the recipient.

She giggled into his mouth. If boys only knew what girls thought about while making out!

'What's funny?' he asked.

'Nothing. I'm just happy.'

The limo pulled over and stopped.

Andrew looked at his watch. 'It's six already. We must be at the restaurant.' He stood up to put his head through the roof. 'Yes, we're here, Penny. My Dad picked it. Is Thai food OK with you?'

'It's fine. Could I have my things from the trunk, please?'

Penny changed in the car while Andrew waited on the sidewalk. When she stepped out, alluring in a long black slub-silk hobble-tight skirt and matching jersey-knit off-the-shoulder top, his attempts to compliment her tripped on his stuttering tongue. Penny smiled and tottered ahead, into the Thai Delight Golden Garden.

A sweet little Thai girl served them green tea. Andrew asked Penny to order, as she'd eaten Thai food before and he hadn't. She chose deep fried tiger shrimp, papaya salad, curry fried rice and peanut red curry seafood, that he insisted they wanted 'extra hot'. Andrew's face was red and sweating before he was halfway through his curry. Penny called for a Singha Thai beer to cool his taste buds and a soothing dessert, mango and lychee sherbet.

During the meal, Penny had selected titbits to offer to Andrew's lips on her chopsticks and made sure to touch his hand frequently. She'd asked him about his courses and did he have his own digs or live in a dorm? Penny said it was such a shame that he'd be leaving in just a week, and she really meant that. Their relationship was blossoming. She didn't want Andrew to forget her and take up with some simpering little co-ed. He'd be a target, she knew. As he was taking extra degrees, he'd be older than most of the other young men. Add that relative maturity to him being athletic, handsome and having a rich Dad, and the girls would swarm him.

Penny had one week to get Andrew so obsessively infatuated with her that he'd be blind to the charms of all other girls. It was a fine line that she had to walk. If she took him to her bed, which she would have *really* enjoyed doing, he'd yearn for her less. Even the best sex can't be as good as it's anticipated to be by the fevered imagination of a celibate young man.

He *was* currently celibate, she was sure. It was even possible he was still a virgin. That was OK, by her.

Andrew said, 'The show Dad got us tickets for is called *Spamalot*. It's at the Shubert Theater, on West 44th Street. Have you heard of it?'

'Lovely! I'm a Python fan. Are you?'

'Python?'

'Monty Python?'

'Oh yes. I've heard of that. British, isn't it?'

Inwardly, Penny groaned. If he wasn't a Python fan, chances were, he wouldn't understand or enjoy the show. She was proved partly right. 'I'm Not Quite Dead' left him cold and puzzled. Penny rested a hand on his thigh in compensation for what he was enduring. Andrew perked up when The Lady of the Lake revealed her skimpy lingerie, as most of the men and many of the women in the audience, would have, Penny thought.

In the interval, he had a Molson Canadian lager and she had a Cosmopolitan, mainly because her Mom didn't like her to drink anything too sophisticated in public – bad for her image – so she was taking advantage of her mother's absence.

They were back in the limo by ten thirty-five. 'How long will it take us to get me home from here?' Penny asked.

'Half an hour, maybe forty minutes.'

'Oh. We don't *have* to be back before midnight, do we?'

He beamed. 'No.' Andrew picked up the phone. 'Through Central Park, please, driver. Take your time.'

Either the passion Penny'd inspired earlier was still hot in his blood or else the chorus line's lovelies had rekindled it, because his kisses were fierce and he didn't wait to take advantage of her off-the-shoulder neckline. He was a quick study. Obviously remembering her preferences from their tryst on the hotel's patio, he turned her to face away from him and worked both sides of her top down to her elbows, baring her delicate young breasts and trapping her arms. His teeth nibbled on her nape. His fingers teased and rolled her nipples until they were hard and then plucked at them in an urgent rhythm. Penny writhed without having to exaggerate her passion. Once again, she considered letting him fondle her between her legs but shook the temptation off. It isn't wise to let lust change a decision you'd made when you were calm.

When she judged it to be about eleven-thirty, she worked her hands back behind her to grope Andrew's cock through his pants. He groaned.

'Andrew,' she whispered. 'Let me go for a second, OK?'

She could feel his reluctance as he released her. Penny reached over to the hamper and opened it.

'You're hungry again?' Andrew asked in a hurt tone.

'No. Andrew, take your pants down, please?'

He asked, 'What?' but didn't hesitate to obey.

Penny turned to him with the pot of butter and a napkin from their picnic in her hands. 'I don't want to spoil your pants,' she explained.

He looked blank, and somewhat ridiculous with his pants around his knees. His expression changed when Penny smeared butter over the palm and fingers of her right hand. Her elbow nudged the tails of his shirt aside. Belatedly, Andrew shoved his underwear down to join his pants.

'Don't do a thing,' Penny told him. 'Just enjoy.' Her slippery hand closed around his shaft. She squeezed as her fingers slithered up to his cock's head and relaxed her grip as they slid down again. 'Is this good?' she asked.

Andrew nodded.

'Faster?'

He nodded again.

'Harder?'

He made a noise in his throat.

Penny pumped, not as hard or as fast as she imagined he'd have liked her to, prolonging the act. It was such a shame that she had to restrain herself. Her body yearned for his seed. It had been a very long time since she'd made love to a boy and even then, she hadn't 'gone all the way', as she'd wanted to. Most young women of her age were getting fucked on a regular basis. In a way, she envied them, but she'd chosen a different path, one that demanded strict discipline of her.

Andrew's legs straightened out in front of him. His thigh muscles bunched. He was making strangled noises. His hips rose and fell, fucking his cock through her fist.

'Please?' she asked. 'Do it for me, Andrew.' She cupped the napkin in place.

Andrew emitted something between a screech and a bellow. His cock throbbed in her hand and spurted a thick rope of liquid ivory into her napkin. Penny pumped some more, drawing out his after-shocks until his expression told her that pleasure was turning into discomfort.

The limo stopped. Penny stood up to look through the roof. 'We're here,' she announced. 'I'll go up and send your Dad down. You'd better be decent by then!'

Twelve

Rolf blinked awake, alone in Trixie's bed. He tried ordering his cock to twitch. It responded, even though it was limp. Good. He wasn't a young man any more and the orgasm Trixie'd given him had been spectacular. It was good to know he was still able to go more than one round in a day, provided he got a break in between.

The room was a bit brighter. The drapes were parted but the gauzy curtains weren't. Trixie's naked body was silhouetted, in profile, gently curved tummy, flaring bottom, slender at her waist, her breasts plump and pouty-nippled. She was on the phone with a martini in her free hand but put the phone down as soon as he saw her. By her body-language, she hadn't enjoyed the call.

'Problem?' he asked.

'No, Lover. The phone's on, at last, and would you believe it – my first damned call is a heavy breather.'

'Not a wrong number?'

She shrugged. Her breasts wobbled. Rolf's cock twitched again, by itself. Trixie said, 'I don't think so, but maybe you're right. I hope so.' She strode towards him like a predator, clicking on the three-inch heels of satin pom-pom slippers. 'Ready to torment me?'

As she came closer he could see that she was still wearing black hose, but different ones. This pair had narrower lace at the tops and didn't come quite so high up her thighs. She'd added a velvet choker with a little bow at her throat.

'I'm ready.'

She stopped close to the side of the bed, posed like a pin-up from a risqué magazine out of the 1940s.

Rolf inhaled musky perfume and talcum powder. 'You're gorgeous!' he blurted.

'Thank you.' She followed his gaze, down to her pubic mound, which was bald except for a tiny golden triangle of sleek fur. 'You like that?'

'Love it!' It was weird, considering that she'd already performed the most intimate and exciting erotic act on him that he'd ever experienced, but this was his first look at her sex. Its outer lips were puffy and a deeper pink than the surrounding skin. He got the impression that they'd be very sensitive. The only sign of her clitoral shaft was a delicate double-crease where her lips united just below the proud pout of her mound.

'It's all yours,' she promised, 'but you *did* promise me an extended teasing.'

'Until you beg for it,' he said, showing that he'd remembered her words. Rolf tossed the bedclothes back in invitation.

'Exactly,' she said. Trixie set her martini aside, turned and sat her dimpled bottom on the edge of the bed. For a moment she didn't move, allowing him to admire the slenderness of her waist and the dramatic curves of her hips. Rolf's hand lifted to touch her but she lay down and wriggled back to sit in his lap, 'spoons' style. Her left leg worked between his. Her right covered his right. Both of her legs moved, subtly, and her bottom wriggled against him. Rolf was intensely aware of the slithering rasp of nylon on his skin, and the slick smoothness of her bare thighs on his hairy ones. His cock responded, straightening and thickening, but her bottom's cheeks trapped it, uncomfortably bent. As if she understood, Trixie squirmed and released its shaft to spring up and press against her tailbone.

'Like this, please,' she said. She pulled his left hand down over her left shoulder and his right one around her side so that a warm plump breast nestled in each of his palms.

'We fit perfectly,' she said.

'As if we were made for each other.'

'I might wriggle, when you get me worked up.'

'I hope you do.' He nudged her with his cock.

Trixie giggled. 'I'm ready.'

Rolf lifted the index finger of his right hand to her lips. Trixie sucked on it and made saliva to wet it. He returned it to her breast, found the difference in texture between her areola and the skin surrounding it, and began to circle its rim, very lightly, very slowly.

'Cruel beast!' Her calves moved on his shins.

'True.' He returned the finger to her mouth for more spit and continued his torment but slowly spiralling in towards the jut of her nipple. His late wife had never been adventurous in bed but she'd adored having her breasts played with. Over the years of their marriage, he'd become quite adept.

Trixie was breathing more heavily, he thought, and she made tiny movements in his arms. He wasn't sure, but she might have been making soft noises with her mouth.

Trixie said, 'Mm.'

He rewarded her by wetting his finger again and smoothing its ball on the very peak of her nipple.

'Bastard!'

'Are you begging?'

'Enduring.'

He gave her nape a long lick and let his teeth close gently on the muscle at the side of her neck, where it joined her shoulder. She *definitely* shivered.

His right hand deserted her right breast to pull the sheet up over her left one. It was time for his left hand to play. His fingers located her nipple through the fine cotton but applied no pressure. With the utmost delicacy, he scratched her nipple's tip.

Trixie moaned and arched. 'I don't know how much of that I can stand!'

'We'll have to find out, won't we?'

'Sadist!'

'Masochist.'

'Harder, please?' There was a whine in her voice.

'Not till you beg.'

'Do I have to?'

'Yes.'

'Then I'm begging.'

Rolf made pincers with the thumbs and index fingers of both hands. Each took a sheet-covered nipple gently by its base and scratched it slowly, from flared base to round-pointed tip.

'That's even worse, you bastard!'

'Really?' He repeated his action.

She writhed against his lap, growing frantic. 'You know what I want! Please, Rolf! Please? I'm begging, damn you!'

Simultaneously, he sank his teeth into her shoulder, pinched hard, and rolled her nipples. Trixie yelped. For a moment he thought he might have misinterpreted her needs but her bottom thrust back at him and she hissed a long, ecstatic, 'Yesssss!'

His fingers increased their pressure. Trixie jerked and juddered and sobbed. Her feet hooked behind his calves as she hitched forward and down, splaying the inner lips of her wet sex on the hardness of his thigh. His arms pushed her down and his leg pressed up. His fingers were unrelenting. She ground and ground and ground against his leg, making desperate little mewing sounds until she let out a great gasp and a shiver, and slumped.

Rolf let Trixie rest, panting, in his arms.

Eventually, she murmured, 'It's been a long time, Rolf.'

'Don't you – er – do it yourself?'

'Of course, but it's not the same.'

'I know.'

She wriggled in his lap. 'We don't have to do it for ourselves any more, do we Rolf?'

'No. Not any more, not now we have each other.'

'Unless we do it *to* each other, or *with* each other, *watching* each other.'

The idea of it clenched Rolf's gut. All his life, his masturbation had been his dirty little secret, always denied, never shared. Now this intoxicating woman was suggesting they do it together, watching each other. If they did, they'd be revealing themselves in a way he'd never even considered.

Her hand reached back to hold his shaft. She shifted up the bed and guided his dome towards her sopping sex.

'Not yet,' he said. Rolf had only performed cunnilingus twice in his entire life. Once had been on a skinny girl in college, at a party, in a closet that smelled of wet wool and rubber boots. He'd never known her name. The second time had been with his wife, Rachel, on their tenth anniversary, when she'd got tipsier than usual. She'd never let him do it again, perhaps because she feared he'd expect her to reciprocate on a regular basis, not just as special and rare treats. All those years, he'd wanted to please a woman with his tongue. Now, at last, he was in bed with one who he was absolutely certain wouldn't object.

Rolf moved back away from Trixie and tossed the bedclothes aside. Rachel would have snatched them back to cover her nakedness. Trixie just rolled onto her back, hands linked behind her head, thighs spread wide, proudly naked, and asked him, 'What did you have in mind, Lover?'

'This.' He reared over her, propped on arms that bracketed her lovely body. Rolf's head dipped to bring his mouth to hers. She, surrendering, didn't wrap her arms around him, as another woman might have. She left her hands under her head, letting him know that she was his toy.

He nibbled her lips, delved into her mouth, sucked saliva from under her tongue. She kissed him back but the only parts of her that moved were her lips and tongue. His mouth grazed from the corner of her mouth, across her cheek, down the side of her neck and over the swell of her milk-skinned left breast. Rolf's lips and tongue nibbled and licked at her stiff nipple, no teeth, in case she was still tender from his earlier cruelty.

From left nipple, back to her mouth, trailing down once more to her right one. His hand cupped her sex. One finger curled, parting and entering her. Trixie moved, just a fraction, lifting herself to him.

His tongue's tip traced the lines of her ribcage. He inched lower. When his tongue explored her navel, Trixie trembled. He smoothed his cheek against the bulge of her mound, brushing his skin with the soft golden triangle of her pelt. Trixie held her breath. Her thighs strained further apart. Her hips tilted. Her voice wasn't begging him but her body was.

Rolf made tight little circles with the finger that was inside her, dabbling in her wetness. He slid down even further, to rest his face on the firm smoothness of the inside of her thigh.

'Are you sure you want to do that?' Trixie asked, with a tremor in her voice.

'*Very* sure.'

'My late husband – he didn't like to . . .'

Rolf thought, 'What a fool,' but he said, '*I* do.'

He inhaled, sucking in her fragrance. There was a hint of the perfume she was wearing, something with mimosa, he thought, and under that, her own wet scent, sweet and heady, newly-mown dewy grass, with traces of bonfire smoke and of the decadent aroma that a white truffle releases if you break it between your fingers.

Her right kneecap was beneath his left hand. He caressed it, enjoying the glossy hardness under raspy nylon. He withdrew his right index finger from inside her and sucked her nectar from it.

'How do I taste?' she asked lightly but with an underlying concern.

'Delicious.' His finger dipped into her once more and then lifted up to her lips. 'Try some.' He wasn't sure how she'd react to being invited to sample her own juices but took perverse pleasure in testing the depths of her depravity.

She sucked with relish and declared, 'Nice, very nice, but I still prefer your come, Rolf. It's fuller-bodied.'

No clever response came to him so he let his tongue run the length of her sex's right lip from bottom to top.

Trixie gasped, 'Oh God!'

He trilled the tip of his tongue in the slit between her lips.

'Yes, yes, yes.'

Rolf's tongue probed, moving from side to side, parting her. He lifted his head and gazed down, down into the livid wet pink gash between her swollen purple-tinged lips. Two fingers spread her, exposing the delicious intricacies inside her sex. Rolf's mouth watered. Once again testing Trixie's depravity, he spat into her. She gasped, in a way he thought indicated pleasure. Maybe he'd impressed her with his inventiveness?

Rolf watched in fascination as his spittle ran and mingled with her own wetness, in her depths.

Trixie moaned, 'Touch me.'

His mouth descended, pressing its lips to the lips of her sex and spreading them wider. Pressing down hard to work his mouth as deeply into her as he could, he extended his tongue and lapped, left and right, up and down, savouring her juices.

Trixie made a soft mewing noise and pushed up at him. Now, her hands left her head and came down to bury their fingers in his hair. Rolf's face moved from side to side, extending the range of his tongue's explorations. When it delved into the delicate cup at the base of Trixie's slot, his nose was enveloped by her lips. Every breath he took was redolent with her essence.

He flattened his tongue and drew it up the full length of her slit, up over the smooth hardness of her pubic bone. His lips found the delicacy they sought, the tiny pink pea of her clitoris, and gripped it. Trixie gasped and froze. Rolf waited for a teasing count of ten before he gave the sensitive nub a forceful lick.

She gasped, 'Yes!'

Encouraged, Rolf worked two fingers up inside her, behind her bone, and fumbled for the area he'd read about but had never had the opportunity to find. As he'd learned, it was round and puffy and slick and felt as if covered in tiny bumps. He palpitated it in an urgent rhythm and matched the pace with flicks on her clitoris with his tongue.

Trixie gasped, 'Lover!' Her thighs strained apart. One of her hands deserted his head. His eyes rolled upwards to peer over the slight swell of her heaving belly. She was pinching and twisting one nipple, then the other, then back, with vicious urgency. Rolf made a mental note.

Her breath came faster, and faster. Rolf's tongue and fingers quickened their pace. She rose up in a taut bow, onto shoulders and heels, lifting half of Rolf's considerable weight with her. Her internal muscles contracted on his fingers. The noises that bubbled from her throat weren't words but they didn't have to be for him to understand her.

With an enormous effort of will, Rolf stopped.

'Bastard, bastard, bastard! Fucking, fucking bastard! Do me, fuck you! Let me *come!*'

He waited.

Trixie babbled, 'I'm sorry, Rolf, dear sweet wonderful Rolf. Please, please, pretty please? I'll do anything you like, just let me come. I'll be your slave. Anyway you want me, anything you want me to do, anything you want to do to me, *anything*, just do more of those wonderful things you were doing and let me come, please?'

Relenting, he licked again, and rubbed again, harder and faster, urging her. His free hand left her knee and reached up to a breast to pinch and tug at a throbbing nipple, knowing he hurt her and knowing that the pain was lancing to her clitoris in spears of exquisite pleasure.

Her thighs twisted under him. Her calves folded inwards. Her stockinged heels drummed on his shoulder blades. The fingers and thumb of his right hand closed into his palm. When he felt her insides begin to contract once again, he pushed and screwed, filling her sex with his fingers as deep as their second knuckles.

Trixie screamed. Perhaps he'd misjudged her needs and had really hurt her? But no, her muscles clamped on his hand, almost crushing it, and suddenly his fingers were bathed in a hot flood.

She slumped, legs flung wide. Rolf carefully worked his hand from her clinging flesh and planted a gentle kiss on her sex's lips. She twitched, from head to toe, and groaned.

'Not yet,' she begged. 'You totally destroyed me, you

wonderful man. Nobody, nobody, has ever fucked me like that before. That was incredible, Lover.'

Rolf lifted his head. 'I haven't fucked you, yet.'

'Yes you have, just not with your cock. I'd like that now, if you don't mind, Lover? Your hard cock – my soft wet pussy – they're made for each other, aren't they?'

'We'll just have to find out, Trixie. Are you ready?'

'Yes, darling. I'm ready for you now.'

He lifted himself up the bed and over her, on elbows and knees. 'Look into my eyes,' he said. Holding her gaze, he lowered his hips. Her fingers wrapped his shaft and drew it towards the heat and wet and softness between her thighs.

'Carefully at first, please?' she asked him. 'After all, you are rather big.'

Three hours later, they shared a shower and the pleasure he took from soaping her body was gentle and affectionate. There was no lust left in him, not even when she lathered his cock. Trixie had sandwiches from the delicatessen in her fridge. In robes, they ate companionably. He sipped a martini. She drank three. After, they dressed and chatted and flirted and she had another martini. Rolf was just beginning to feel he might be persuaded back into Trixie's bed when a chime sounded.

Trixie checked a clock. 'That's Penny already,' she said. 'She has a key but I asked her to buzz up, to warn us.'

'She's a good girl,' he said.

'Yes she is, thanks. She's very fond of you, you know.'

'But fonder of my son.'

Trixie didn't respond to that.

Thirteen

At nine the next morning, Andrew wanted to phone Penny.
Rolf explained that it wasn't polite to make social phone
calls before ten, and if a man has kept a woman out till
midnight, not until after lunch. Andrew decided that
twelve-thirty was close enough to 'after lunch'. All he got
was Trixie's machine.

Rolf tried the number at two and four. Andrew had used
up one and three. By six, each man was wondering if he'd
done or said something to offend his lady but neither
father nor son confided that to the other.

At seven, Rolf phoned out for a pizza. He and Andrew
had just pushed the empty box aside and opened their
second beer each when the phone rang. Andrew beat Rolf
to it.

'It's for you, Dad.' He covered the mouthpiece with his
hand and stage-whispered, 'It's *her*.'

Rolf took the phone. 'Trixie?'

'Hi, Lover. Got your messages.'

Rolf wanted to ask where she and Penny had been all
day but that would have sounded both needy and possess-
ive, so he just waited.

She continued, 'You drained me yesterday, Stud. I
turned the phone's ringer off so I could sleep in some and
recover, and I didn't wake up till after noon. Then, of
course, I didn't think to turn the phone back on till just
now, when Penny wondered why you men hadn't called
us.'

'Well, we had, of course.'

Trixie's voice changed, as if she was cupping the phone and whispering. 'You were *fantastic*, Rolf.'

Not looking at Andrew, who was hovering, Rolf replied, 'Ditto.'

'Not alone?'

'No.'

'Shame. We could have had phone sex. Would you like me to talk dirty to you, Rolf?'

He twisted to one side in his chair in case his growing erection was showing. 'That'd be nice.'

'I wish your cock was in my mouth right now, all hard and hot and throbbing.'

'Me too.'

'Is it awkward for you?'

'Very.'

'Then we'll save it. Can you call me later, say about half an hour after midnight? Penny should be in bed by then. So will I, most likely *naked*, unless I decide to wear something naughty.'

'That sounds fine.'

'It will be, I promise.'

Andrew, who'd been jittering, couldn't wait any longer. He interrupted with, 'Can I talk to Penny, please, Dad?'

'Just a minute.' Into the phone, Rolf said, 'Are you busy tomorrow, Trixie?'

'Sorry, Lover, but yes. You know how it is when you move, particularly if it's to a new state. We have to see that nice banker of yours and arrange an account for Penny and I'll have to sign things, then there's the changes of address, drivers' licences, insurance, all those boring chores.'

'Evening?' he suggested.

'We'll be exhausted, no fun at all.'

'Even exhausted, you'd be fun, Trixie. I could be happy just watching you sleep.' Rolf realised that Andrew had heard that and scowled. Andrew turned away as if he hadn't caught a word.

Trixie asked, 'How about the next day? If you two were to come over right after lunch and bring your swim-things, there's a pool in the building that hardly ever gets used. We could make an afternoon and evening of it.'

'Minute.' Rolf turned to Andrew. 'You OK for a swimming date, the day after tomorrow?'

'Of course. What about tomorrow?'

'They're busy.'

'Let me talk to Penny, *please?*'

'Hold on. Trixie, we're good for Thursday. I'll call you back, er, later, as you suggested. Can Andrew talk to Penny now?'

He passed the phone to his son and went to pour himself a Johnny Walker Gold. The prospect of two dates with Trixie called for a more celebratory drink than mere beer, even if one of the dates was to be by phone. Even so, while he was mentally picturing Trixie's mature lushness, naked, he couldn't help but wonder how revealing Penny's bikini would be.

They had two phone lines that connected with every phone. Lights came on to show if a line was in use. Just in case, once Andrew came off the line, Rolf sneaked into Andrew's room and unplugged his phone. He didn't want his son to be woken by a tell-tale light and he *certainly* didn't want Andrew listening in on the sort of conversation he was expecting to have with Trixie.

He and Andrew watched TV together. Rolf allowed Andrew two scotches, 'To celebrate – whatever.' Scotch was likely to make the boy sleepy. At eleven, Rolf announced, 'I think I'll take a shower.'

'You had one this morning.'

'Well, now I'm going to take another.'

Fresh from his shower, Rolf checked the living room. Andrew wasn't there. Good. He was likely in bed and asleep already. Padding noiselessly on bare feet, Rolf went to his bedroom and closed the door. He went to bed naked, with a box of tissues on the nightstand beside him.

Not to seem too eager, he waited until twelve thirty-three before he punched 'one' on his speed-dial. Rolf counted eight rings before Trixie picked up. Her drawled 'Hello' was like velvet being drawn across the nape of his neck.

'Hi!'

'Hi yourself. All alone, in bed?'

'Yes. You?'

'Yes. Wearing?'

'Me? Nothing at all.'

'I am – wearing something.'

Rolf swallowed. 'What?'

'Black stay-up nylons. You like those, don't you?'

'Oh yes, very much.'

'And that black choker.'

'Lovely.'

'And a waspie.'

'A what?' he asked, though he was pretty sure he knew what a waspie was.

'Like a corset, but briefer – no bra part and it doesn't go down so low.'

He said, 'I wish I were there.'

'Me too, Rolf, but you're not, and that can have advantages.'

'I don't understand.'

'Rolf, before we go on, I'd like to get something straight.'

'What?'

'Phone sex – it's fantasy. That means that we can do things over the phone that we wouldn't really do, if you were here, right?'

'I understand.'

'Good. I wouldn't want you to think, just because I talk about them over the phone, that I'd really do all the things I describe. In fantasy, there are no limits, no inhibitions, OK?'

'Of course. Is your waspie real or just part of the fantasy?'

'It's real. You'll see it, someday.'

'I look forward to that. You were going to describe it?'

Trixie's voice became deeper and huskier. 'It goes from just under my bust, down almost to my navel.'

'Pretty navel,' Rolf interrupted.

'Thanks. It's made of leather, vertical red and black

stripes, and it's very stiff, very constricting. It pinches my waist – makes it very small. Do you like that, Rolf?'

He had to clear his throat before he said, 'Yes.'

'My maid, Yvette, pulled it so tight I can hardly breathe.'

Rolf flashed back to an erotic drawing another student had shown him, back in university, of a French Maid in a short-skirted uniform, her knee in her Mistress's back, tugging on the strings of a corset. He croaked, 'Yvette?'

'She's fantasy, Rolf. I don't *really* have a maid to dress and undress me.'

'Of course not. I understood that.'

'Shall I tell you about her?'

'If you like.'

'She's half French, half Vietnamese, slender and supple, with waist-length black hair and sloe-eyes. She's young, just about Penny's age, but totally depraved. I bought her from the Madame of a brothel in Tangiers, where she was the star attraction.' Trixie chuckled. 'How do you like her so far, Rolf?'

'Lovely, but she's nowhere near as attractive as her Mistress.'

'Thank you, kind Sir. Oh – one other thing – she's very flexible. Yvonne can eat her own pussy.'

'Really?'

'That's rare, Rolf. I've tried but I can't bend enough.'

'You've *tried?* Is that for real, or imagination?'

'For real. A woman has needs, Rolf, and it's been lonely for me since my husband passed on. There's only so much a vibrator can do.'

'Vibrator?' he prompted.

'Every widow's best friend. Mine's a "classic" – a nine-inch smooth ivory cylinder. I got it from a mail order catalogue. I wouldn't dare go into one of *those* stores.'

'I see.'

'He's here in bed with me, Rolf.' She giggled. 'Want to say hello?'

Rolf said, 'Hello,' and heard a buzzing response.

'He's not jealous, Rolf. He knows you're better than him in bed but he doesn't mind.'

'Big of him.'

'You're better. You aren't jealous of him, are you Rolf? You wouldn't mind watching while he made love to me?'

'No, of course not.' He thought for a moment. 'I think I'd enjoy that,' he confessed.

'And I'd enjoy watching you stroke yourself. Are you doing that, Rolf?'

'Not yet.'

'Please do. I'd love to be there, watching you, watching those big strong fingers lovingly stroking that lovely hard smooth cock of yours. You *will* let me watch, one day, won't you? I want to learn how you like to do it, so I can do it the same way for you.'

'You do it just fine,' he said.

'Are you doing it now?'

'Yes.'

'Would you like to know what we're doing?'

'We?'

'Me and Yvette, remember?'

'Of course. Your exotic young maid. I'd almost forgotten her. What are you two naughty girls up to?'

'I'm lying on my bed, in my waspie, on my back. Yvette is leaning over me. Her head is moving to and fro, stroking my bare skin with the tips of her silky black hair. She's naked. Her breasts are quite tiny, with sharp little nipples. I'm pinching one right now. She likes that.'

'Like you do.'

'Don't interrupt.'

'Sorry.'

'No, I'm sorry. Can I carry on?'

'Please.'

'I'm pulling her down by her nipple, bringing her mouth down to my breast. Her lips are on my nipple, sucking hard, *very* hard, like I'm her mother and she's suckling.' Trixie paused. 'Are you stroking yourself, Rolf?'

'Yes.'

'Yvette is so bad, she'll do absolutely *anything* for me. She will for you, too. You'd like that, wouldn't you, Rolf, being in bed with both of us, me telling Yvette what to do to you.'

84

'All I need in bed is you, Trixie. You're more than enough for any man.'

'But you've thought about being in bed with two women, haven't you. All men do. Have you ever done that, in real life?'

He confessed, 'No.'

'Me neither, with two men. I don't even fantasise about that.'

'What *do* you fantasise about, when you . . .?'

'Masturbate? A big strong masterful man, like you, Rolf. In fact, it's always been about you, ever since the night we met.'

'Really?'

'Really – and Yvette, sometimes. She's sort of my alter-ego, who does the things I wouldn't do, for me. She's a dirty little girl, Rolf, the kind men dream of fucking.' Trixie paused. 'You don't mind me saying that word do you, Rolf? "Fucking?"'

'No, not in our fantasy, I don't.'

'How about "pussy?"'

'No, I don't mind.'

'"Cunt"?'

'I . . .'

'I'm pushing Yvette's face down, Rolf. Eat my cunt, you nasty little bitch!' In a conversational tone, Trixie asked, 'Did that offend you, Rolf?'

'That's the language she understands, right?'

'Exactly. I knew you'd get it. Rolf?'

'Yes?'

'When I'm bad, really bad, will you use that sort of language to me?'

'Like "cunt"?'

'And "bitch", and "slut".'

'Would you like me to?'

'Yes.'

'Then I will.'

'Thank you.' Trixie gave a little sigh. 'My slut, Yvette, has her tongue in my cunt, Rolf. She's slurping away – can't get enough of my juices. You're still stroking yourself?'

'Yes.'

'Is there anything you'd like Yvette to do to me, for you to watch?'

'Such as?'

'Don't be shy, Rolf. Such as I roll over and have her work that long pointy tongue of hers up my tight little bum-hole. Would you like that?'

Rolf managed to get a 'Yes' out. Trixie was amazing. He'd never dreamed that a real woman could be so uninhibited. His fist tightened on his cock and pumped faster.

'Oh yes,' Trixie continued, 'lick my bum-hole, you bitch! Work that nasty tongue of yours deep into me. Tongue-fuck my bum! She's so bad, Rolf. The more I degrade her, the more she likes it. Would *you* like to degrade her?'

'How?'

'Ever bugger a woman, Rolf? Ever shoved that big hard cock of yours up a young girl's tight little rear and fucked her till she screams? Ever *made* her take it?'

The 'young' threw him for a moment but he managed, 'Um – no.'

'Then now's your chance. Yvette's kneeling up behind me, licking my bum-hole, with her bottom up in the air, ready for you. Fuck her bum, Rolf. Force your way into her. Sodomise the nasty little slut!'

Rolf heard Trixie's vibrator buzzing again, loud and then muted, as if it'd been muffled by her flesh. Her own dirty talk had to be getting to Trixie. He could see her in his imagination, likely on all fours to fit her fantasy, with her vibrator in her hand, pumping it into herself, into her *cunt*, as she would say.

She'd done all the talking, so far. He owed it to her to contribute.

'I'm kneeling up behind Yvette, Trixie. I'm spreading the cheeks of her bum. I can see her hole. It's too small, but I'll make it take me, all of me.' He made a spitting sound. 'Hear that? I've spat on it, Trixie. Now I'm putting my cock to it. I'm forcing it, Trixie. It's *so* tight, but it's stretching.'

'Make her take it, Rolf. You know the bitch wants it.'

'I'm in, and I'm fucking her.'

'And she's licking my bum-hole and fingering my cunt, Rolf. She's working her whole hand into me. Oh fuck! She's fisting me! Good job she's got small hands, Lover. If you ever did this to me, it'd be devastating. Fuck her hard, Rolf!'

'I am!'

'And I'm – and I'm . . .' She squealed and sighed.

Rolf let the climax he'd been holding back flow. Too late, he remembered the box of tissues by his bedside. Oh well! He'd change the sheets before Mrs Chow, his cleaning lady, came on Friday.

'Did you?' Trixie asked.

'Yes. You?'

'Yes, thank you, Rolf.'

'Trixie?'

'Yes?'

'How much of that was fantasy, that you'd never really do, and how much was fantasy that you *would* do, under the right circumstances, with the right man?'

'A woman is entitled to her secrets, Rolf. Goodnight, dream lover.'

Her phone clicked off, twice. Rolf wondered why, for just a moment, before he drifted into sated sleep.

Fourteen

Rolf knuckled the door to the women's apartment. It swung open.

Trixie called from what sounded like a couple of rooms away. 'Come on in you two! We're just getting ready for you.'

Rolf and Andrew lugged the picnic hamper into the dining room and started to unpack it. They had the table pretty well covered when Trixie and Penny emerged from the main bathroom wearing skimpy but opaque wraps and raffia wedgie sandals.

Penny clapped her hands to her face and squealed, 'Oh my God! Are you feeding us all for a week?'

'I wish,' Andrew said.

Trixie checked the label on a quart of Tanqueray. 'Sorry to keep you two waiting but we had to decide which swimsuits to wear, "for your viewing pleasure".'

'I'm sure it'll prove worth the wait,' Rolf said.

'We do our best.'

Andrew asked, 'You have a lot of swimsuits?'

Penny grinned. 'You know how some women are with shoes? That's how my Mom and me are with swimsuits. No matter how many we have, we always want more.'

Rolf tore his eyes away from Penny's long slim legs, hoping that Trixie hadn't noticed that he'd been staring at her daughter's thighs. 'I'd be very happy to take you ladies on a shopping expedition, someday. There must be a hundred places to buy bikinis in town.'

Andrew jumped in with, 'Count me in.'

'You'll be at university, my boy, sorry.'

His son scowled.

'Do we get changed down at the pool?' Rolf asked.

'No. Use our bathrooms,' Trixie offered. 'That'll give me time for a little drinkie before we go down.'

'*Mother!*'

'Just to warm me up, in case the water's cold.'

Rolf and Andrew changed quickly and came out in the terry robes they'd brought with them and flip-flops.

Trixie greeted them with, 'As there's hardly ever anyone at the pool, we thought you men wouldn't mind if our swimsuits were a teeny bit more daring than we'd usually appear in, in public.'

Rolf swallowed. The swimwear they'd worn at the resort had been pretty daring, by his standards. He asked, 'They don't allow nude bathing in this building by any chance?'

'Naughty!' Trixie scolded. 'Where'd the mystery be in that?'

They split up at the entrances to the pool, the men going through the men's locker room and the women through the women's. Rolf wasn't the least surprised that he and his son emerged at the pool before the women did. The men made for the deep end.

Andrew suggested, 'Race?' and dived in.

Rolf followed him in under half a second. They were close enough reaching the other end that both could claim to be the winner. Andrew won the second race but by no more than an arm's stretch.

Rolf asked, 'Best of three?'

Andrew began, 'In that case, I've already . . .' but the women arrived and the rivalry became irrelevant.

They still had their wraps on. As if it were choreographed, they tossed them aside and posed, obviously waiting for the applause that the puzzled men gave them. Where was the 'more daring than they'd usually appear in, in public'? Each was wearing a simple one-piece. The men climbed out of the pool for closer looks.

Trixie's 'more daring' became apparent. Her halter-neck suit with French-cut legs alternated vertical stripes, black-on-black. Seen closer, half the stripes were narrow, about an inch and a half wide, with a glossy satin finish, but the other, wider, two and a half-inch stripes were made of a very fine mesh, as transparent as black nylon hose. The stripes that barely covered her nipples and her sex were opaque, but Rolf couldn't help but wonder what would happen if she were to twist or turn, moving her body under the fabric. Even immobile, the effect was deliciously erotic. As she'd suggested in her apartment, mystery can be much sexier than nudity.

Whatever it was that was specially daring about Penny's suit, also halter-neck and with equally high-cut legs, stumped Rolf. It was very glitzy, with alternating diamonds of gold lamé and of some plain white fabric, perhaps silk, but it wasn't dramatically revealing.

'You both look gorgeous,' Rolf said.

'Super hot,' Andrew agreed.

Penny smiled knowingly. 'You'll see.' She ran to the deep end, up onto the single diving board, and executed a perfect long flat dive.

Trixie jumped into the shallow end with a squeal. Penny raced in a fast crawl to join her. Andrew looked at his Dad, shrugged, and jumped in. Rolf followed.

Penny stood up, with the water barely up to her hips, and posed again. The white diamonds had turned so transparent that they were virtually invisible. Like Trixie's satin stripes, the gold diamonds covered the more intimate parts of her anatomy, but only just, and even if the subtle curves of a young breast aren't quite as exciting to a man as a naked nipple, they are still powerfully erotic. The crease of a groin isn't the same as a bare pussy, but . . .

Rolf realised that he'd been staring at Penny too hard for too long and turned to Trixie.

She said, 'I'm going to try the whirlpool.' She started to heave herself onto the side but seemed to find it a struggle.

Rolf helped, boosting her with one hand on the cool flesh of each half-bare cheek of her bottom. By the time she was kneeling on the side, his erection was fighting the fabric of his Speedo. Somehow, he clambered out of the water with one hand concealing his lust.

Behind him, he heard Andrew challenge Penny to a race, the show-off! Relieved that the youngsters were too busy to notice his embarrassing bulge, he joined Trixie in the lightly steaming water.

'Can you push the button?' she asked.

He found it beside the railings of the steps. When he thumbed it, the water roiled from the thrusts of a dozen powerful underwater jets. Trixie made for the nearest one and sat on the ledge beneath it. Rolf joined her.

'Sit by a jet,' she told him. 'It feels wonderful on your back.'

'I'd rather sit by you, Trixie.'

'Sweet.' Her hand found his thigh under the water.

Rolf twisted and craned. The kids were splashing around in the deep end. He ducked down enough that they wouldn't be able to see him and turned to kiss Trixie.

When they parted for air, she asked, 'Do you still respect me, Rolf?'

'Respect you? Of course I do. Why do you ask?'

'On the phone? I was pretty raunchy.'

'So was I. I guess we're two of a kind, Trixie.'

She leaned close and whispered, 'Randy as teens but with the know-how they lack, right?'

He grinned and cupped her right breast.

'You like me to be naughty, don't you, Rolf?'

'Of course.'

'I'm going to be naughty right now.'

'You are?'

'Keep an eye on those two for me. Warn me if they head this way.'

Rolf turned. Kneeling on the ledge raised his head and shoulders above the edge of the whirlpool. 'I'm watching them. 'Now what?'

Trixie joined him, kneeling on the ledge. A big grin spread across her face. He didn't understand why until he looked down through the water. Trixie had spread her knees far apart, bringing her sex lower and just a few

91

inches from the throbbing water-jet's outlet. The crafty little minx was being masturbated by it.

Remembering what she'd told him she liked, he leaned closer and whispered, 'You little slut!'

'I am, aren't I. Want to help?

'How?'

She worked three fingers under the crotch of her swimsuit and pulled it aside. Rolf was fascinated. The pulsating jet was fluttering the lips of her pussy. No wonder she was grinning. The water had to be penetrating her at the same time as it beat on her clitoris.

'Hold me open,' she said, 'but don't block the flow.'

It took him a moment to understand. He reached down with one hand, laid two fingers together between her pussy's lips, then spread them wide, opening her sex up and further exposing her clit.

'That's *so* good,' she gritted out. 'You're so much fun, Lover.' She stretched a hand out towards him, to the waist of his Speedo, and shoved it down. Rolf gulped. It was a public place and their kids were fooling around not a hundred feet away. Still, he reasoned, no one could see and if anyone came close, he and Trixie could be decent in seconds.

Her fist closed around his shaft. Her eyes misted, as if she were intent on the sensations she was enjoying. She pumped him, hard and fast for half a dozen strokes, then gently and slowly for half a dozen more. Her fingers tightened on him, and tightened more, as if she was intent on strangling his cock. Rolf thought of complaining but the expression on her face was so rapturous that he couldn't bring himself to spoil the moment for her.

She said, 'Oh fuck!' and slumped.

Rolf thought she would have slid underwater if it hadn't been for her grip on his shaft.

After a while, she told him, 'That was *so* nice. Your turn, Lover.'

'My turn?'

'Try it. Here.' She shimmied over, pulling him after her.

It wasn't easy, getting his cock to the same level her pussy had been at, but with her encouragement, he managed. She pointed the eye of his cock directly into the pulsating stream of water. It was nice, but men aren't built the same as women. A clit is far more sensitive than the head of a cock. The vibrations would never have taken him to climax, but the way she was stroking him at the same time would have, and that moment was getting very close. Rolf was in conflicted torment. His cock was desperate but his conscience would never forgive him if he climaxed in a public pool.

He was still struggling with the dilemma when Trixie said, 'Oops!' and yanked his Speedo back up over his straining shaft. 'The kids. They're coming.'

Rolf timed it very carefully, so that as Penny got in, he was climbing out, with his back to her. There was no other way to hide his erection. He executed a long flat dive into the shallow end, against the posted rules. Rolf really *needed* cool water to flow around his cock. An icy shower would have been even better.

He'd swum ten vigorous lengths and his cock was beginning to soften when he found Trixie swimming beside him.

She gave him a wry smile. 'Another few minutes and you'd have been there, huh?'

'That would have done it,' he agreed. 'The kids?'

'Still in the whirlpool.'

'They'll be all right in there?'

'I'm sure they won't be doing anything we wouldn't do.'

'Or that we would, I hope.'

'They'll be necking, no more, except maybe a little fondling. Nothing serious. I trust my Penny. Rolf?'

'Yes, Trixie?'

'If you were to hang onto the side, I could finish off what I started. I hate to think of you suffering.'

He shook his head. 'I'll be OK. I couldn't enjoy it, wondering if we'd be interrupted at any moment.' Rolf couldn't reveal his real reason, because he didn't want to pollute the pool. Trixie'd likely think he was being silly.

'Maybe later?' she asked him.

'Maybe. I can wait.'

93

'Tough guy, huh?' She eeled away and down to the bottom of the pool, to reverse and shoot up like a dolphin, so close to Rolf's body that her fingers trailed up his legs and over the front of his trunks.

'You're a terrible tease, Trixie.'

'Yes, but I always deliver in the end, and you *love* to be teased, don't you.'

He grinned. 'Lust feeds on lust, doesn't it.'

'True. The more you want me, the more I want you, and vice-versa. That's the way it works.'

'Then you must be horny as hell right now, Trixie, because I want you so badly, it's agony.'

'Poor Rolf. The minute we're alone, I'm yours, anyway you want me.'

He glanced towards the whirlpool. 'But we've got the kids.'

'Yours will be away at university next week.'

'Can we find some course or something for Penny to take?'

'We're awful, Rolf, wishing our kids away.'

'Yes, we are. We'll find a way to be alone, Trixie. Love can't be denied.'

Her eyebrow lifted. 'Love? I thought we were talking about raw lust.'

'Lust, for sure, but you've come to mean a lot to me, apart from that, Trixie.'

'I don't want to trap you with my "feminine wiles".'

'But I want to be trapped.'

'Are you sure?'

He paused a moment before saying, 'Sure I'm sure.'

She cocked her head on one side and gave him a sadly considering look before turning and swimming away from him. Rolf cursed himself. His hesitation had hurt her feelings, he thought, and she was the last woman on earth that he wanted to hurt. How to make it up to her? He knew, of course, but acknowledging what he knew was hard. Somehow, he had to show her that he had genuine feelings for her, apart from lusting after her body. That'd mean holding back on the physical side of their relationship while still showing her lots of affection.

He could do that, he decided. Of course he could.

Rolf swam for another introspective half hour, planning how to 'make nice' to Trixie, before he realised she wasn't in the pool with him. Hell! *That* wouldn't go down well.

He found her back in the whirlpool with Andrew and Penny.

Trixie said, 'I've had enough. I think I'll go up.'

Fearful that she was avoiding him, Rolf said, 'Me too.'

Simultaneously, Andrew said, 'Not me,' and Penny said, 'I'm coming too.' Andrew pouted. 'Well, I don't want to stay down here all alone.'

It was a little awkward, riding up in the elevator. Back in the apartment, the women seemed in no hurry to get changed out of their swim things, so the men took the lead. Rolf busied himself with the food he'd brought, opening pots of pâté, unwrapping cheeses, cutting the pie and the cake. Trixie mixed martinis. As they nibbled and sipped, the atmosphere defrosted, or so it seemed to Rolf. Perhaps the coolness had been in his imagination.

Penny suggested, 'Scrabble?'

'Not in these clothes,' Trixie said. 'Let's all go get dressed first.'

When the men emerged from the bathrooms, the women were already waiting, to Rolf's surprise. Penny was in Capris, with a cropped top that left just a four-inch band of her svelte torso bare, innocently sexy, unlike her mother. Trixie had changed into a brief blue polka-dot sundress with what would have been a modestly high Peter Pan collar, if it hadn't been unbuttoned to deep between her braless breasts.

They sat boy-girl-boy-girl around the card table. Trixie sorted her tiles with one hand and rested the other on Rolf's thigh. It seemed he was forgiven, if he *had* offended her. Perhaps he'd imagined it. Perhaps her warmth had returned as a result of the drink beside her being her third or fourth martini since their swim. Whatever, he was glad it was back.

Penny got off to an excellent start with 'comment', with a fifty-point bonus for a seven-letter word.

95

Rolf said, 'Wow! What a way to start!'

Andrew scowled.

Trixie said, 'My daughter is brilliant. Didn't you know that?'

Penny mock-slapped her mother's wrist.

Trixie added 'hun' to the 't' to make 'hunt' and leaned to whisper in Rolf's ear. 'I could have built on the "c" but it'd have made a naughty word.'

Penny said, 'No swear words allowed, Mom.'

The first game ended with Penny a clear winner, followed by Rolf, then Andrew, with Trixie a distant fourth, perhaps because of the number of martinis she'd consumed. She said, 'You and Penny, Rolf, best at bridge, best at Scrabble, maybe you two . . .'

Penny interrupted with a quick, 'Let me get you another drink, Mom.'

Rolf and Andrew exchanged embarrassed looks.

By the time the second game was halfway through, Trixie was slurring her words, dropping tiles and would have been earning penalties for words she'd made up, if they'd been counting penalties.

Rolf looked at his watch. 'It's after nine. We have an early start tomorrow, Andrew. We'd better say goodnight.'

Andrew opened his mouth as if to ask 'what early start?' but Penny put a finger to his lips. At the door, Andrew turned his back on his Dad and Penny's Mom, to kiss Penny goodnight. Rolf took advantage of the private moment by stooping to kiss Trixie. He was half-holding her up by then. She wasn't too tipsy to return his kiss with passion, though. She took his hand and pulled it up under the short skirt of her dress, directly onto the shocking hot wetness of her naked pussy.

'It's all yours, Rolf,' she hissed into his ear. 'Any time you want it.'

On the drive home, Andrew asked, 'What do you think of Penny, Dad?'

Rolf composed his thoughts before he replied. 'I think she's a sweet girl, son, very bright and very pretty. Why do you ask?'

'I – um . . .'

'Out with it, son. You can talk to me.'

Andrew blurted, 'I proposed to her, Dad.'

'You haven't known her long.'

'Long enough.'

'OK. What did she say?'

'She said that if I still felt the same when I finished university, and if I asked again, I could probably guess what her answer would be.'

'You took that as a deferred "yes"?'

'Yes.'

'Then, congratulations.'

'You're OK with it?'

'Sure.'

'It has to be kept a secret, Penny says, just you, me, her and her Mom.'

'My lips are sealed. Son, on the same subject, how do you feel about Trixie?'

'Trixie? She's a bit of a ditz and she seems to drink a lot, but she's fun, and nice. Dad? Dad, do you mean . . .?'

'Yes. I'm thinking of proposing to her. I think she drinks out of nervousness.'

'That'd make Penny my sister!'

'Stepsister, son. And if you married her, she'd be both my stepdaughter and my daughter-in-law. That'd funny but it's no problem.' And, Rolf thought, Penny being married to his son and being the daughter of his wife should put an end to the indecent feelings he'd had for her but had been denying, shouldn't it?

The next day, Rolf waited until noon to call Trixie. The tell-tale for the first line was lit, so Andrew had to be on the phone. When Rolf dialled on the second line, he got a busy signal. So, Andrew was on the line with Penny.

At four, when Andrew was still on the phone, Rolf decided not to wait any longer. He rapped on the boy's door. 'Son? I want to talk to Trixie – see if we can all get together this evening.'

His son said something that Rolf couldn't hear and then called out, 'Tonight's no good, Dad. There's a party of some sort at their co-op – like a welcoming party or something – for residents only. Trixie's still asleep but Penny says they'd like to come to the airport to see me off tomorrow, OK?'

'Sure.' Rolf felt a chill in his gut. If that was the effect not seeing Trixie for one whole day had on him, he'd better do something about making her a permanent part of his life, and soon.

Fifteen

People are expected to hug and kiss at airports. Andrew and Penny took full advantage of that licence. While the youngsters were embracing, Trixie turned to Rolf and in a loud theatrical voice said, 'I'll be heartbroken until you return to me, my darling. Stay safe. Come back to me as soon as you can.'

Rolf blinked. He wasn't going anywhere. What on earth . . .? Oh! Right! Joining in Trixie's little game, he said, 'Six months isn't so very long, darling,' and scooped her into his arms for a lingering kiss.

The loudspeaker announced that Andrew's flight was boarding. Penny thrust a gift-wrapped box into his hands. He gave her a bulging plastic shopping bag. Andrew stole a final kiss goodbye. The boy turned to shake his father's hand and disappeared through the gate.

Rolf asked, 'If you ladies aren't busy for the rest of the day . . .?

'Sorry, Lover,' Trixie said. 'We have some boring legal stuff to take care of. If you could drop us off on Madison Avenue?'

'Of course.' It wasn't so far from his office and he knew there was work backed up, waiting for him. Work would keep his mind off Trixie – and off Penny.

'It was nice of you to give my boy a going-away present,' he said to Penny.

'It's a camera – a Nikon D80, the same model that I use. He doesn't have a good camera, does he, Rolf?'

'Not one that good. That's very generous of you, Penny.' He put his arms around both of the women's shoulders as they walked towards the exit. 'So, if I may ask, what was Andrew's present to you, Penny?'

She hugged the plastic bag and blushed.

Trixie chuckled and said, 'I know!'

'Mother!'

'Don't be ashamed. It's romantic, I think.' Trixie turned to Rolf. 'It's nothing, really, just an old shirt of Andrew's she asked him for, as a keepsake.' Leaning close, she whispered, 'To keep under her pillow, I think.'

Penny was obviously embarrassed by her mother's revelation so Rolf changed the subject. 'After your "boring legal stuff", what are your plans?'

Penny said, 'Our lawyer insists he's taking us out to dinner. He has quite a thing for my Mom, Rolf, but don't worry. I'll protect her for you.'

Trixie snorted. 'He's seventy, bald and obese. I hardly need protection.'

'He's not seventy by several years and he's heavy-set, not obese,' Penny corrected her mother, and drove a spike of ice into Rolf's heart.

First the co-op party, now this damn lawyer? Trixie seemed to have a full social life, apart from him. There were predatory men everywhere. Trixie, being the way she was, giving off the vibes she did, would have those wolves sniffing around her like she was a bitch in heat, which in a way . . . He didn't finish that unworthy thought.

When he let them off, Rolf looked intently into Trixie's eyes and told her, 'I'll call you tomorrow. How early will be OK?'

'I'll call you, Rolf, but it won't be very late, I promise. Our lawyer keeps early hours. I expect us to be home and in bed by ten-thirty.'

'Then perhaps we could talk on the phone, tonight, say about *twelve-thirty*?'

She grinned wickedly. 'Not tonight, Lover, but . . .'

An impatient horn blared behind Rolf's car. He was holding up traffic. Rolf blew Trixie a kiss and pulled away.

In his rear-view mirror, he saw that they were waving and blowing kisses after him, both Trixie and Penny.

The next day, Rolf was up at seven instead of his usual eight. He was showered and shaved and cologned and dressed by seven-forty. He toasted a bagel and made a pot of coffee, which he took to his table with the *New York Times*, a pen, and the phone. The crossword would keep his mind busy for a while. After that, he'd find a book. He *wouldn't* keep checking the time. That'd be pointless. She'd said, 'Early'. With her, that could be any time, even 'early' afternoon.

His phone chimed at four minutes after nine.

Trixie's molten-caramel voice said, 'Good morning, Lover. Guess what? Penny's off to some dull old museum. I've given her a fistful of money to go shopping with, after. She won't be back till five, at the very earliest. Are you busy?'

'No. I'll be there as fast as I can. Is there anything I can bring?'

Trixie's voice dropped to a low purr. 'Your stiff cock, Lover. That's all I need, but I need it bad.'

It hadn't been stiff until she'd said that, but it stayed hard as he brushed his teeth for the second time that morning, splashed on more cologne, dropped a pack of mints into the pocket of his Otterburn tweed jacket and rushed out. It was still hard when he rapped on her door. It was amazing, and delightful, how often he got erections, and quality ones at that, since he'd met Trixie and her daughter.

When Trixie opened the door, Rolf's cock suddenly got a lot harder.

She posed like a pin-up, as he'd learned she always did when she thought she looked particularly sexy. One hand was on her hip, where the towel she was wearing was loosely knotted. Apart from that towel, all she wore was her pom-pom mules. 'As we don't have a lot of time,' she said, 'I was warming myself up for you. I hope you don't mind.'

She turned. Her towel fell. Trixie's lush hips swayed like a harem dancer's as she led Rolf towards her bedroom. In six steps, he managed to shed his jacket and tie. He was still unbuttoning his shirt when he heeled her bedroom door closed behind him.

'We don't have a lot of time?' he asked.

'Like I said, just till five.'

'Oh.' That was a relief. Seven hours of love-making seemed ample to him, even if it wasn't to her. He kicked off his loafers. Rolf hadn't worn socks. No man can look sexy while taking socks off. His shirt sailed across the room. His pants fell for him to step out of.

'Nice!' Trixie exclaimed, her eyes on the bulge in his boxers. Those followed his shirt. Trixie clapped her hands in glee at the sight of his wagging erection. 'That's *just* what I need!'

Rolf felt strangely awkward. He'd enjoyed some pretty wild sex with Trixie before but here they both were, stark naked, and they hadn't so much as touched each other yet. He felt as if he was on public display.

'Remember when I said I'd like to watch you play with yourself, Rolf, and you said the same about me?'

He nodded, voiceless.

'Can we do that, please?'

Trixie's exhibition at her door had driven an essential part of Rolf's mission out of his head. Belatedly, he remembered. 'I've got something important I need to talk to you about, Trixie.'

'Is it *really* important?'

'I think so.'

'Then it should wait till later. I'm horny. You're horny. We shouldn't talk about important things while we're horny. Horniness makes it difficult to think. Maybe that's why I'm always chattering such nonsense, because I'm always so damned hot. Can we play first and have our important talk after?'

'Sure.'

'So? Want to watch me and let me watch you watching me watching you and so on?'

'I'm game.'

'Then we're all set up for it.' She perched her pretty bottom on the edge of her bed. Three feet opposite her, there was an oversized Cheval mirror, tilted slightly forward. To her left on the bed was an assortment of lotions and sex toys. They were mainly what they call dildos, or so Rolf suspected. He was far from being an expert on the subject. One toy in particular caught his attention. It had a cord that was plugged into the wall. It was a shaft of about eighteen inches that had a textured sphere the size of a tennis ball at one end. Surely it wasn't designed to penetrate a woman? At least, he hoped it wasn't. It'd be a hard act to follow.

Trixie patted the bed to her right. 'Come on!'

Rolf sat beside her, feeling the heat from her body on his thigh.

Trixie looked at him. 'No. I think kneeling up beside me would be best. Do you mind?'

Rolf was puzzled but Trixie was 'mistress of ceremonies' so he knelt up on the bed.

'Legs apart a bit, please Rolf.' She lolled back on one elbow, half-turned towards him, her face behind his clenched bottom. Her left leg folded up to bring its heel onto the edge of the bed. Her right leg stretched, toes pointed, and swung aside to press its thigh against Rolf's knee. The mirror's view was straight up between her thighs, directly at her sex.

'Do I have a pretty pussy, Rolf?' she asked.

'Gorgeous.'

'And you have a beautiful cock, Lover. They make a handsome pair, don't they.'

He grunted his agreement. Trixie picked up a cylindrical container and squirted clear fluid into one hand. 'This is just a lubricant, Rolf. It gets warm on your skin, which is kind of nice.' She massaged oil into her pussy and passed the container up to him. 'See how it feels on your cock.'

As he self-consciously rubbed the oil onto his stiff shaft, *very* aware that she was watching what he was doing in the mirror, she opened a small jar.

'Clit cream,' she explained. 'It tingles – makes my clit more sensitive.'

'Oh?'

103

'Maybe we could try it on the head of your cock sometime, but not right now. It feels nice but it doesn't taste so good.'

Rolf absorbed the implications of that remark.

'Watch me, Lover. Watch the naughty things I do to myself.'

'You're a bad girl, Trixie. Show me how bad you are.'

'Oh, I will!' Her left hand went behind her. Its fingers reappeared from below and between her thighs and caressed the sensitive spot just below where her pussy's lips met at the bottom. Her right hand gripped the bulge of her sex, covering it, and compressed, kneading the deeper pink plumpness, squeezing hard and manipulating the tender flesh mercilessly.

Rolf's hand began to pump.

Her voice deeper and huskier, Trixie said, 'Watch. Watch this.' Her right hand cupped her pussy, the heel of her palm pressing on her pubic mound. One finger curled down and penetrated her inflamed sex. Another followed, and a third. The skin over her knuckles whitened as she crushed her own flesh against the hardness of her pubic bone. Her hips and thighs trembled. The muscles in her tummy bunched and relaxed.

'Does that feel good?' Rolf asked, in awe at the privilege he was being afforded.

'Mm. Stroke yourself more, Lover. I'm watching you.'

Rolf's hips pushed forward. Suddenly, he was proud of doing something he'd been ashamed of for most of his life. That was *her* gift to him, erasing his shame.

'Your balls sway,' she told him. 'Nice balls. Nice *big* balls.'

'They're all yours,' he said.

She giggled. 'I'll cherish them, Lover.' The three fingers that'd been buried inside her withdrew. She lifted them to her lips and sucked the glistening juices from one before stretching up to offer the other two to his mouth. She really was delicious. When he released her fingers, they took his left hand and guided it down to her lolling right breast. 'Play with my tit, Rolf. I'm a greedy little bitch.'

He rolled her nipple.

She said, 'Watch the mirror. Watch closely.'

Rolf concentrated. For a moment he couldn't see that she was doing anything but then the subtle movements of the middle finger of her left hand became apparent. Its pad was making tight little circles, right on the striated pucker of her bottom's hole. She really liked that? It had been in their phone fantasy, of course, but he'd thought she'd introduced it just to please him and that in real life it was only for gays or was something brutal men forced women to endure. He stared in disbelief as the tip of her finger disappeared, then one joint, then two, then she pulled it back and thrust it in again, finger-fucking her own bum!

Rolf forced his right hand to slow down. The exhibition of wanton and perverse lust that Trixie was putting on for him was so exciting he might come at any moment, but he wanted to make the intense pleasure last.

'Would you lick me there, some day, Rolf?'

'Lick you?'

'My bum hole. Would you?'

He croaked, 'Yes.'

'Me too – you. You'd like that, Rolf?'

'Yes.'

'Am I shocking you?'

He admitted, 'Yes, but I'm loving it.'

'Me too. I like to talk dirty and I like it that I can still shock a sophisticated man of the world, like you.'

Rolf wasn't about to argue but doubted that his adolescent fumblings and his rather sedate love-making during his marriage qualified him as a 'sophisticated man of the world'.

She lifted the three fingers of her right hand and held them immediately above her pussy. 'I'm bad, Rolf. I've got a very bad *cunt*. Can you say that word, Rolf, "cunt"?'

'Cunt.'

'Thank you, Lover.' Her three fingers slapped down, making a 'splat', and rose and fell, again and again. 'I'm punishing my cunt for being so bad, Rolf. *Bad* cunt, bad,

bad, bad, bad!' Her breath came faster. 'Rolf? Rolf, Lover? I'm going to come, but you mustn't, please. I can come again, fast. Rolf, my hair, please? Take hold of my hair. Tight!'

He released the nipple he'd been torturing and gripped a fistful of her hair. She strained against his hold, making it hurt, and accelerated the tattoo of slaps she was raining on her sex. Rolf was fascinated by her image in the mirror; by the way she was punishing her pussy; by the livid marks his fingers had left around her nipple; by the way the tendons stood out on each side of her neck, but mostly by the way her wet mouth was working and by the fury of lust that blazed from her eyes.

By instinct, he twisted his left wrist, forcing her throat to arch as her head was dragged backwards on her neck. His right hand abandoned his cock. *His* pleasure could wait. *Her* ecstatic convulsions were a miracle that he was privileged to be allowed some small participation in.

Her eyes went staring blank. Her lips distorted and parted in a silent scream. Without knowing why, Rolf clamped his right palm over her mouth, sealing it, bottling her orgasmic shout inside her heaving chest.

Trixie spasmed. Rolf released her, suddenly afraid that he'd hurt her. She toppled back, rigid, legs straining, and slowly relaxed. Her sparkling blue eyes blinked open and gazed up at him, filled with both tears and love.

'Lover,' she gasped, 'that was incredible.'

'I didn't . . .?'

'Hurt me? Only in a good way, Rolf. Everything you did to me was absolutely perfect, as if we'd made love a thousand times before and you knew my every need.' She eyed his cock. 'You didn't . . .?'

'No.'

'Thank you. I don't want to miss it, when you do. Could you get me a martini, Lover? There's a pitcher already made, in the fridge. It'll take me just long enough for us to drink one each, to recover, and then I'll show you what some of my little friends here . . .' She waved at the array of toys and lotions beside her. '. . . can do.'

No longer self-conscious about walking around naked, Rolf went to the kitchen. That was some selection of sex toys she had. It was understandable, her being such a sensuous woman and having been celibate for so long. Not that she'd actually said she hadn't had any men in her life since the death of her husband. He just *knew* she hadn't. It was *important* that she hadn't, even if that was unreasonable.

Hadn't she said that she didn't dare go into sex-shops and had bought her vibrator from a catalogue? It had to be a very interesting catalogue, if she'd bought all those gadgets from it. Maybe he could get a copy and buy her a treat or two. Maybe he'd just call the company and have them send her one each of everything they had.

Trixie consumed her martini in two swallows. She smacked her lips. 'Ready for round two, Lover?' She eyed his cock, which was still close to rigid, and added, 'That was a silly question. I can see how ready you are. *This* time you will come, OK?'

She patted the bed again. Rolf resumed his kneeling position beside her. She half-turned, to lean back on his thighs, and rubbed her cheek against his shaft. Trixie said, 'My *cunt* is a greedy little cunt, Rolf. It likes me to use three toys at once. Would you like to see that?'

He nodded and added a 'Yes', in case she hadn't seen his head move.

'First . . .' She took up the bottle of lubricant. The fingers of her left hand parted the lips of her sex. She jetted copious amounts of oil all over her sex, and *into* it. Both of her hands massaged the liquid into her skin. When she stopped, the entire deep pink area was glistening and dripping.

'Slippery,' she said, with relish. She wiped her hands on his thigh and selected two vibrators from her collection. One was likely the one she'd described over the phone, a simple cylinder. She twisted its base. It began to hum. Unceremoniously, she slid it between the lips of her cunt to two-thirds of its nine-inch length. Holding it there with the fingers of her right hand, she picked up another length of plastic in her left, about the same length but flexible and no thicker than a pencil except for its handle, with a cherry-sized ball at the end.

Rolf started stroking his cock again. His free hand caressed the soft warm skin of Trixie's cheek and neck.

Her left hand reached down behind her. This time, Rolf expected it when it reappeared from underneath her, between her thighs. He held his breath. The ball rotated on the pucker of Trixie's anus. She pressed, and it disappeared into her. Bit by bit, she worked at least five supple inches of plastic up into her rectum.

Holding both toys by their bases in one hand, from beneath her, she pulled them back a couple of inches and then worked them back in.

Rolf rubbed his cock harder. Trixie had shown him enough obscenities in the brief time he'd known her that this one didn't shock him very much, but it still had the power to excite him.

And to think he'd secretly lusted after her daughter! Penny was certainly beautiful and seductively innocent, but a mere girl just couldn't compare with this experienced woman for sexiness. He was sure that Trixie'd cured him of any perverse feelings he'd had for her daughter. Come to that, if he had Trixie, he'd never look at any other woman again, ever.

'Pump that stiff cock, Lover,' she encouraged. 'Stroke nice for me.' Her right hand took up the giant shaft with the tennis-ball end. Her thumb flicked a switch. It trembled, growling in her hand like a leashed tiger. Trixie bit her lower lip and pressed the vibrating ball against the base of her pubic mound. Her thighs parted further to accommodate it. As best Rolf could see, it was squeezed against the left side of her protuberant clitoris.

In a very matter-of-fact voice, she said, 'I can't take very much of this, Rolf. I'll be coming quite soon.' Her tone changed, becoming strangled. 'I'll be . . . Oh God, this is *so* good.'

Rolf's thumb found the corner of Trixie's mouth. She twisted her head to take its pad between her teeth. She bit down as she worked the big vibrator harder against the polyp of her clit. Strained noises came from her throat. Rolf pumped himself as hard as he could, thinking it might be special if they climaxed at the same time.

They didn't. A coughing grunt wracked her tiny body. Trixie toppled back, letting her three toys fall, two to the floor but the big one onto the bed. No sooner had she collapsed than she bounced back up, avidly intent on Rolf's cock.

'Give it to me!' she commanded, brushing his hand aside. '*This* time, you are going to come!' Her left hand took over. Her mouth opened to take the head of his cock inside, on her tongue. She nodded, hard and fast, fucking his cock with her mouth. Her right hand lifted the big vibrator off the bed and pressed it up behind Rolf's balls.

He came instantly and so copiously that although she gulped as fast as she could, his jism trickled from the corner of her mouth. She poked her tongue out to show him his own cream, pooled on it, then swallowed and licked her lips.

She gazed up at Rolf. 'So, there was something you wanted to discuss?'

Rolf took a deep breath. His mind slowly cleared. He slid off the bed and knelt before Trixie. 'Trixie,' he asked, 'will you marry me?'

She giggled.

'What's funny?'

'Sorry, but there you are, kneeling, stark naked, your lovely cock dangling between your thighs, and here I am, just as naked, with the taste of your come still fresh in my mouth. You have to admit, Rolf, that it isn't the classical image of a proposal.'

'I guess not. Anyway, will you?'

'Of course I will, Lover. I've been hoping you'd propose but I didn't expect it so soon. I was ready to work for it much longer.'

'Work for it?'

'Work that I love, I promise you. Yes, I'll marry you, Rolf Carmichael, but on one condition.'

'Anything. What condition?'

'A pre-nup. I'm comfortably off but you are much wealthier than I am, Rolf. I don't want anyone to think I'm a gold-digger who's married you for your money.'

He grinned. 'That won't be necessary, Trixie. My wife – she was the best estate lawyer in New York. Everything I own is entailed in a trust that it'd take a Presidential order to break. I have an ample income but the capital is safe, even from me. Only Andrew possibly can inherit.'

'Well, that saves time, doesn't it? Lunch break, Lover? There's lots of left-overs from that hamper you brought, and we'll have a couple of drinks to celebrate, and then we can resume our fun and games. You, my mighty bull, are going to be ridden like no bull was ever ridden before, and *that's* a promise!'

'Oh!' he said. 'I'm forgetting. I have a ring for you. It's in my pants pocket.'

Sixteen

Penny didn't get back till half after five. When she arrived, both her Mom and Rolf were respectably dressed, although both had damp hair. She oohed and aahed over her Mom's antique engagement ring; nine flawless half-carat diamonds set in white gold. She congratulated the betrothed couple and hugged them both with bubbling enthusiasm.

When Rolf phoned him, Andrew wanted to come back for the wedding. Rolf told him, 'You can't take time out from your studies at this crucial point, son. Anyway, it'll just be a City Hall quickie, to make us legal. Trixie and I plan to have a great big church wedding, with a fancy reception, but not until after you graduate. You've only got one last semester to wait. Son, maybe we'll make it a *double* wedding then, huh?'

They set a date, in just four weeks. While Penny was in the kitchen preparing supper, Trixie perched on Rolf's knee and put her lips to his ear.

'Lover,' she whispered, 'I want our wedding night to be *really* special.'

'It will be.'

'What I mean is, if we're making crazy love day and night from now till then, that'd be our honeymoon, done and over before we're actually married. Would you mind terribly if we saved ourselves from now until after we're married?'

'You mean?'

'No actual – you know. We can kiss and cuddle and pet all we like, but no actual *penetration*?'

He must have looked dubious because she added, 'I won't let you *suffer* too much, Lover, I promise. I wouldn't count any small services my *hands* might be able to perform for you as breaking our deal.'

Well, that'd be better than nothing, and after he'd endured a brief period of abstinence, there was sure to be more wild sex than he'd ever enjoyed, every night, for the rest of his life.

'It won't be easy,' he told her, 'but I can wait if you can.'

The following twenty-eight days were hectic. Rolf had to put in extra time at his office, just to clear his desk. If they were going to honeymoon abroad, Trixie needed a passport. Her co-op was to be put on the market. They decided to keep Rolf's apartment as a town residence but to live in the Hamptons, in a 'real house'. They found a relatively modest six-bedroom home on five and a half very private acres, mainly wooded and backing onto a conservation forest, not far from the village of Sag Harbor. It had five bathrooms, including an en suite to the master bedroom that was big enough to live in, with a sunken Jacuzzi whirlpool bath made for two. Trixie loved the stainless steel kitchen, though she admitted to not being much of a cook. In particular, she admired the garbage compactor and the garborator. Rolf couldn't understand why, unless she liked them because both vibrated when in use.

Penny fell for the pool in the back, which was kidney-shaped, surrounded by rock gardens and enclosed by a ten-foot privacy fence on three sides. The fourth side consisted of a shed for the pool equipment, a changing room and a dry sauna. 'I'll be able to tan all summer, and no strangers are going to be able to see me if my bikini happens to be a bit revealing.'

Trixie added, 'That's right! Maybe I'll get an itsy-bitsy bikini, too. You'd like that, wouldn't you, Rolf?'

Given the choice of anywhere in the world for their 'first' honeymoon, Trixie opted for two weeks in Paris. 'Penny speaks fluent French,' she explained. 'That'll be handy.'

That was the first hint Rolf had had that Trixie expected Penny to accompany them on their honeymoon. Still, he and Trixie would be sleeping together, legitimately, so having Penny along wouldn't have to spoil things for them. It wasn't as if he didn't like the girl. If anything, he liked her far too much.

Trixie had started referring to Penny and herself as 'Rolf's women'. At first, that made Rolf vaguely uncomfortable but he gradually came to like it. There was something very 'alpha-male' about the expression.

Most of the women's furniture was to go into storage, with just a few special pieces going to the new house. Penny volunteered to take care of those arrangements, plus putting the co-op on sale, and of the travel plans. She really was both useful and very competent, in contrast to her ditzy mother. Between them, Rolf considered he had everything a man could possible ask for in 'his women'.

The three of them shopped for furniture together. They found most of what they needed at Lost City Arts, in Cooper Square, but not until they'd spent the previous four solid days scouring the City and buying nothing but an eighteen-inch bronze reproduction of Michelangelo's *David*. Trixie fondled it and said that it turned her on, which was good enough for Rolf.

The women would need cars once they moved. They settled on a pair of matching metallic-blue Lexus LX 460s.

Rolf gave them his Black American Express card and sent them shopping, Trixie for her trousseau and Penny for 'travelling clothes'. Penny pointed out that once Trixie was in Paris, there'd be no stopping her raiding the fashion houses, 'So why shop beforehand?'

Rolf assured her that 'his women' could buy finery 'before, during and after' the honeymoon, with his blessing, 'and don't forget to check the bikinis.'

They took him up on that and giggled when they made oblique references to the sexiness of the swimwear they'd found. 'You're teasing me,' he complained.

Penny stroked his cheek. 'Poor Rolf! Mom, shall we give him a sneak preview, just one of yours and one of mine?'

'If he'll promise to be good. No ravishing until we're legal, right, Rolf?'

He agreed, of course. To 'show their suits in the right setting', the women insisted on going down to the pool. When they threw off their wraps and struck their poses, Rolf suspected that once again, there'd be more, or less, to the suits than it seemed at first glance.

Both suits came from the same manufacturer, obviously. They were in matching leopard prints. Trixie's was another one-piece, but four-inch strips down both of her sides were left bare, with the front and back of her suit lacing together. Penny's was a bikini, with the bottom lacing at the sides like Trixie's.

'And the secret is?' he asked.

Trixie pouted. 'You guessed!'

'Just that there has to be a secret, not what it is.'

'Come into the whirlpool and you'll find out,' she challenged.

Rolf led the way into the swirling water, followed by Trixie and, to his disappointment, Penny. He had memories of that whirlpool that he'd have liked to renew.

The 'secret' was one he'd secretly suspected. When wet, the leopard spots stayed opaque but the rest of the fabric turned transparent.

'His women' giggled and exchanged whispers frequently, often with sly glances at him. Coming up to his wedding, those are things a man has to endure. They were teasing little minxes, both of them, and he loved it that they were, even though it became hard to bear. Between them, Trixie with blatant intent and Penny by just being her natural self, they kept him in a constant state of arousal. It was an exquisite torment.

They 'forced' him to accompany them to a lingerie fashion show. Trixie's cooed comments, into his right ear, 'How would you like to see my tits in that wispy little bra? – Imagine running your fingers up under the legs of those French knickers', and the like, didn't embarrass him too much. Penny's simple, 'Do you think that'd suit me, Rolf?' whispered into his left ear, did. He was *supposed* to be

114

imagining his bride-to-be in flimsy frippery. He *wasn't* supposed to be thinking about his soon-to-be step-daughter's body draped in scraps of black lace.

Trixie took to wearing wrap-around skirts. If, in a restaurant, or when driving, Rolf didn't take advantage by sliding his hand under her skirt's flap and caressing her thigh, she grabbed his wrist and put his hand exactly where she wanted it. She couldn't lean past Rolf, it seemed, without her elbow nudging his erection. She whispered to him a lot, and each whisper ended with her nibbling on the lobe of his ear. Often the whispers were things like, 'My nipples are getting hard from me thinking about you sucking on them, Rolf', or, 'My pussy's soaking wet for you, Rolf. Can you smell it?'

Trixie kept her word about using her hands on his cock and took advantage of every chance she got to do so. Unfortunately, those chances somehow never lasted for long enough for him to climax. Rolf felt as if he was fast approaching critical mass. Ten more days. Nine . . .

Seventeen

The ceremony was booked for ten. It started at ten-twenty and lasted sixteen minutes. Married and legal, the happy couple plus Penny stopped off at their two apartments for their luggage, to change into casual travelling clothes and for the rented limo to pick them up. They had time to stop for a celebratory champagne lunch on the way to Newark.

Rolf was a member of Continental Airline's Presidents Club. That meant free snacks and drinks in a luxurious lounge while they waited for their flight. Rolf had coffee. Penny had a white wine spritzer. Trixie managed to down three martinis, 'Because I'm deathly scared of flying.'

In Business-First, the drinks are free and unlimited. Trixie fell asleep after her first two on-board martinis but woke in time to dine with her daughter and her new husband on an excellent bouillabaisse, followed by assorted cheeses and a large dry sherry, and a cointreau, and another cointreau and another cointreau.

After an in-flight shower, that she'd taken because she 'wanted to be wide-awake and squeaky clean for you when we get to the hotel. It'll save time getting to bed, Lover', Trixie was ready for more martinis.

A flight attendant arranged for a wheelchair that Rolf pushed Trixie in through French customs and as far as their waiting limo. At their hotel on the *rive droite*, he and Penny half-carried her up to their suite. Rolf allowed Penny to get Trixie undressed and into bed. After all, the girl didn't have any idea how familiar he already was with her mother's body.

Penny gave Rolf a hug and a quick kiss on the corner of his mouth. 'She'll be fine tomorrow,' his new step-daughter assured him. 'She's always been afraid to fly. The only way she can manage it is if she's a bit tipsy.'

He said, 'Totally plastered, you mean.'

Penny gave him a sympathetic shrug.

Rolf slid into bed as carefully as he could. Trixie was naked and facing the other way. He put a loving arm over her but that brought his aching cock into contact with her warm bare bottom. A gentleman doesn't *do* things to a woman who has passed out, not even if it's his wife. Not even if it's his wedding night. Not even if he's spent a month in an agony of frustration and has been promised, fervently promised, that it was going be the most exciting night of his entire life.

Rolf backed away, leaving just his fingertips gently on Trixie's shoulder. She shrugged them off in her sleep. He rolled over and tried not to think of the sumptuous womanly body that lay inches behind him, nor of the supple girlish one that slept just one room away.

In the morning, both Trixie and Rolf were jet-lagged, although Penny was bright and perky. Rolf said he'd be fine if he got some fresh air and sunshine. Trixie took three aspirins and two sleeping pills with her coffee and went back to bed.

'So how do we amuse ourselves?' Rolf asked Penny.

'Seeing that you're an engineer who specialises in stress in large structures, I thought we'd go see the Eiffel Tower.'

Rolf smiled, pleased. 'You know about my speciality?'

'Of course. So?'

'Won't your Mom want to see the Eiffel?'

'If she does, I won't mind seeing it twice.'

The cab dropped them a hundred yards from the Tower. The roads don't go any closer. Rolf bought himself and Penny hot-dogs from a street-vendor to supplement their continental breakfast. In the open elevator going up, Penny asked Rolf intelligent questions about the structure

117

and was incredibly impressed by his knowledgeable answers. On the top platform, she was intimidated by the height and clung to his arm until she got used to it.

The view helped. Below them was the École Militaire, the French military school. Beyond that, Paris was a maze of rooftops that looked to be close enough that you could step from one to the next. There were rain clouds to the west. They could see shimmering silver curtains of rain divided by brilliant beams of golden sunshine. Gradually, Penny relaxed. Before long, she was running from side to side of the platform, gleeful as an unleashed pup.

Something distant caught her eye. To Rolf's alarm, she hitched herself up onto the wide iron balustrade, her feet off the floor, balancing on her tummy. Her skirt was short, very short, and he was behind her. Even as he rushed to hold her in safety, the image of her squirming young thighs burned into his libido.

'I won't fall, silly,' she said. 'But if you feel better holding me, that's OK.'

His hands were on her hips. Her bottom and the backs of her legs were pressed against the front of his body. Rolf edged back a few inches, slowly, so as not to draw attention to how close he'd been, but he still held her hips and they were vibrantly mobile under his palms as she twisted and craned for better views.

After, they walked the Champs Élysées and found a sidewalk café for a late lunch. Rolf ate most of the best and biggest ham sandwich he'd ever been served: a fresh eighteen-inch crusty baguette, slathered with sweet butter, filled with a slab of tender ham half an inch thick and smothered in very mild Dijon mustard. Penny was content with a croissant and apricot preserves, though she opened the third of Rolf's sandwich that he couldn't finish and devoured the ham from it.

He said, 'Mustard, corner of your mouth.'

Her tongue lapped out, giving Rolf a guilty reminder of the way her mother had licked his semen from her lips.

Penny eyed a pair of slender mademoiselles who were strolling arm-in-arm as elegantly as if they'd been on a catwalk. She said, 'They say you'll see the most beautiful women in the world, in Paris.'

Rolf said, 'That's true now, ever since you and your Mom arrived.'

Penny beamed. 'What a charmer you are, Rolf. No wonder my Mom adores you.'

'And I her.'

'Rolf?' She gazed into his eyes with an intensity that made him uncomfortable. 'Rolf, thank you. Thank you for being so kind and for understanding my Mom. I know she drinks too much, sometimes, but it's only because she's been so lonely since my Dad died. That'll change now she's got you taking care of her.'

'She's very special, Penny. I'm a lucky man.'

'And she's a lucky woman. Me too.'

'Because of Andrew?'

'Yes, but because of you, too.'

She reached over to rest her fingertips on the back of his hand. Her nails weren't painted but they were almond-shaped and quite pointed. He'd never noticed that before. They'd leave deep scratches down a man's back, if . . .

'Shall we walk some more?' he asked, keeping his voice as light as he could.

They got back to their suite at five. Trixie was already up, made-up, dressed in a clinging black velvet pantsuit, and vivacious, though languorous as a cat. When she walked, she padded. A yawn elongated her torso, narrowing her waist and exposing a three-inch strip of skin between her pants and her top. Rolf had never seen her look so desirable, not while fully dressed.

Penny announced, 'Our reservation at The Crazy Horse is for seven, so we'd best get ready.'

'We're going out?' Rolf asked.

'I've got us reservations at three shows and a couple of clubs, spread out over our two weeks,' Penny told him. 'The Internet is a wonderful tool.'

He turned to Trixie. 'Are you up for it, darling?' he asked, hoping she'd say she wasn't. The consummation of their marriage was long overdue.

119

'Doesn't that show have a reputation for being rather risqué?' Trixie asked her daughter.

'We're in *Paris*, Mom.'

'So it does? Good. Rolf will enjoy that, won't you Rolf?'

He nodded, with reservations. Yes, he liked to look at beautiful female bodies but right then, the body he desperately wanted was Trixie's. His appetite didn't need stimulating.

'And we'll be back here by eleven, for an early night, you lovebirds,' Penny promised.

There was ample nudity in the show but it was elegantly presented. Rolf was concerned Penny might be shocked by the display of so many naked breasts but she passed Trixie's opera glasses to and fro and didn't blush or giggle. The showgirls were of all ethnicities. When a statuesque ebony beauty, sporting a peacock's tail of feathers and wearing nothing else but an elaborate mask, strutted across the stage, Trixie whispered into Rolf's ear. 'Ever had a black girl, Rolf? Ever made love to one?'

He coughed. 'No.'

'Me neither, a black man. A lot of women crave "midnight love" because black men are reputed to have such enormous cocks.'

Rolf popped a shrimp into his mouth to avoid having to comment.

'I'm very happy with *your* cock,' Trixie continued. 'When we get back to our suite, I'll show you just *how* happy.' She reached under the cover of the table cloth and squeezed his cock through his pants.

Rolf covered her hand with his and moved it aside. 'Penny,' he reminded Trixie.

'She's watching the show – the one on stage. I bet she wouldn't even notice if I was to . . .' Her fingers moved to the tab of his fly's zipper.

'Trixie! No!'

'Am I bad?' she asked, almost giggling. 'Are you going to spank me?'

'I've a good mind to do just that,' he threatened.

'And I've a good mind to let you.'

For the rest of the show, Trixie seemed content to rest her hand on his thigh and press her leg against his.

They didn't get out until eleven, and then had to wait in line in the drizzle for a taxi. It was after midnight by the time they let themselves into their suite.

Trixie said, 'You shower first, Lover. I'll be quick with mine, I promise. I'm as eager to get to bed as you are.'

Penny said, '*Mother!*'

Trixie tapped her daughter's wrist. 'It's our honeymoon, remember.'

Penny flounced off to her room with a brief 'Goodnight!'

Rolf asked, 'Is she OK?'

'Just jealous, Lover. At her age, her hormones are beginning to seethe.'

'And at your age?'

'They're boiling, Lover. Now go shower before I rape you right here and now!'

'Promises!'

He shaved and showered and brushed his teeth and cologned in record time. Naked under the bedclothes, he strained to hear Trixie's progress. Keeping to her promise, she joined him only fifteen minutes later, in a pale-blue chiffon garment that reminded him of baby-doll pyjamas, but without the bottoms and with the ribbon-tied top cut below her breasts, cradling them. True to form, she was carrying a pair of martinis. When she gave him his, she stole his olive and rolled it up under her nightie, in her navel, while he gulped his drink in two swallows.

'Your cock and I need to get reacquainted,' she announced.

Rolf threw the bedclothes aside, showing off his rigid erection. 'Trixie, meet my cock. Cock, meet my wife, Trixie. You'll be seeing a lot of her from now on.'

She sat on the edge of the bed, her eyes hot on his shaft. 'God, but you've a beautiful cock, Rolf,' she husked.

'Thank you.'

'No, thank *you*!'

She took hold of its base, leaned over and parted her lips around its head. Her mouth closed, warm and wet. Her tongue lapped. Bobbing, Trixie started to pump Rolf's shaft. He reached down to get a breast into his palm, a nipple to roll between his fingers. It'd been four long weeks, plus a full day, and this was what had obsessed his every moment.

Trixie pushed down, taking him deep, and kept bobbing, making obscene wet noises around the head of his cock.

Rolf gasped, 'Slow down, Trixie. I can't take much of that without . . . Oh! Trixie!' His hand knotted in her hair and tried to drag her head up but the feeling he recognised as the sign it was past the time to stop tingled in the base of his shaft. His hand fell from her head. Rolf lay back and let it happen. The spurting started in his balls, thickened his shaft as it rushed through and burst into Trixie's mouth.

'I'm sorry,' he murmured. 'I wanted you so much – I just couldn't . . .'

'My fault,' she claimed. 'I was desperate to taste you and got greedy. Don't worry, Lover. We'll do *everything*. There's no rush. You just lay back and close your eyes for a little while. I'll watch over you until you're ready again.'

Rolf was determined not to rest for more than ten minutes but the after-climax warm contentment swallowed him. When he woke, there was daylight in the room. Trixie was sitting up, wearing a fresh satin nightgown, and Penny was perched on the foot of their bed, drinking coffee, wearing a short towelling robe and dewy from her shower.

'Do you want to do the Louvre today and tomorrow,' she asked, 'or today and some other day, later on? It'll take at least two full days and even then we won't do it justice.'

He said, 'Today's good by me. We can decide about a second day, after.' Penny wouldn't have planned anything for the evening, not after a day looking at art. They could have an early night and he'd be able to make up to Trixie for his performance last night, or his lack of one.

It didn't work out that way. By five in the afternoon, Trixie's ankle, the one he'd helped her injure at the resort, was painful. They went back and had a room-service supper, with Trixie eating off a tray in bed, a pillow under her foot. Pain-killers and sleeping pills and martinis took care of the ache – and put her to sleep.

Eighteen

Rolf had imagined that their honeymoon would be two solid weeks of orgiastic bliss. After all, he and Trixie were hot for each other and there'd be no external interruptions. Penny might restrict their freedom to make love by day, but there'd be nothing to keep them apart at night.

He soon learned that a lusty man and a passionate woman can go to bed, alone, and things can still come between them and love-making, things that he could never have predicted. There'd been jet-lag coupled with booze. There'd been a sore ankle and pain-killers. And then there were emotional problems and misunderstandings, mainly caused by his own stupidity. He *did* get nights of uninhibited love, but only three of them out of the fourteen he'd counted on.

Penny managed to get them into Man Ray, Johnny Depp's restaurant, on a Friday, when it's transformed into a dance club. Penny danced a lot but both Rolf and Trixie felt out of place and preferred to watch. Rolf made the mistake of letting his eyes linger for too long on a diminutive oriental girl who gyrated in a spotlight wearing a tiny black-net tent dress over nothing but her golden skin.

Trixie started with 'I don't care how many *women* you ogle, Rolf Carmichael, but that's a *child*! She can't be a day over fourteen. What are you, some sort of secret paedophile?'

'I beg your pardon! I wasn't ogling, and if she weren't of age, she wouldn't be allowed in here.'

'Should I be worried about leaving Penny alone with you, Rolf?'

That hurt, mainly because it was something he was worried about himself. They sulked until two in the morning and then dragged Penny away from her fun. That night, they used both of the double beds in their room.

The next day they 'did' the Musée Rodin in the morning. Trixie was disappointed that there weren't more erotic nudes, like *The Kiss*. They left much earlier than Penny had planned so they took a double-decker bus tour in the afternoon.

At supper in their hotel's restaurant, Trixie told Penny, 'You've brought books to read, I hope. If not, I'm sure you'd be interested in watching French TV. I hear there are some good shows on tonight.'

Penny tossed her platinum ponytail disdainfully. 'Sure there are. I've always wanted to watch old black-and-white westerns, dubbed, and there's a Jerry Lewis marathon that runs till dawn. Whoopee!'

'Penny!'

'I get it, Mom, I get it. You and Rolf want some steamy alone-time. I guess I can survive on my own for a night. Maybe I'll go clubbing and pick myself up a suave French stud, perhaps a *pied noir*.'

In a flat tone, Rolf said, 'No you won't.'

'Joking – just joking. I'll be fine, honest. I could do with some time away from you love-birds, anyway. You two are so sweet, you make my teeth ache.'

The ice that the hotel's machines dispensed was in spheres and half the size Rolf was used to. Trixie sent him to fill a bucket for them to take to bed. When he was back and in bed, she appeared from the bathroom fully made-up but naked, and tossed the bedclothes off him.

'On your back, please, Rolf? Hands by your sides? Can you just lay there, doing absolutely nothing, unless I tell you?'

'I can, but remember the last time? I don't want to . . .'

'Don't worry, Lover. It's going to be a very long, very *hard*, night, I promise.'

She picked up the ice-bucket and climbed onto the bed to sit astride his chest with her knees clamping his arms to his sides and her sex warm and wet on his skin.

'Nice view,' he commented, looking up her breasts.

'I'll make it even better.' She hollowed her back, pushing her breasts forward, and picked up a ball of ice. Her left hand held her left breast. Her right rubbed ice round and round her nipple, turning it into a rigid spike. 'Fuck, but it's cold, Lover. It's like ice needles, stabbing into me. I can feel it biting right down deep into my poor boob. See how stiff it makes my nipple, Rolf? I'm hard and numb. Will you defrost it for me, please?'

She curled her body, bringing her chilled nipple down to his lips. He sucked ice-water off her engorged nub and mumbled it into his mouth to suck on, hollowing his cheeks as he drew.

'The pain of the cold is *such* a turn on, Lover, but it's the defrosting that melts me inside. If we're ever cold to each other, Rolf, remember that, will you?

She sat up, plucking Rolf's treat from his lips, and selected another sphere of ice. Trixie rose high, pubes pushed forward, so that her pussy was directly above Rolf's face. Two fingers of her left hand parted her sex's lips and pulled them up and back, exposing both the pink inner surfaces of her outer lips and the unsheathed tip of her engorged clitoris. When she pressed ice onto that exposed polyp, her entire body cringed.

'It's unbearable,' she exclaimed. 'Well, almost unbearable. I can take it, just. It hurts like hell, but I can take it.' After a few shivering moments, she slid the ice down between her sex's lips, to where she opened, and pressed the ball into herself. When she let go, her pussy's lips held it, three-quarters inside her, with just a new-moon sliver showing.

Trixie walked forward on her knees and lowered herself, presenting the ice to Rolf's lips. With a giggle, she teased, 'Try a Trixie-pussy daiquiri, Lover. I hope it's to your taste.'

His tongue explored, trying to hook past the

obstruction. Trixie squeezed. The melting ball was ejected into his mouth.

'Taste good?' she asked.

'Mm.' He crunched the ice between his teeth.

'You're supposed to suck, not chew, silly. Now I have to give you another one.' Once more, the ice had to be rubbed on her clit and stroked down between her lips before her pussy held it and offered it to him. This time, he sucked it out and then pushed it back into her with his tongue.

'Clever man, clever, clever man,' she gasped. 'I've never been fucked with an ice ball before, Lover. I *do* like to try new things, don't you?'

He nodded with the ice held between his teeth, rubbing it on the inner surfaces of her splayed labia.

'Keep still,' she said, and dismounted him. While he watched, she worked three balls of ice into herself, one at a time. He reached out to stroke her hip but she batted his hand aside. 'Be patient. This game is only just begun.'

She bent over his hips and rubbed her cheek on his cock. 'Nice and stiff. Good.' Her hands scooped ice-balls from the bucket. Trixie clamped a double-handful of ice to his burning shaft. 'Is it cold, Rolf? My nipple managed to stand it. So did my clit. Can your cock do the same? Can it, Rolf?'

It was cold, much colder than he'd have been comfortable with under different circumstances, but it was far from unbearable. She massaged. The numbness crept deeper. Rolf's main concern was that he might lose his erection, but ice couldn't compete with the proximity of Trixie's lips, even if he couldn't feel the gentle pecks she treated his cock's head to from time to time.

'The ice inside me has melted,' she announced. 'That means it's time.'

'Time for?'

'This.'

She threw a leg across him and lowered herself, steering his cock towards her pussy. 'You thought I was pretty hot stuff, didn't you, Rolf. Well, right now, I've got the coldest damn cunt you are ever going to fuck, Lover.'

126

Once more, her crudity shocked him but excited him at the same time. Trixie was so damned hot! A woman who talked like that – a man could do *anything* to, no matter how taboo. She'd stripped herself naked in front of him, not just her body, but her animal self, her libido. That took incredible courage.

He saw, but didn't feel, his cock meet her pussy's flaccid lips, part them, and sink into her depths. Trixie worked down until her pubes were pressed against his. He gave a little upwards jerk.

'No, Lover. I'll do all the moving, please. For now, we'll just wait and let ourselves thaw out. Concentrate on feeling it, OK?' She stared down at him.

Rolf read love and lust and soaring happiness in her eyes. It occurred to him that acts of passion that some people might think perverted could be expressions of the purest, most intense, love. What he felt for Trixie, at that moment, and what he was sure she felt for him, transcended any emotion he'd ever felt before. Tears came to his eyes.

'Did I hurt you, Lover?' Trixie asked.

'No. I'm just so happy.'

She grinned. 'Good. That's the way I intend to keep you, my man, my special man, so happy that it hurts.'

Feeling slowly returned to his cock. He twitched it. She gave him an answering squeeze. Her hips moved, just a little, rocking on him.

'My nipples,' she said. 'Play with them, please.'

He pulled his arms out from under her and reached up to toy with her cool stiff nubs, coaxing warmth into them. She dipped into the ice bucket again. One ball was for pressing against her clit. Two more she accommodated by leaning forward, reaching back, and wedging them in the cleft of her bottom, against his scrotum.

'I'll never come with ice on my balls,' he observed.

'Nor me, with my clit frozen. It's going to be a long night, Lover.'

And it was.

The next morning the women let Rolf sleep in while they shopped on the Rue de la Paix, which Penny warned him was the most expensive street in the French version of Monopoly.

'Rest up for tonight, Lover,' Trixie told him. 'It's going to be a wild one. Shopping always makes me horny.'

The night started well, not kinky, but passionate, with breathless kisses and fervid caresses. Trixie inspected his cock again, eyes and fingers, taking her time. Rolf fondled Trixie's outer pussy until its lips parted and wept and then he explored, learning her inner intricacies, probing deep.

She said, 'Ouch,' and jerked.

'Sorry,' he said. 'Did I hurt you?'

'Your nails. When did you last have a manicure?'

'Just a few days ago.'

'Well, there's a jagged edge there, somewhere.'

He curled his fingers so that his nails wouldn't touch her and withdrew his hand. 'You OK?'

'I don't think I'm bleeding but I don't want anything inside me, Rolf, not now, not for tonight, just in case. If you really need it, I could give you a blow-job.'

He *did* need it, but he wasn't going to say so, not when she offered like that, without lust, just out of pity. 'I'm fine,' he said.

'I should be healed by tomorrow.'

'And I'll get another manicure.'

'Thank you, Rolf.'

He did get a manicure, but he didn't get the benefit. Trixie blew hot and cold. There was too much garlic, either in the potato salad or on the escargots they ate at a deli-restaurant for lunch. Trixie retired early, with an upset stomach. Out of consideration, Rolf slept in the other bed.

One night Trixie knelt, bum up, back hollowed, hands stretching her cheeks apart. Rolf took that as a request for analingus. He was willing, even eager. It was such an intimate, *forbidden* caress, that giving it and receiving it had to be strongly bonding. His tongue rimmed her and then probed and he felt her opening to him but he couldn't get in as deeply as he'd imagined he would. He settled for tongue-fucking her bottom shallowly but as hard as he could. She responded with delighted squeals, so he had to

128

be doing it right. Assuming it naturally followed, he knelt up and pressed the head of his cock to her pucker.

'No, Rolf! I don't do that.'

'But – on the phone . . .'

'That was Yvette we pretended you were buggering, not me, if you remember. Didn't I explain to you that we could do things in fantasy that we'd never do in real life? Didn't I make that clear? Didn't you understand that?'

'But, that toy of yours, the long thin one . . .'

'That's different, Rolf. Surely you can see that?'

He couldn't, but he wasn't going to say so. Women are sensitive to subtle nuances that men aren't. He sat on his heels, not sure what to do next. Trixie rolled over, took his cock in her hand and jerked him off with a stroke that was fast and almost impersonal, or so it felt. Perhaps he imagined that.

And then there was the night they discussed Penny. After all, even if he'd never take the place of her dead father, he'd volunteered to take on some of the responsibilities of a parent. Trixie was concerned about the lingering effects of Penny's teenage trauma. The way she saw it, a sensitive girl who'd almost been raped might go either way. It might make her frigid, unable to enjoy sex, ever, or it could make her promiscuous, over-compensating. Trixie didn't want either for her daughter. Nor did Rolf. Trixie went over her daughter's ordeal again, and again, adding details that he didn't want to know about, just to make sure that he understood. They agreed that it was terrible but he was at a loss to see where their discussion was going. He wasn't a shrink, but if Trixie thought that Penny should see one . . .?

That was an offensive suggestion. Only crazy people saw shrinks, and her Penny was far from crazy.

There was no sex for Rolf that night, not that he was in the mood for it, not after a long discussion about what swine men in general were.

He decided, or hoped at least, that once they got back to the States, into a normal life, with a routine, there'd be more sex, more love. Maybe he would get what he'd expected to get on his honeymoon, once their vacation was over.

Nineteen

Exhausted, they'd just dropped their bags in the hall of their new home. Penny had run upstairs, declaring that after all that travelling she'd need an hour or more in a scalding hot shower to wash the grime off. Trixie was fixing herself a 'welcome home' martini. The phone rang. She picked it up, frowned, gave the receiver a hate-filled look and hung up sharply.

'What was that?' Rolf asked.

'Another heavy breather, or the same one.'

'I thought we'd left that nonsense back in New York.'

'Just like I thought I'd left it behind in Ridge River.'

'The same one, you think?'

'It's hard to tell just from the breathing, but I think so.'

'Did you try checking caller ID?'

'Several times. Either it's blocked or he's calling from a cell phone.'

Rolf frowned. 'This is getting serious, Trixie.'

'For Penny and me, it's been "serious" for over a year.'

'Sorry. If it keeps up, I'll talk to the police.'

'Thank you, Lover. I knew you'd know the right thing to do.'

That night, Trixie came into the bedroom wearing just the bottom half of a pair of lavender satin pyjamas that she'd bought in Paris. 'I lent the top half to Penny,' she explained. 'She hasn't unpacked yet.'

That made no sense, considering that Trixie had six feet of closet space dedicated to nothing but nightwear, if

Penny needed to borrow something to sleep in. Rolf knew better than to question Trixie's logic. Not that he wanted to. She looked absolutely stunning. Her breasts were magnificent and seemed much more naked because she was wearing pants. Those were tied around the widest part of her hips, inches below where her navel indented the subtly erotic swell of her belly. Rolf was sure that if she sucked in, her pants would slither to her feet. The pyjamas were man-style, with an open fly that was slightly parted, baring a narrow V of skin down to her mound, pointing the way.

His cock, which had already been half erect in anticipation of her joining him, stiffened instantly. She slid under the covers. Rolf reached for her.

'Not tonight, if you don't mind, Lover? I'm beat. I'll make it up to you, I promise.'

'No problem,' he lied. 'I could do with a good night's rest, myself.' Mental images kept him awake till past one – of Trixie's breasts – and of Penny's legs as they'd be displayed with her wearing just a pyjama jacket.

He woke at about three, with Trixie's warm cheek on his stomach and his cock's head in her mouth. She released it to say, 'I was being selfish, Rolf. I'm sorry. You're a good man, better than we deserve. Hold my head by my hair, Lover. Use my mouth. Just fuck it. I'd *really* like that.' She took him back between her lips, pressed the head of his cock against the roof of her mouth with her tongue, and waited.

Rolf took two fistfuls of her curls and rocked, slowly, plopping in and out between her loving lips. Gradually, his strokes went deeper and became faster. Trixie made little encouraging noises. Her fingers cupped his balls and urged him, demanding that he let loose the frenzy of lust she'd inspired. When he came, she gobbled and slurped, making the most delightfully obscene noises he'd heard in what seemed like ages.

He woke in an empty bed to the aromas of coffee and frying bacon. For the first time since they'd been married, Trixie was up before him. He jumped out of bed, quickly brushed his teeth and hair, put a robe on and went down.

Trixie, with a wrap over her pyjama pants, was already eating. Penny was at the stove, cooking, and yes, the pyjama top was dangerously short and her slender legs were impossibly long, just as he'd imagined they'd be.

Trixie excused herself, 'To go change into my working clothes.'

Penny served him a plate with three sunny-side eggs, six crisp rashers of bacon and a stack of buttered whole wheat toast.

'I'll get fat,' he said.

'My Mom will work it off you, right?' She winked.

Rolf coughed and dug into his breakfast. The phone rang.

Penny said, 'I'll get it.' She picked it up and said, 'Hello?' Her face crumpled. She hung up and burst into tears.

'The breather?'

She nodded. Her slender young shoulders were heaving. Rolf had no choice but to go to her and hug her, patting her back and murmuring, 'There, there', and fighting the growing erection that holding her slender body close to his inspired. What sort of monster was he? The girl was in terror and suffering from a past trauma. How could he be so aware of the way her sobs made her small breasts quiver against his chest and of the way the sweet curve of her hip felt under his 'comforting' hand? As soon as her sobs subsided, Rolf backed off, sure his face was crimson, and finished his cold breakfast.

Penny drove her new car into Sag Harbor, to take her mind off things and pick up a few groceries. Rolf got dressed and went looking for Trixie. He found her in the room they'd decided would be his home office, cum library, cum den, cum TV room. In a tiny flared skirt and a gingham blouse that tied between her breasts, she was busily unpacking and sorting his books. His heart melted. What an angel she was! If he'd ever harboured an unkind thought towards her, he swore he never would again.

They unpacked and sorted and shelved, together. Even doing that; even with a wisp of hair falling over her forehead and needing to be puffed away; even with a

132

smudge of dust on the tip of her nose, his bride was still incredibly sexy. She allowed him an occasional kiss. She let him hold her thighs when she climbed onto his desk to reach a high shelf. Trixie didn't let him go beyond that, 'Or we'd never get your books put away!'

They lunched on crackers and pâté. He offered to mix her a martini.

'Are you trying to seduce me with strong drink, Mr Carmichael?' she accused.

'If that's what it takes.'

'Try again, later, after supper,' she said. 'I promise it'll work.'

For the rest of the afternoon, Rolf whistled, off-key. Trixie didn't object.

His mood crashed when Penny returned, shivering and hugging herself.

'What is it?' her Mother demanded.

'Him!'

'The Blair boy?'

'One of the Blairs, I think. I never got a good look at him, but he followed me all over Sag Harbor village.'

'Come on,' Rolf said. 'We'll go back and find this bastard and I'll have a word with him.'

'You won't do anything rash?' Trixie asked.

Rolf made tight fists. 'Of course not. I'm not a violent man.'

They drove to Sag Harbor and scoured the surrounding area for hours, but neither Trixie nor Penny were able to catch sight of Penny's persecutor. Rolf pulled into a crab-shack for a late supper and they called it a day. When they got home, neither Trixie nor Rolf were in the mood for love-making.

The next morning, Rolf took them to the police. The desk sergeant opened a file but apologised that there wasn't much more he could do unless they could make a positive ID of the shadowy figure that Penny had *thought* she'd glimpsed, and not unless the alleged stalker actually *did* something.

That night, Rolf was nuzzling between Trixie's thighs and she'd just started to squirm and pant when there was a rap on their bedroom door. Trixie rose, put on a robe and answered it. Penny'd had a nightmare. Trixie returned with her daughter to her bed, to comfort her.

Rolf tried to sleep.

134

Twenty

Rolf announced, 'We should get a dog – a big dog – maybe two. Having dogs around would make Penny feel more secure.'

Trixie shivered. 'I'm afraid of big dogs.'

Penny said, 'You're scarier than any dog, no matter how big, Rolf.'

His chest expanded. 'But I can't be here watching over you all the time. I still have work to take care of.'

Penny asked, 'How about a gun?'

'I could never shoot one,' Trixie declared. 'Horrible things!'

'I could,' Penny claimed, 'if Rolf would teach me how.'

'I have a revolver at my office,' he said. 'My work has sometimes taken me into places where carrying one is a good idea. I could bring it home. It's legal – I have a permit.'

Rolf's revolver was a double-action, .38 calibre, Ruger GPF-840, seven pounds of blued metal with a rosewood and rubber grip. Trixie claimed it was the most repulsive thing she'd ever seen. Penny seemed to find it fascinating. Rolf knew enough pop-Freudian psychology to understand why her admiration for his deadly weapon pleased him, and to try to dismiss it.

Most youngsters would have been impatient to take the gun outside and try firing it. Penny impressed Rolf by accepting that a revolver isn't a toy, and has to be learned about. Trixie provided latex gloves to protect her daughter's pretty hands and spread newspaper on the kitchen table. Rolf taught Penny how to strip the weapon, clean it and reassemble it. He lectured her about safe usage and showed her how to adjust the trigger pressure and what 'cocked' and 'half-cocked' meant. Trixie giggled at those words and snorted when he told Penny, 'You've picked up stripping and cleaning very quickly.'

Trixie's snort warned him that he'd committed a *double-entendre*.

Penny said, 'I've taken every camera I've ever owned apart, and I've fixed a few, so I've had some practice.'

On Rolf's insistence, she went up to change into jeans and a top with long sleeves. The wooded area in the back of their property was pretty wild and there'd be bugs. He found a hollow, so they had natural 'butts', and push-pinned a sheet of paper to the trunk of a dead tree, at about the height of a man's crotch.

He strode off six long paces and scratched a line in the dirt with the edge of his boot. 'This is far enough away, and that's where you aim,' he said.

'To hit his – um . . .'

'No. The bullet will often go high, until you've had a lot of practice. Aim down there and you'll be likely get him somewhere in the torso. If you *do* happen to hit him there, that'll take care of him just as well.'

Penny took a two-handed grip and slowly squeezed the trigger, as Rolf had told her. She hit another tree, three feet to the side and five feet higher than her target. 'Oh!'

'Like this.' Rolf put his arms around her, from behind. As he was so much taller, he had to bend his knees. His arms went round her and his hands took hers.

Penny leaned back against him, her bottom against his lap, the scent of her hair in his nostrils. '*Now* I feel safe,' she whispered.

Rolf said, 'Provided you've a firm grip, if you point at the target with your index finger and squeeze with your second finger, the bullet will go where you point. Try it.'

Her second shot hit the right tree but seven feet up. Her fifth clipped a corner off the sheet of paper.

'If that tree had been a man,' Rolf said, 'you just killed him, or at least took him down.'

'Really! Oh, Rolf, you are *such* a good teacher!'

'It's you who are a fine pupil.'

She twisted round and flung her arms about his neck. As he was half-squatting, he lost his balance and toppled backwards. Penny's lithe little body thudded on top of him.

She sat up, astride his hips. 'Oh! Did I hurt you, Rolf? I'm so sorry.'

He should have lifted her off, but where to get hold of her? Sternly, he told her, 'I'm fine, but no horseplay when there are guns around, OK, Penny?'

She grinned. 'Horseplay?' Her hips moved on him. 'Gee up, Rolf, my fine stallion.'

'Penny!' he warned.

'Sorry.' She climbed to her feet. 'Can we reload, please, Rolf?'

A box of ammunition later, Penny could hit the paper with almost every shot and without Rolf holding her hands.

'Once a week, you come out here and practise, OK?'

In a Western drawl, she said, 'Sure thing, Wyatt. We still on for that little upcoming fracas at the OK Corral?'

When they got back to the kitchen, Trixie looked them up and down and plucked a dry leaf from Rolf's hair. 'Target practice, huh? You shooting from a horizontal position, Rolf?'

He retreated upstairs to change.

After six more 'breather' phone calls in one week, Rolf had their number changed. That seemed to work.

Commuting was a bitch. Rolf decided he'd go into the City on Wednesday mornings, sleep over at his old apartment and return on Friday evenings. Penny and Trixie started to go riding at a local stables once or twice a week. They also took up antique hunting, scouring the surrounding towns and villages. As they lived near what had once been a major whaling port, Trixie decided to collect scrimshaw and read up on the subject, to Rolf's pleased surprise. She surprised him again when she got Penny to teach her photography, and applied herself to that, as well.

They started by photographing sea- and landscapes but together they developed an interest in portrait photography. Trixie presented Rolf with a small portfolio of glamorous shots that Penny had taken of her. Some of them were very sexy – not nudes or even close – but with costumes and poses reminiscent of the 'cheesecake' pin-ups of the forties and fifties. Usually there were generous lengths of her stockinged legs on display.

'For your eyes only, Rolf,' Trixie told him, to his relief.

Every week, Penny gave Rolf a letter to Andrew to mail for her. One week it was a large manila envelope marked, 'Do Not Fold.'

Rolf raised an enquiring brow.

'It's pictures Mom took of me that I thought he'd like,' she explained. '*Nothing* like the ones of her that I took for you, I promise.'

'Maybe he'd like some like those, of you.'

'Should I?'

'Within decent limits, why not? After all, you two *are* engaged.'

Two days later she showed him a picture Trixie had taken of her, to see if he approved. In it, she was posed looking cute, sitting on a fence, in a tied gingham shirt and a wind-blown skirt that had lifted high enough to show a few inches of her golden thighs above the tops of her dark stockings. Obviously, Penny's pose had been inspired by the same era of pin-ups as her mother.

'Mom told me that men like to see a girl's legs in stockings,' she said, coyly.

'I think your mother is right.'

'Is it OK to send this one to Andrew?'

'He'll find it – inspirational – I'm sure.' He looked closer. 'There's a tiny mark, Penny, down in the bottom left corner.'

'I know. My fault. I spilled something on my camera's lens. I've ordered a special solvent. I don't want to chance scratching the glass. Does it spoil the picture?'

Rolf grinned. 'That little smudge is the last thing Andrew is going to look at when he sees this. He's a lucky boy.'

But Rolf wasn't such a lucky man. The pattern that he'd hoped he and Trixie had left behind in Paris continued. She complained about being very busy, though Rolf couldn't imagine what with. Antique hunting, riding and photography couldn't consume *all* her energies. She and Penny shared the cooking, Penny taking the lion's share, except for when he barbecued. Two cleaners from a service came in three days a week. There was a laundry service that picked up, so the hi-tech washing machine and dryer were hardly ever used. It wasn't that Trixie was *avoiding* sex with him. In fact, sometimes she complained that he was neglecting her that way. It just seemed to work out that once a week was all they could manage, at first, then once every two weeks, and then once a month . . .

Trixie and Penny returned to the police station. They explained to the desk sergeant that he could close that file. Trixie said she was embarrassed to admit it, but looked like her daughter might have been imagining things. Penny was sorry if she'd caused a problem. The sergeant ran his eyes up Penny's long bare legs and down into Trixie's deep cleavage and assured them that they'd caused no problems and to stop by any time.

Penny adjusted to having a man around most of the time, though Rolf didn't get used to Penny's constant presence. As a rule, she didn't get fully dressed before noon. In the mornings, she wore wraps or robes that would have looked sexy on a sedate young lady. Penny wasn't sedate. She was athletic and full of energy. She bounced around the house. Stairs were for bounding up and down, two or three steps at a time. When the garment a girl wears is short and only closed by a belt, vigorous movement leads to exposure, usually briefly, but exposure none the less. Rolf took to avoiding the stairs in the mornings, unless he knew where she was.

It wasn't that he didn't like the flashes of Penny's long slender thighs or the quick peeks into her tender young cleavage. The problem was, he enjoyed them far too much.

The pool service sent a team to clean and open up the pool. Penny was delighted. Her vacation tan had virtually disappeared. Now she'd be able to swim, which she loved to do, and she could sunbathe. The pool was very private, so she wore her skimpiest bikinis, or sometimes just the bottom halves.

Rolf accidentally discovered that the ten-foot fence didn't block the view of someone looking down on the pool through the windows of the spare bedrooms. He thought about mentioning that to Penny, or maybe talking to Trixie about how the pool could be seen from upstairs, and have her warn her daughter. If he did, though, they'd know he'd looked down on Penny, sunning herself when almost naked. They'd guess that he hadn't averted his gaze, because, to his deep shame, he hadn't. He decided to say nothing. It'd be easier to simply avoid those rooms. Rolf had no reason to enter them, after all. No reason at all. Ever.

Twenty-one

At the ungodly hour of six in the morning, Trixie made her face up and tried on the swimsuit she'd kept hidden at the bottom of one of her lingerie drawers. It was a glossy black 'sling-shot' by Cici that she'd bought on-line from Bikini-Beach. The suit was little more than a G-string pouch, with straps that widened to almost two and a half inches where they passed up over her breasts en route to the back of her neck. There, they were joined to a third narrower strip that ran down her back and disappeared between the cheeks of her bottom. Even with the straps adjusted to be as tight as they could go, it was difficult for her to move without fully exposing one breast, or more likely, both.

She practised, finding how to walk holding her body still, so that the straps still crossed her nipples, and how to move to 'accidentally' expose them. Trixie stepped into raffia wedgies that rose five inches at her heels and checked herself in the mirror again. The way she was dressed shouted, 'Fuck me, I'm a slut!'

Perfect.

She'd been planning today's outing ever since she and Penny had got lost and had stumbled across a golden beach where you could rent cabanas to change in. There'd been several beautiful young people playing volleyball on that beach, so she wasn't likely to forget it.

It was important that she be appropriately dressed. Trixie covered her body with a little pink sundress and her head with an enormous pink straw hat. With a pink parasol in her hand and her pink sunglasses dangling around her neck, she crept downstairs. Rolf had left for Manhattan yesterday. He wouldn't be back till suppertime tomorrow. Penny was still fast asleep. Trixie might get into trouble about how she planned to spend her day, but that was in the future. A woman has needs. She was perfectly prepared to pay, later, for satisfying hers today.

In the kitchen, she filled a quart thermos with icy gin and added a splash of dry vermouth. The thermos came with a carrying case that had styrofoam compartments for two martini glasses and a small jar of olives. She wrapped a third glass in a thick fluffy towel and added it to the contents of her oversized pink raffia bag. There! She was all ready for her teensy little 'walk on the wild side'.

Her Lexus purred around the driveway and turned east onto the blacktop. There were no clouds. The sun was up and beaming benevolently. It looked like it was going to be an absolutely perfect day.

After an hour's drive and only two wrong turns she found the beach she was looking for. The tide was out. There weren't many people about yet. Trixie paid the grizzled old man in the wooden booth and was given a key to cabana number twenty-eight, the furthest and most isolated little hut. The sand dragged on her sandals but Trixie was sure-footed and stronger than she looked. When she got to number twenty-eight, she judged it ideal for her purposes. There were grass-crowned dunes behind it and between it and the other cabanas, that protected its privacy.

It was about eight feet-by-eight, with one door and two narrow windows. Inside, it was bare except for the deep wooden bench that ran around three sides. There were hooks on the wall for people to hang their things on. Trixie unpacked her bag, hung her dress up and went outside, ready to be bait in her own trap.

The cabana came with two deck chairs that were chained to its front wall. Both were patched and rickety. Trixie chose the soundest and stretched out. The only negative was the sun. She hated to discolour her pure talc-white

142

skin. The hat helped some but her parasol was woefully inadequate. Perhaps she wouldn't have to wait too long.

A young couple passed, hand-in-hand, giggling, obviously heading into the dunes to find their own privacy. A ragged-looking man of about Rolf's age made his way along the beach swinging a metal detector. The sun rose higher. Trixie was considering whether to head back into the cabana for a little drink when she heard two young male voices bellowing, as young male voices often do. She lifted her sunglasses to her forehead and put her binoculars to her eyes.

They were tossing a beach ball back and forth. One was a tow-head with too much chin and not enough forehead. The other had a Mediterranean look, with raven hair pulled into a pony-tail. They looked to be about Penny's age, or maybe a year younger. More importantly, both obviously worked out. They were tanned and had muscles that rippled, with hard pectorals, ridged abdominals and thighs that bulged like jodhpurs. They'd be tireless lovers – probably not sophisticated – but tireless.

Trixie licked her lips. A glance down assured her that although her nipples were *almost* exposed, technically, she wasn't actually indecent. She sucked her tummy in and raised her binoculars again.

They'd seen her but were pretending they hadn't. It was strictly by chance that their strolling game of toss-the-beach-ball stopped strolling right in front of her cabana. Trixie smiled to herself and crossed and recrossed her legs. She was the perfect lure for teenaged males. All she had to do was wait.

Trixie was relying on a law of nature. When young males throw a ball about idly and there is a pretty female nearby, sooner or later the ball will inevitably roll to her feet. In this case, it rolled so close that she was able to lift her legs and trap it under her heels.

Tow-head bounded towards her, flexing his muscles as he ran, and said, 'Sorry. May we have our ball back, Ma'am?'

Trixie looked him up and down, very slowly, until he shuffled and blushed.

143

'Ma'am?' he asked again.

'You look – very hot.' Let him interpret that as he liked.

'Ma'am?'

'My name is . . .' Trixie paused. She should have chosen a name earlier. '. . . is Bambi,' she decided. 'You are?' She rolled the ball under her heels, flexing her own muscles, the long sleek ones in her shapely thighs.

The boy said, 'I'm Randy.'

Trixie smiled. 'I'm sure that you are, but I wanted to know what your name is.'

His face went blank as he processed her words. When he'd interpreted her weak pun, a broad grin spread across his young face. 'That's my name – Randy.'

'Not the way you're feeling?' She stretched like a cat.

'Well, I am, randy, I guess, and my name's Randy, both.'

His black-haired friend loped up to join them. 'I'm Dirk,' he announced. Nice to meet you, Ma'am.' He extended his hand.

Trixie set her parasol aside and took his fingers and held onto them, keeping him bent awkwardly over her legs. 'Randy, introduce me properly to your charming buddy, please?'

Randy scowled and said, 'Dirk, Bambi. Bambi, Dirk.'

That was a relief. Trixie had momentarily forgotten whether she'd called herself Bambi or Candi or Sandi or some other bimbo-esque name. 'You two local?' she asked

'We're from Chicago, on vacation,' Randy told her.

It was good that they weren't local. She really didn't fancy running into either of them at the supermarket. She doubted they were from Chicago, though. Their accents placed them further south. Their names were likely as fictitious as the one she'd given them. That was fine, by her. She said, You may help me up, *Dirk*.'

He tugged. Trixie writhed to her feet, somehow without letting her breasts slip from under their straps. She turned and bent for her parasol. All there was of her slingshot, behind her, was a ribbon-wide strip of glossy fabric that ran down her back and between the cheeks of her bottom. *That* view should interest a pair of teenaged boys.

When she turned back to them, both were standing awkwardly, in positions she recognised well. They were trying to hide their erections.

'I was saying to Randy that you both look hot. Would you like something cold? I hate to drink alone so you'd be doing me a favour.'

Both nodded eagerly. Dirk added, 'Thanks, Ma'am.'

'If we are all to be friends, remember to call me by my name, please. "Ma'am" makes me feel old.'

'You sure aren't that, *Bambi*,' Randy said.

'That's settled, then. We're Bambi, Randy and Dirk, all good friends, on vacation, out together for some fun on the beach, right?'

'You said it, Bambi,' Dirk agreed.

Trixie opened the cabana door. 'So let's have some fun, shall we, boys?'

They somehow managed to squeeze through the door after her, both at once, side-by-side.

'Close the door,' she said. 'This is a private party, for just the three of us.'

Randy pushed the door shut. Dirk found the bolt and shot it. Trixie poured three martinis, added olives and gave two to the teens. 'To fun times, right boys?'

Randy spluttered his drink but Dirk managed to down his in one long swallow, following Trixie's example.

'So,' Trixie said. 'Let's all sit down and get to know each other. Let's play "Truth", shall we? Any question, you have to answer with absolute honesty, no matter what. After all, we're all friends here, aren't we? I'll start. You boys obviously work out.'

They preened.

'What are your sports?'

Randy said, 'Tennis.'

Dirk told her, 'Track. I run. The hundred yards dash is my best.'

'A sprinter? Not in everything, I hope. In some things, the marathon is better.'

'I can keep going for a long time,' Dirk boasted.

'How about football?' Trixie asked. 'Either of you play?'

Both shook their heads.

'Neither of you are "tight ends"?'

Seeming unsure what she meant, though by their nervous grins they perhaps suspected it was salacious, they shook their heads again.

Trixie raised her eyebrows. 'Are you gay?'

'No! 'Course not. No way.'

'You've neither of you ever kissed another man?'

They looked at each other. 'No!'

'There'd be nothing wrong with it if you had. I've kissed other women. Do you think that's strange?'

Both hastened to assure her that women kissing women was just fine, or maybe more than fine.

'So you've neither of you ever touched another man's cock?'

That question rendered them both speechless.

'Back to kissing, for now. Neither of you has ever kissed another man, but *would* you? What if someone male was to offer you a million dollars for a kiss – a hot wet one – with tongues?'

Again, they looked at each other. Both shrugged.

Dirk said, 'For a million bucks? I guess I might, just a kiss, nothing else.'

Trixie smiled. 'That's interesting. How about for something different? A new car? A vacation abroad? What if I said that if you two kissed each other, right here, right now, I'd kiss you both?' She twisted to pour more martinis. The movement exposed her left breast completely.

Dirk gulped. 'If I kissed Randy, you'd kiss me? I dunno, Bambi. I'm tempted, but he wouldn't, I know.'

'Would you, Randy?'

'I don't think so.'

'What if I offered you more than just a kiss?'

'More?' Dirk asked. His eyes were intent on Trixie's naked nipple.

'What is it you kids say? Second base, third base? Is there a fourth? I never could get the hang of that.' She cupped her left breast and gave it a squeeze. 'How about if I let you play with this little toy for a while? That's called "second base", isn't it?'

146

Randy clutched at his crotch.

'Well, would you kiss each other, passionately, if I gave each of you one of my tits to play with while you did it? That way, it wouldn't be a gay thing, would it? More of an orgy thing.'

Randy looked at Dirk. 'What do you say?'

Dirk thought for a while, looked at Trixie's breast longingly, and nodded. 'OK.'

'Now?' Randy asked Trixie.

'Not just yet. I haven't finished the game. My next question is, what would I have to offer you to get you to suck each other's cocks?'

Dirk shook his head. 'No way!'

'It's nice, sucking cock,' she assured him. 'I *love* it.'

Dirk croaked, 'You do?' Growing bold, he pushed his hips forward and added, 'Want to try mine?'

'Don't rush me,' she scolded playfully. 'OK, you don't want to suck each other, but how about jerking each other off? Would you do that?'

Dirk looked at the floor and blushed.

'You've done it, haven't you, Dirk,' Trixie accused. 'Maybe not to Randy, but you've done it.'

Randy looked a question at Dirk, who confessed, 'One time, at camp. Everyone was doing it. It don't mean I'm queer or nothing.'

'Of course it doesn't,' Trixie consoled him, 'and if you did it right now, just to amuse me, it still wouldn't mean that you're gay.'

Randy shifted further away from Dirk.

Trixie said, 'You never know what you might like until you try it. Dirk, you jerked another boy off. Was it terrible?'

'No, not *terrible*.'

'And he jerked you off?'

'No.'

'Another boy did? Was it a "circle jerk"?'

He nodded.

Trixie leaned forward. Her other breast swung free. 'When the other boy jerked you off, did you come?'

'I guess.'

'So it felt good?'

'I guess.'

Trixie licked her lips. 'You know, just talking about you young boys jerking each other off has made me so *hot*. Can you imagine how horny I'd get if you two were stroking each other's cocks, right now? I bet there's nothing I wouldn't do.' She pushed two fingers down under the diminutive scrap of fabric that covered her sex.

Dirk looked her up and down. 'You'd fuck us? Both of us?'

Trixie chuckled. 'For starters, yes.'

Dirk looked at Randy, who said, 'I don't know, buddy. I've never . . .'

'You wanna fuck Bambi or not?' Dirk demanded.

'For starters,' Trixie reminded them.

'Can I have another of those fancy drinks?' Randy asked.

'After,' she said. 'If we do this, we do it stone cold sober.'

Randy toed the floor and threw quick glances at Dirk. In Trixie's judgement, Dirk was now ready to play but Randy, who'd been the bolder at first, was still teetering on the edge. All he needed was a little push.

She set her glass aside and stood. 'No pressure. No one should do anything they don't want to. Let's start the party with a little friendly kissing, shall we?'

Even in five-inch heels, she had to stretch up to get a hand to the back of each boy's neck. She tugged Randy's head down first and lanced her tongue into his startled mouth. As they kissed, she felt Dirk's hand fondle her left breast, compressing it at first but soon moving to tweak her nipple. As a reward, she twisted to kiss him but she kept her hold on Randy and pulled his face closer. The boys, growing bolder, toyed with a breast each. Trixie would have liked to have dropped her hands to their cocks but she needed to control their kisses for a little longer if she was going to get them to do the things she wanted to do to each other.

Her lips turned from Dirk's mouth to Randy's, and back again, gradually drawing them closer together. Before long she had them cheek-to-cheek, mouths touching corner-to-corner, and was able to stab from one mouth to the other without turning her head. Her boy-toys were getting very horny. Her tongue flicked from Randy's mouth into Dirk's and she twisted both of their heads by their hair. Both strained their tongues towards hers and both achieved their goal, but met the other boy's tongue at the same time.

Trixie let the three-tongue kiss continue until she felt that they were growing accustomed to it. Her hands dropped to the waistbands of their trunks. Still kissing them, she eased their swimsuits down their thighs. Two erections sprang free.

Pulling her mouth back, she said, 'Keep kissing each other, boys, and I'll amuse myself a little lower down, if that's OK by you.'

One of them grunted something. Trixie squatted, drawing her hands down their torsos, fondling their firm young muscles, until she sat on her heels.

Hard young cock! There's nothing like it, particularly when it comes in twos. She pawed their suits down to their ankles and tapped their calves to tell them to kick their Speedos aside. Her fists wrapped two shafts. A glance upwards told her that they were still kissing each other, but in earnest now. Teenaged boys tend to lose all of their inhibitions when lovely women take hold of their cocks.

She *had* them! By the time these two left the cabana, they'd be transformed. There are few things so powerful as a lovely woman who is also utterly depraved, and Trixie prided herself on the depth of her depravity.

Her right fist slowly pumped Dirk's cock. She twisted to take Randy's between her lips, just to gently tongue it at first but temptation overcame her and she mumbled down its length until it filled her mouth. She slurped off it, lubricating it with her spit, and turned to suck on Dirk's.

Pump and suck, she went from cock to cock, all the while pulling them closer and closer together. Eventually, cock touched cock, side by side, wrapped in both of

Trixie's hands and being pumped simultaneously. She felt Randy's legs stiffen, as if he wanted to protest, but by then she was stretching her lips wide, gradually working both cocks' heads into her mouth. There was a limit to how deep she could force them both in at once but she got enough of their lengths trapped that she could nod on them without holding them in place with her fingers. She cupped and jiggled their balls, slid her fingers back between their muscular thighs and worked a finger up into the cleft of each steely teenaged bum. Trixie found their clenched knots and caressed them gently, letting them get used to the play.

Dirk began to thrust into her mouth. Randy froze for a second and then followed suit. Trixie stiffened her fingers and probed. Dirk's sphincter relaxed, and then Randy's. Trixie's fingers eased into them, just one joint. Their bum-holes were hot and clinging and when she pushed deeper, they clenched on her fingers.

One of them, she thought it was Dirk, grabbed the back of her head and fucked into her mouth. Trixie twisted her fingers deeper into their bums, seeking and finding their prostates. Both reacted to her perverse caress, thrusting harder and deeper. The cock in her left cheek, Randy's, let go, flooding her mouth. Trixie gulped. She twisted her head sideways, dislodging Randy's cock, unplugged her finger from his bum and reached up to pull him down to his knees.

Still holding and pumping Dirk's cock, she pulled her mouth off it for long enough to ask Randy, 'Give me a hand, here.'

She worked the crotch of her slingshot aside, took both of Randy's hands and guided them, one to his friend's shaft, the other to her cunt. 'Make him come on my tongue!'

Bemused, Randy pumped Dirk's cock with one hand and fingered Trixie with the other. She opened her mouth wide and extended her flattened tongue. Perhaps that sight triggered him, for Dirk came almost instantly, shooting a long pearly jet into Trixie's eager mouth.

She pushed her dangling slingshot to the floor and stood up, licking her lips. '*Now* we'll have another little drink, boys, and after that, we'll get *really* dirty, right?'

The young men looked at each other, as if to seek approval for the things they'd done to each other, then at Trixie, as if to ask what could be more obscene than the acts they'd just performed. She ignored their unasked question and poured three fresh drinks.

'Here!' She sat down in the corner, where two benches met, and lifted her feet up, one on each.

Dirk looked at her exposed cunt and took half a step towards her.

'Don't be shy,' she said. 'Take a close look. Have a taste. Do you like eating pussy?'

He dropped to his knees, stared intently at the parting between her lips and slowly put his mouth to it. Trixie'd had better, a lot better, but even unskilled cunnilingus is better than none. While he licked and slurped, she downed her martini and beckoned Randy closer.

'Are you bad, you two? Really *bad*?'

Randy frowned. 'How do you mean, "bad"?'

She gave him her best innocent wide-eyed look. 'Well, I wouldn't want to be accused of corrupting you boys. You aren't virgins by any chance, are you?'

''Course not!'

'So you've done everything, have you? Intercourse and so on?'

'Like I said.'

'So I won't shock you, either of you, if I ask you to do things that adults do?'

Dirk lifted his face from between her thighs. 'We're adults. We've done it all,' he assured her.

Trixie pushed his head back down. 'Don't stop licking, sweetheart. I like what you're doing. If you keep it up, I'm liable to come all over your handsome face. Would you like that? Do you like it when your girlfriend comes on your tongue? You like the taste?'

He didn't reply but his ears turned red.

Trixie continued, 'I bet she *loves* it when you get her off

151

by licking her, right?' She turned to Randy. 'If you look in my bag, you'll find a tube of lube. Fetch it, please. I want to play with your bum.'

He stepped back. 'My bum?'

'I've had a finger up it already, silly, and you loved it.' She looked down at Dirk. 'Lap higher, Dirk. See that little pink thing? Lick that.' Returning to Randy, she said, 'I'm going to play with your bum some more, and after, I want you to bugger me. Do you like doing that?'

He nodded.

'You've buggered lots of girls, I bet. No boys, though?'

He handed her the lube and shook his head.

Trixie squirted oil over three fingers of her left hand. 'Boys' bums and girls' bums feel just the same to a stiff cock, I promise. "A bum is a bum is a bum is a bum," as Gertrude Stein might have said.'

He looked blank.

Trixie shrugged. 'Come here!' One hand behind him pulled him closer. His cock was stiff again already. Trixie took its head between her lips. Randy sighed. The fingers of her left hand probed between his cheeks. He rested his hands on top of her head. Later, perhaps, she'd teach him how to direct a woman by her hair.

Her index finger rimmed his bum-hole, slowly and gently. His cock thickened. She probed, easing his ring open. Her tongue flickered on the knot below his cock's head. Around his cock, she managed to say, 'Dirk's tongue is getting to me, Randy. He's hot, isn't he. I bet he could suck you real nice, if you'd let him.'

Dirk's protesting eyes looked up at Trixie but his tongue didn't stop lapping.

Trixie pushed a finger into Randy's bottom, revolved it, working to enlarge it, and eased a second finger in. His thighs stiffened and he made a gurgling sound. Trixie pushed her lips down his shaft, mumbling on it, working it deeper and deeper, as she slowly finger-fucked his bum.

Her free hand dropped to Dirk's head. She held it in place and humped at it, deliberately spreading the lips of her pussy across his cheeks. Her stiffened clit worked under his upper lip. Trixie fucked at his mouth, willing herself towards a climax. His clumsy licking certainly wasn't going to get her there by itself.

Her third finger joined the other two. Randy seemed to have adjusted to the invasion. His eyes closed in concentration. His fists knotted in Trixie's hair. The boy's muscular thighs shuddered.

He grunted, 'I'm coming!' and he was right. His cream flowed across Trixie's tongue.

She concentrated, telling herself how wicked she was and how debauched the scene was and wallowed in her own depravity, and *forced* herself over the edge.

Randy staggered back.

Trixie told Dirk, 'That was wonderful!' She looked at Randy. 'You too. I love fingering your tight little bum and when you come, it's absolutely delicious!'

Dirk said, 'You too, Bambi. Your stuff tastes pretty good.'

'You'll get more, I promise.' As if absently, she reached out to scoop the jism that still drooled from the eye of Randy's cock onto her fingertip and put it to Dirk's lips. Without thinking, he licked.

'Your friend tastes good as well, right?'

Dirk mumbled something, looking away from Randy.

'You've only come once today, right, Dirk?' she asked. He nodded.

'Would you like to fuck my bum?'

Dirk swallowed hard and nodded.

'Randy,' she said, 'you know what it feels like to have your bum-hole lubed. Do you think you could do mine?'

Dirk writhed to his feet. 'You said that I . . .'

'Am going to fuck me there. So you will. Randy will oil me and you'll fuck me. Fair?' She turned and bent over, her hands flat on the slats of the bench. 'You spread me, Dirk. That'll make it easier for Randy.'

'Spread?'

'Hold my cheeks apart. Maybe, if you're up for it and as you've such a good tongue, you could lick me there first.'

153

'Lick your . . .?'

'If you won't, I know Randy will.'

'I'll do it!' He squatted behind her. His friend eased Trixie's cheeks apart. Dirk saw that the ring around her anus was a shade darker pink than the rest of her skin, about as dark as her nipples. Dirk took a deep breath. His face worked between her cheeks. His tongue stretched out and explored.

'Down a fraction,' she told him. 'That's it, right there. Ring me, sweetheart. Oh God! That feels *so* good! Now probe. Work the tip of your tongue in. Make it really wet. That's it, tongue-fuck my bum, Dirk. Tongue me good.' She squealed, not faking it. The sensations were utterly delectable. She could have submitted to Dirk's tongue all day but he'd get bored, eventually, and she hadn't finished corrupting the handsome boys.

'Let Randy oil me,' she said. 'Two fingers, Randy. Work them in deep and then spread them to open me up. I'm really tight there. You nice and stiff, Dirk? You'll need to be.'

'I'm stiff,' he assured her.

Randy's two fingers twisted into Trixie. She clamped at first so as not to betray her ability to relax her internal muscles. As she was tilted forward, the lube trickled in even deeper, which was always a nice sensation.

Randy asked, 'Enough?'

'Plenty. Dirk, my bum's all yours. Fuck me hard. Fuck me deep. Randy, you come here, on the bench in front of me. Bring the lube. I want you to play with my clit while Dirk buggers me, OK?'

Despite having come already, Dirk's cock proved stiff enough to force its way into Trixie's bum-hole. Once its head was lodged beyond her tight ring, he took hold of her hips and surged into her. Trixie winced, for Randy's benefit. Men prefer it when being buggered hurts the woman some. As Dirk slow-fucked her bottom, Trixie reached down and lifted Randy's hand to her cunt. She let him play for a while, enjoying it more than she had Dirk's tongue, before she steered his fingers into her, where he'd be able to feel his friend's cock.

'Feels good, doesn't it?' she asked.

'What does?'

'Dirk's cock, moving inside me. You're making it better for him, you know, making me tighter. It's dirtier, as well, you feeling your friend's cock.'

'I don't mind,' Randy told her. 'I'm game for anything.'

'You are?'

He nodded.

'In which case . . .' She leaned down and whispered softly into his ear.

Red faced, Randy nodded and ducked under Trixie's arm. As if casually, he rounded Dirk. Trixie reached back between her own thighs to take a firm hold of Dirk's swaying balls. Randy, as he'd been directed, poured lube over his own cock and presented it to Dirk's bum.

Dirk jerked. 'What the fuck!' He tried to pull back but Trixie had him by the balls.

'This is what the lady wants us to do,' Randy told him. He leaned into his friend, forcing his way between clenched cheeks and past the tightness of his virgin sphincter.

'You'll like it,' Trixie promised. 'A bum is a bum is a bum, remember.'

'No!'

It was too late. His friend was buggering him and he was buggering Trixie and the sensations had no morals, no standards. Within seconds, he climaxed, filling Trixie's bum, and then he endured the humiliation of what his friend was doing to him until, to his surprise, his cock hardened again, still inside Trixie, and that time both young men climaxed at about the same time.

Randy and Dirk sank onto the bench, not looking at each other.

'That was nice,' Trixie chirped. 'But neither of you has fucked my cunt yet.'

Randy shook his head. 'Sorry, Bambi, but I'm done. I couldn't get it up again to save my life.'

'You will, I promise. Then we'll try a DP.'

He looked blank.

155

'Double penetration? You fucking me up my bum while your buddy fucks my cunt?'

'Oh.'

Dirk looked up. 'I'll take her bum again if you don't want it,' he told his friend.

'No – I'm down with it.'

Dirk's face fell.

Trixie said, 'Don't squabble, boys. It's early. There's lots more we can try.'

Randy said, 'Huh?'

'Both of you fucking my cunt at once? I *really* like that.'

Six strenuous hours later, on the way back to the kiosk to return the cabana's key, Trixie had to walk with her legs apart. She was pleasantly sore in some places and feeling nicely dilated in others. Luckily, she had good muscle tone. Her cunt would be tight again long before Rolf returned but the bruises and bite marks around her sex wouldn't have faded by then. She'd have to avoid getting too intimate with him until they were gone. That'd be no problem. She was adept at avoiding sex with her husband. Trixie had Rolf trained to the point that he expected disappointment and was grateful for any sexual sops she tossed him.

The bigger problem would be Penny. No matter what clever lies Trixie concocted, her daughter always knew when her mother had been on one of her little adventures. There'd be disapproving looks from Penny, at least, maybe worse, much worse. Penny could be quite the little tartar when she was roused.

Oh well! She'd played her game and she'd enjoyed every moment of it. She was prepared to pay the price if she had to. Perhaps, if she was very sweet to her daughter, took some flowers in with her, maybe, she could wheedle her way past Penny's stern looks?

Twenty-two

They were all three, Rolf, Trixie and Penny, in the kitchen, sampling ginger muffins that Penny'd made, when the phone rang. Trixie picked up. After a moment, she said, 'Of course. As soon as I can. Don't worry.' She hung up, pale as parchment.

'What is it, Mom?' Penny asked.

'Aunty Elizabeth. Cancer. She's dying.' Tears spilled from her eyes.

Penny hugged her mother and patted her shoulder.

Rolf said, 'I'm so sorry. Is there anything we can do?'

In a voice that crackled with grief, Trixie said, 'She needs me, Rolf. I have to go to her. It's a long way – in Colorado – a tiny place – Wishburg – almost in Wilderness country.'

'Of course you may go, wherever it is.'

'Thank you. It might be for quite a while. You never know how long these things will take and they'll need me to take care of *everything*. She's all alone. I'll have to arrange the funeral, when . . .' She broke down, sobbing.

When a large brandy had helped Trixie compose herself, Penny told her, 'You aren't to worry about us, Mom. I'll look after Rolf for you.'

'And I'll look after Penny,' he said, and then it sunk in. For some time, for an indefinite period, he was going to be left alone with the young girl who, he suddenly realised, he lusted after even more than he lusted after her mother, his wife.

The Friday after Trixie left, coming back from Manhattan, a traffic tie-up delayed Rolf. He didn't get home until

157

half past nine. Penny greeted him at the door with a warm hug. 'I'm so grateful you called me to tell me you'd be late. I'd have been worried sick, otherwise. I've run a bath for you. You must be famished as well as exhausted, so how about I bring your supper into your den for you?'

'Thanks. Wonderful.'

She took his briefcase. He trudged up the stairs.

Rolf had long considered that one advantage of his mature years was that he'd encountered most sorts of situation and knew how to react to them – how to *feel* about them. That wasn't the case when he entered the ensuite bathroom.

The air was steamy and fragrant. The room was lit by two score or more candles, everything from stocky wax pillars to tapers to votives. The underwater jets were on. The tub was filled to overflowing with thick rich foam. There was a glass of scotch on the ledge, with an ice cube melting in it.

What did it mean? How should he feel about this, whatever it was?

Was this simply a dutiful stepdaughter's way of showing him he was loved, *platonically*, and that she simply wanted to help him unwind from the ordeal of three days' work? Or had she set the scene for seduction?

Nonsense! If, in the unlikely, impossible, event that Penny had designs on his body, she'd have been waiting *in* the tub, posed prettily. He was being foolish. Penny was just being her sweet considerate self and he was allowing his forbidden feelings for her to paint her innocence as corruption.

Sin is in the eye of the beholder.

Rolf dealt with his confused thoughts by blanking his mind and letting his subconscious take care of them, if it could. He'd luxuriated in the suds for about half an hour when Penny rapped on his bathroom door. 'Supper in ten, Rolf, please.'

He pulled on pyjama pants and a robe. When he was ensconced in his favourite chair, Penny, in one of her shortest and flimsiest wraps, brought him a tray and a beaded glass of Chablis. 'Blackened cod, Cajun style,' she announced. 'You said you'd had it in San Francisco once and liked it.'

'Wonderful! Do you memorise *everything* I say, Penny?'

'Most of the time. I just want to please you.'

'Well, you do. You please me a lot.'

She blushed and skipped to plop into the chair opposite him, where she curled up and watched him enjoy his special supper. He ate and tried not to let her see that he was watching her. Penny had lovely legs. Her ankles were slender; her calves sleek; her knees dimpled and her thighs were surprisingly full at their tops, tapering in intoxicating curves.

They were very mobile, those young legs, so that even if he tried not to watch them, they drew his attention back by crossing and recrossing or sliding on each other in a way that was innocently sensuous. Penny was likely unaware of the effect her legs had on men. Male lust was probably still a mystery to her.

No sooner had he finished than she was up, clearing his tray away and fetching another large scotch. 'You have your book?' she asked.

'I've got *everything* I need,' he assured her, and quickly added, 'except for your mother, of course.'

'She called today. Aunty Elizabeth is in pain but being very brave. Mom sends her love and said to tell you she misses you. We aren't to call her because of the medical equipment, like in a hospital. She'll call us whenever she can.' Penny took a book from his shelf. 'Do you mind if I stay here and read with you? I won't disturb you, I promise.'

That was a promise she couldn't keep. Her mere presence disturbed him. He said, 'I'm delighted to have your company, Penny.'

She refilled his glass before he realised he'd emptied it. His book was one he was forcing himself to finish because of the time he'd already invested in it. After about an hour, it slipped from his fingers. It didn't seem worth the effort to pick it up.

When he woke, his den was dark except for his reading lamp, which had been turned aside so as not to shine on him. Rolf sat up. He realised that his robe was dangling loose and the fly of his pyjama pants was gaping. He must have disordered his clothes by squirming in his sleep. Penny would have gone up to bed long before he'd done that. She had to have.

Penny woke him at ten in the morning with the promise of flapjacks with Vermont maple syrup and real English sausages with fried green tomatoes for breakfast.

'I'm going riding later,' she told him. 'Want to come?'

After the disturbed and disturbing night he'd had, he had two choices. He could crawl back to bed or he could snap out of the blahs with some invigorating exercise. 'I'd be delighted,' he told her. 'It's been years since I was on a horse.'

Penny rode well. Again, Rolf found it a pleasure to watch her. Riding beside her, he could see the muscles in her bare midriff flex. When he dropped back, her jeans were tight enough that he could follow the clenching and relaxing of her bottom's cheeks. He tried pushing ahead of her but she was the better rider and always caught up.

'I *love* riding, don't you?' she said with glee in her voice.

'All girls do, don't they?' he commented. 'I wonder why that is?'

Penny giggled. 'Rolf! Isn't it obvious?'

'Obvious?'

'We take great powerful beasts between our thighs, and rock . . .' She exaggerated her hip movements. '. . . like this. Girls get off on it, of course. When I was at school, we used to argue which was best, a canter or a trot, for . . . Well, you know.'

'Penny!'

She pouted. 'Well, it's true. Better we should ride horses than stable boys, right?'

'Does your mother know you talk like this?'

'I have no secrets from Mom and she has none from me.'

'I hope you're wrong about that.'

She giggled again. 'Well, I don't get all the *details*, of

course. She *has* told me that you are a fantastic lover, though, Rolf.'

In self defence, he urged his mount into a gallop. Penny chased after him, whooping.

When they got home, after a sandwich lunch, Penny announced that she was going to take a swim, to cool off, and invited Rolf to join her.

'I'm too stiff. I think I'll take a nap.'

When Rolf got to the top of the stairs, the spare bedroom door was ajar. *He* hadn't been in there, not since he'd discovered the view from the room's window. He'd better go in, just to check. Once inside, it was only natural that he'd glance out the window.

Penny was floating on her back, on an inflatable raft. She wasn't wearing the top of her bikini. Her hand looked as if it was tucked into the front of her bikini's bottom. Rolf turned aside. There, in front of him on a chest of drawers, was a pair of binoculars. Either Penny or Trixie must have been looking at birds, or something.

Rolf bit his lip. His hand reached for the glasses, drew back, and reached again. It was just too damned *opportune*! There was Penny. There were the binoculars. He knew what he should do and he knew what he was tempted to do. Temptation won.

When he focused the lenses, he saw that he'd been right. Penny's hand *was* pushed down under that scrap of fabric. It seemed she found the cloth restricting because she pulled her hand out, undid the tie at her hip, yanked the fabric aside and put her hand back, right on her sex. Her thighs spread. The middle two fingers of her hand bent under and disappeared. Penny's body tensed. She arched, straining up against her hand.

Rolf felt his face reddening and his cock hardening. Penny, sweet innocent Penny, was masturbating! He put his hand to his own crotch. What he *wanted* more than anything at that moment, was to take his cock out and jerk off, joining Penny in her pleasure. Somehow he forced himself to lay the binoculars aside and go to his bathroom for a long cool shower.

When would Trixie be back? When?

That evening Penny made stir-fried jumbo shrimp with a medley of baby vegetables on a bed of wild brown rice, with Hoi Sin sauce. Rolf mumbled his thanks. He couldn't look at her without seeing her on that floating raft, legs spread, head thrown back in ecstasy. As soon as he could, he retreated to his den and his boring book. After a while, Penny followed him, poured him a scotch and settled into the chair opposite. She was wearing that goddamned pyjama jacket again, and not even properly done up.

He kept his eyes on his pages, even when she brought him refills for his drink. At eleven, she made hot chocolate. Rolf hoped it was a sign she was going to go to bed but after they'd drunk, she poured him another scotch.

'May I have one?' she asked.

'Does your mother let you?'

'I'm nineteen, almost twenty, Rolf. I'm legal, in every sense.'

'Then help yourself.' Perhaps a scotch would make her sleepy. It wouldn't seem right if he went to bed before she did but it was getting late and his eyes were heavy.

Once more, Rolf woke in the wee small hours, alone in his den. By reflex, he checked his crotch. Damn! Not only was his fly gaping but his naked cock was lolling out. How in hell's name had that happened? Could he have touched himself in his sleep?

For the rest of that week, Rolf changed his habits. He didn't prepare for his evening's relaxation by showering before supper. He stayed fully dressed until he went up to bed and he rationed himself to one small scotch a night.

After his three-day stint in the City, the open-fly incidents had faded from his mind and he'd convinced himself that he'd spied on Penny scratching herself, not masturbating. He was home on time on Friday and was treated to a dozen oysters, two lobster tails, duchess potatoes and a Greek salad. He had a new book about one of his favourite historical characters, Sir Richard Francis Burton, the translator of *The Arabian Nights*. Penny brought him a scotch and took up her usual place opposite him, but wearing both the top and bottom to her pyjamas for a change. As Rolf'd shed no more than his jacket, tie and shoes, the scene was totally respectable.

Even so, at some point, he nodded off. He was woken by a delicious but alarming sensation, that he denied was possible. His eyes cracked open. He hadn't been dreaming. Penny was kneeling by his side. She'd unzipped his fly. His cock was cradled between her hands, being gently stroked and closely inspected.

He *dared* not let her know he was awake. If she knew, he'd have to react. What on earth would could he do? There was no appropriate response to the situation. What *could* he do that wouldn't destroy his relationships with both Penny and her mother? His eyes closed. Rolf did the only thing he possibly could, under the circumstances. He denied that anything was happening.

Twenty-three

Rolf might have been in denial about waking up to find his innocent young stepdaughter playing with his cock, but his cock wasn't. Despite his mental commands, it thickened and lengthened under the manipulation of Penny's slender fingers. Her face, as much of it as he could see through slitted eyes, was rapt, as if she was witnessing a miracle. Her eyes glistened. Her lips were slack. She wet them with a pink and pointed tongue. Her head moved closer. Rolf held his breath. If those virginal lips were to touch his cock – he didn't know what he'd do.

His shaft was so stiff it resisted when she tried to bend it towards her. Penny's right hand worked his foreskin. She spat into her left palm and glossed her spit over his dome. Rolf clenched his sphincter and ran the periodic table through his head. She'd get bored with her obscene game, or grow nervous of waking him. If she stopped *now* and left the room, he'd be able to pretend that it hadn't happened. If she stopped *now*. Or *now!*

Penny didn't stop. She smiled, a knowing little smile, and pumped harder. He could feel his shaft throbbing in her hand. Whatever, he had to hold back. He had to.

Penny murmured, 'I know you're awake, Rolf.'

Inside his head, he screamed. What his willpower had failed to do, the sudden shock achieved. Overwhelmed by *his* guilt about what *she* was doing to him, his cock softened.

Penny sighed a disappointed 'Oh!'

164

'What do you think you're doing?' he demanded.

'I was curious.'

'Are you *mad*?'

'Perhaps I am, with desire for you, Rolf.'

'I'm your mother's husband, your step-father.'

She drawled, 'Yes. Forbidden fruit, right, Rolf? You know what they say about that. Am *I* forbidden fruit, to you? Does that make me more desirable? I hope it does.'

'This is crazy.'

'Am I bad, Rolf, really bad? If I am, I should be punished. Will you punish me, Rolf?'

She stood. For the first time since her perverted caresses had woken him, Rolf realised that she'd discarded the pants to her pyjamas. Her legs, her incredible long legs, were bare. They were within his reach. Rolf knew, and the knowledge terrified him, that if he reached out and stroked her thigh, she'd welcome the caress.

She threw herself flat across his lap. 'Punish me, Rolf. Spank me. Make it hurt!'

He hated, desired, loved her. There was relief in his mixed emotions. He'd desired Penny, and had been tormented by the shame of that. That she desired him made his guilt less. Guilt shared is guilt halved. Guilt punished is guilt dissolved. There was nothing he could do about his own guilt, but he could assuage Penny's.

In compassion, in anger, his hand rose – and it fell. The clap of his palm on her bottom's smooth cheek shocked and inspired him. He slapped again, and again. Penny writhed. Her legs flailed, but none of her wriggles was so violent as to dislodge her.

At the sixth blow, she screamed, 'Harder!' and infuriated him. If she wanted harder, then harder was what she'd get. The blows that he'd been pulling, despite his anger, rained down with furious force. Her body stilled and tensed. She started to pant, short sharp breaths that came faster and faster, synchronised with his slaps.

Rolf was filled with malicious glee. Her bottom was red and mottled with purple. Flaunt herself, would she? Tempt him, would she? Play sweet and innocent when secretly she was utterly depraved, would she? Take *that*, and *that*, and *that*!

He slowly became aware that she was sobbing, that tears were streaming down her face. She babbled, 'Stop, stop, please stop! I can't take any more!'

A different sort of guilt flooded through him. Overcome with compassion, he lifted her up and turned her into his arms. Rocking her, and only vaguely aware that his rigid cock was trapped beneath her naked bottom, he crooned comforting sounds into her ear.

Penny wriggled, bearing down hard. 'Feel how burning hot my bum is, on your cock?'

'Penny, don't,' he almost begged.

'Your cock's like iron. You need me, Rolf.' Her arm snaked down between their bodies.

Rolf's recoil enabled her to get her hand back onto his shaft. He said, 'No, Penny,' as she gripped and stroked, pumping frantically. Rolf lifted her bodily from his lap and dumped her on the floor but she still clung to him, still urged his cock. He stood up awkwardly and grabbed her wrist. She changed hands. Rolf realised that he'd have to hurt her, really hurt her, to stop her. The fragility of her body was her weapon against him.

And part of him didn't want to resist.

His dilemma was resolved. Without warning him, Rolf's cock spurted. His semen splashed in a diagonal line across the jacket of Penny's pyjamas and onto her throat.

'Thank you, Rolf. *That's* what I wanted. Now I know that you want me, and that I can satisfy you, even if you fight it. Now *I* know that, and *you* know it. I think that's important, don't you?'

She climbed to her feet and sauntered from his den, leaving Rolf in a state of shock.

After an hour of bewildered thoughts that took him exactly nowhere, and two more very large scotches, Rolf went up to bed.

He woke in the dark, confused, with a warm and naked body in his arms. 'Trixie?'

'No, Rolf, silly, it's me, Penny.'

He inched away to break the contact of skin-on-skin. 'Penny, you shouldn't be here. Last night should never have happened.'

She wriggled back into his lap. 'I know what we did was wrong, Rolf, but we can't pretend we aren't wild for each other.'

'Yes, we can!'

'No, we can't. What we *can* do is burn our lust away by doing *everything*, and often. We should act out our wildest fantasies. That way, we'll get tired of each other before my Mom gets back.'

Rolf couldn't imagine ever getting tired of Penny's body but if he *were* to accept her logic, it would justify him indulging his lusts to the fullest. Stalling, he asked, 'What would *your* wildest fantasy be, Penny?'

She whispered, 'To be *forced*, Rolf. What I want, more than anything, is for you to make me perform the most obscene sexual acts a man could possibly want a girl to do, against my will.'

With those words, she conquered him. He knew that. He knew that there was no going back. Sooner or later, he was going to do perverse things with and to Penny, depraved things. His only chance was to put those acts off for as long as he could, in the hope that Trixie would come home and put an end to this nonsense before it went any further. Even though that is what he hoped for, a part of him wanted Trixie to stay away for a long, long time. Rolf said, 'Go back to your own bed, Penny. I'm not going to do what you want.'

She sat up and turned to lean over him, just an erotic silhouette against the moonlit room. 'Yes, you are, Rolf. Not right now, maybe, but you can't resist me forever. We'll play the game but I'll win. From here on, it's open season on Rolf Carmichaels, and I'm a huntress.'

In a flash of naked limbs, she swung off his bed and disappeared.

Twenty-four

Rolf got up late. He took a long cool shower and got fully dressed except for a jacket, taking his time. By then it was well past eleven. Penny might have gone out, riding or jogging, or something. He wasn't avoiding her but if it happened that they just didn't bump into each other, that'd be fine.

Who was he kidding? They lived in the same house. It was a big house, but she'd threatened to seek him out and seduce him. He could always go into the City and stay there, but that would be admitting defeat. He wasn't going to run away from a mere girl!

Whistling bravely, he ran down the stairs and strode into the kitchen.

She was there!

She was there, in strappy black sandals with four-inch heels; cut-off jean shorts that were faded and frayed and torn enough that her skin showed between stretched threads even where the denim covered her; and a drastically cropped white cotton T-shirt.

Penny turned from the pan she was tending and gave him a big smile. 'Like my outfit? I warned you, didn't I.'

Rolf said, 'Good morning, Penny.'

'Denial, Rolf?'

'No. I remember what happened. I'm ignoring it.'

'Brilliant strategy!' She turned back to her pan. 'It's late, so I'll make this a brunch. Eggs and bacon and home-fries and mushrooms, toast and coffee, OK?'

'That'll be fine, thanks.'

'And what shall we do after? Do you want to spank me again? You *really* got off on that, didn't you.'

'No.'

'Liar! You *are* going to do it again, sooner or later, and we both know it. When you do, don't stop just because I beg you to, OK? Never stop doing anything just because I beg, or cry, or scream even.'

He shrugged.

'It's part of the *game*, you see,' she continued. 'I'd like to be forced, as I told you. If I'm being forced, I have to protest to make it seem real. Don't worry, if I *really* want you to stop, I'll call "Red Light!" That's something I read about in a book once, a very naughty book. Can you remember that, Rolf? Don't stop unless I call "Red Light"?'

'I don't have to remember it. It isn't going to happen.'

'Another thing – I'd like you to call me bad names, "Whore" and "Slut" and so on.'

Rolf wondered if that could be in her genes? That's what her mother liked. How much alike were they, mother and daughter? Trixie, back then, had promised to do *everything* for him, just like Penny was promising now. When he'd knelt up to bugger Trixie, he'd found that 'everything' had limits. Would Penny renege on her word, if he pushed her far enough?

He shook his head. That was no way to think. He wasn't going to do *anything* to Penny, not even kiss her. Not even touch her hand.

'Imagination working, Rolf? Mine is. I'm remembering what your cock looked and felt like, and I'm imagining . . .'

He jumped to his feet. 'Enough!'

'You aren't going to run away from me, Rolf. It isn't in you. You're the sort of man who confronts his fears and defeats them. You'll either conquer me by carrying on as usual, no matter what I do, or you'll *conquer* me and bend me to your wicked will. You can't lose, can you?'

She swayed to the table, heels clicking on the wooden floor, with two heaped plates. Rolf sat back down, not looking at the pale undersides of the delicate little breasts that her T-shirt exposed.

Penny cocked her head and gave him a sad smile. 'I'm really sorry I'm putting you on the spot, Rolf, but I'm only being honest. I've wanted you ever since that first night, since that tango. You took me in your arms and I was pressed against the masculine power of your body. Every step I took, every move I made, was in obedience to you. You made me feel small and weak and helpless – and I *loved* it. All of my fantasies, since then, have been about surrendering my body to you.'

'How about Andrew? Don't you love him?'

'I love Andrew for the man he will someday become. I lust for you because of the man you *are*. After all, Rolf, you wanted my Mom and you also wanted me, right from the beginning. I'm no different, with you and Andrew. We're both greedy, you and I.'

'What makes you think I've wanted you?'

'I've seen it in your eyes. They eat me up, Rolf. You stare at my legs. Every chance you get, you're peeking at my tits. How about yesterday, when I was in the pool and you were spying on me from upstairs? Did you think I didn't know? Who do you think left those binoculars nice and handy? I know you used them because they were in a different position when I checked, later. You know what I was thinking about, when I was fingering my pussy? You, Rolf, you looking at me. I was doing it for *you*.'

Rolf almost spluttered his mouthful of egg.

Penny continued, 'Rolf, let's both be honest. You enjoy looking at me. I enjoy being looked at, if it's you doing the looking. I confess, I deliberately gave you chances to look up my skirts and down my tops. I got off on it. I loved it that I made you hard. Now we are all alone for a while, living in our own private little world. While we can, I'll show my body off to you. You can enjoy looking at it. If you won't let us have what we both *really* want, we can at least have that. Then, when my Mom gets back, we can go back to you getting nothing but sly peeks, just as if nothing happened while she was away. Otherwise, I'll just be your obedient little stepdaughter, OK?'

'Do I have any choice?'

'Not really.'

He laid his knife and fork aside. 'In that case, do your worst, Penny. I admit I'll enjoy looking at you. What man wouldn't? I won't do more, though. I won't touch you. Sooner or later you'll tire of your game and we can go back to being normal.'

'"In that case,"' she quoted him, and lifted the hem of her cropped shirt up to rest on her breasts' upper slopes, baring her pale pink puffy nipples.

'Very nice.' Rolf busied himself cutting bacon.

'Maybe I should twist my ankle.'

'What do you mean by that?'

'To seduce you. It worked for my Mom.'

'Are you telling me she faked that?'

'She walked just fine when she and I were alone. It was clever of her, I thought. How long did it take from you resting her foot on your knee to her toes tickling your balls, Rolf?'

'You don't know what you're talking about,' he insisted, knowing full well that she knew *exactly* what she was saying.

'One last thing,' Penny said. 'If you *do* decide to make love to me, I know I said I'd like to be forced but the very first time, I'd like you to be slow and gentle. A girl's first time should be romantic, at the hands of an experienced and sophisticated lover, don't you think?'

'Now you bring the subject up, didn't you swear to remain a virgin until your wedding night?'

'That was an empty promise. In what sense "a virgin", Rolf? I've ridden horses since I was eight. For a while now, I've been borrowing Mom's secret little toys and experimenting with them. I think I'm still pretty tight, but there's no barrier left, no hymen. There hasn't been for years. Mentally, well, I've been doing it in my imagination for ages, even before you came along. Now, as you know, I've held a man's cock in my hand – yours. What's left of my "virginity" to lose? You pushing your cock into my pussy? That's one small step that'll end a journey I've been on for years.'

She grinned. 'As for Andrew, I hope he won't still be a virgin when we get married. He'll be a much better lover if he's had some experience, preferably with an older woman.' Her face brightened. 'I know! We could sic my Mom on him!'

'Penny, you're sick!'

'I know. The cure's in your hands, Doctor Carmichael. You could spank my sickness out of me, or you could *fuck* it out of me.'

'Penny!'

'You don't like my language? I've heard the way you and Mom talk to each other in bed.'

'All the way from your bedroom?'

'No, from right outside your door. It's been educational.'

His mental image of Penny crouched outside his bedroom door, listening and maybe peeking in on his and Trixie's most intimate moments, proved to be the last straw. He threw his cutlery down and stormed outside, into the woods behind the house. To his relief, Penny didn't follow him.

To punish himself, he deliberately marched to where the trees and underbrush were thickest. Twigs whipped his face and arms. Burrs clung to his pants. When he stepped into a mud puddle, his feet shot from under him. He landed on his tailbone and sat in pained shock for long enough that the wet seeped right through his pants and underpants. When he got up, his right shoe had come off. He didn't bother finding it. Rolf pressed on, limping. His right sock got dragged down and trailed his foot in a soggy mess, held on only by his toes. Eventually, he came to a low fence and beyond the fence, a four-lane highway. If there'd been a truck coming along, perhaps he'd have thrown himself under it. There wasn't one, so he sank to his knees and sobbed.

It took about an hour for him to realise what an idiot he was. He was healthy, wealthy and successful, with a son he was proud of and a beautiful, even if maddening, wife. There was only one problem in his life, that a lovely young girl was desperately in lust with him. Ninety-nine per cent of the male population of the world would have envied him. He ordered himself to get a grip. Determined, Rolf stood up and marched back into the woods, intending to go straight back home, where he would take care of the Penny-problem for good, one way or another.

After forty minutes he came to the fence again. By then, his right foot was bare and bleeding. What an idiot he was, to get lost in what was virtually his own backyard. Where was the sun? Rolf peered into the sky. It was overcast with scurrying ominous grey clouds. The brightest spot was just right of directly overhead. Depending on the time, either *that* way was west, or *that* one was. He hadn't put his watch on. Was this the same section of fence as before? He couldn't be certain. Was the fence straight, or did it curve, or did it turn corners?

A fat drop of rain fell on his right instep and rinsed some of the blood away. Another drop hit his left eyebrow and made him blink. Within a minute, it became a downpour. Soaked, miserable, and beginning to imagine he was getting hungry already, Rolf trudged back into the forest.

An age of deep despair and stumbling misery later, he heard Penny's voice faintly, through the drumming of the rain. 'Rolf? Where are you, Rolf? Come on home, please?'

'Here,' he croaked.

She'd changed into boots, jeans and a long-sleeved check shirt but was soaked and dishevelled. He outweighed her two-to-one but she half carried him, him hopping and with his arm heavy across her slender shoulders. In the kitchen, she pulled his clothes off and sat him naked on a towel on a straight chair. Her own wet clothes followed his, into a saturated pile. Penny knelt to wash his right foot and pluck a long black thorn from its heel. Mercurochrome stopped the bleeding from a dozen small scratches. She found a cut on his right cheek and another on his left forearm, that had to be cleaned and disinfected. His left shin was bruised in two places but the skin wasn't broken.

By the time she was done, the proximity of her naked

body was beginning to affect him. Penny glanced at his semi-erection and announced, 'Bath time.'

She helped him up the stairs, her soft hip against his hard thigh, his arm across her shoulders again. He was lowered into steaming and bubbling water. As he soaked, she washed his hair. Her nipples traced lines across his back when she bent him forward to rinse him but that might have been accidental.

'Can you stand up OK?'

'Of course.' He stood, unsteadily. She braced him with both hands on his hips and her face a foot from his swaying genitals. When he was steady, she fetched warm towels and dabbed him dry, thoroughly but impersonally. Rolf was almost disappointed by her coolness. She was, after all, supposed to be desperate for his body.

He hobbled to his bed with hardly any help from Penny. She tucked him in. His eyes closed.

When he opened them, she was curled up on a chaise, watching him. She was wearing a white cotton *broderie anglaise* nightie with cap sleeves. It wasn't long but neither was it daringly short. It laced down to her waist, but the ribbons had been pulled tight and tied in a bow at her throat, to close it demurely. Her platinum ponytail gleamed as if from a thousand brush-strokes. Her face was innocent of make-up. Penny smiled and asked, 'Dinner? Here or downstairs?'

'In the kitchen would be fine – save laying the table.'

'Can you make it, in say, fifteen minutes?'

'Sure.'

She'd laid pyjama pants and a cotton robe out on the foot of his bed. Rolf dressed in those, brushed his teeth again, shaved again, spritzed with cologne and went down. Somehow, despite all that had happened that day, Penny'd managed to roast a rack of lamb with rosemary and prepare baby potatoes and peas with mint.

He sat down. She poured two modest glasses of a Californian rosé. 'To us!'

'To us! Penny, I have to thank you.' He chuckled. 'I was getting into quite a state out there. If you hadn't come looking for me . . .'

'I know those woods well. You were distraught when you left here. I shouldn't have let you go off like that.'

'My fault,' he insisted.

'No, mine.'

They ate in awkward silence for a while. Penny broke the quiet by asking, 'Did your sojourn in the wilderness bring you any insights, Rolf?'

'Now you're making fun of me.'

'No, I'm not. I'm making light of something that is very important to me.' She got up from her seat and went round to Rolf's chair, where she knelt and took his hand. There were tears in her eyes. 'Rolf, a girl likes to know if tonight is the night she's going to offer up her virginity to the man she loves.'

Rolf had been braced against any wickedly seductive gambits she might have made. She could have dressed up as a whore or as a harem slave, and he'd have steeled himself against her. This, though, this modest maiden, imploring him, he wasn't at all prepared for. Before he'd considered his words or the implications, he said, 'I'd be honoured, Penny.'

She kissed his fingers. A tear dropped onto his knuckles. They abandoned their half-eaten meals. At the foot of the stairs, Rolf scooped her up into his arms. He was relieved to discover that his strength had returned enough for him to carry her up to his bedroom without panting. Reverently, he laid her in his bed and turned to switch the lights off.

'Please, Rolf? Leave them on? I want to see you, and for you to see me. We don't need darkness to cover our shame, not when we are shameless.'

He dropped his robe. 'Are we?'

'For the first time,' she said, 'I'm feeling a bit nervous about you looking at my body.'

'Silly girl. You're lovely.'

'Should I unlace my nightie, or take it off, or did you want to do it? Tell me what you want, please.'

Rolf climbed into bed. 'Just leave everything to me.'

'Thank you, Rolf. Rolf, if there's anything you want me to do, anything at all, just tell me and I'll do it, OK?'

'Relax.'

'Whether it's true or not, could you tell me that you love me?'

'I love you, Penny.' He wasn't lying. At that moment, he loved her so much it almost broke his heart. Rolf leaned over her. His fingers found a stray lock of hair and lifted it from her brow. His lips traced the place it had been and drifted to her temple and down her cheek. She turned to meet his kiss with lips that were soft and yielding but not aggressive. She accepted his tongue but didn't invade his mouth in return. He explored, tasting her, tracing her tongue with his, under and over and side-on-side. Her mouth responded by becoming wetter and opening wider. The liquor of her mouth intoxicated him. It'd been a long while since just kissing could bring him to full throbbing erection, but her kisses did. Their passive acceptance was a spur. He kissed harder, drawing her lower lip between his teeth and nipping just hard enough to make her suck in a sharp breath.

'Did I hurt you?'

'You know you can do anything to me, Rolf. If it hurts me, provided it pleases you, that's fine.'

'I don't want to hurt you.'

'Thank you. I don't want you to either, at least, not tonight.' She smiled up at him. 'Tomorrow will be another story.'

Unsure how to respond to that, Rolf let his lips trail down the side of her neck, to its crook. She shivered under him. His fingers found the trailing end of her ribbon's bow and tugged it loose. He sat up and unlaced her nightie, working down to her waist and brushing the cotton away to each side. Penny's lovely young breasts, that he'd once thought might fit into martini glasses, were bared for him. Perhaps he'd underestimated them. Only Trixie's over-sized cocktail glasses could have contained them.

To dismiss any thought of his wife, Rolf brushed his fingertips over one of Penny's pale and puffy peaks.

She sighed, 'Yes,' and in that one word told a tale of long-pent longing.

176

'May I kiss your breasts?' he teased.

'Don't ever ask permission, please, Rolf. Not even tonight.'

He nibbled and sucked gently. There was something in him, something primitive that Trixie had resurrected, that wanted to bite Penny's nipple until she whimpered for mercy. He resisted that urge.

Penny moaned and pushed up at him. He took as much breast-flesh into his mouth as would fit. His hand brushed down the cotton of her nightie and up under it. Her thighs parted for him. As he'd suspected, she was bald there, totally, without even the token patch of fuzz that her mother sported. Somehow, that made her more virginal, more vulnerable. His fingers caressed her with infinite gentleness, not parting her but persuading her to part for him.

Rolf was hesitant to explore inside her. Her maidenhead might be long gone but she'd still be sensitive and tight inside. The more aroused he made her before he penetrated her, even with a single finger, the easier it'd be for her. Keeping his weight off her, he slithered down under the bedclothes and lifted her nightie, so that he could rest his cheek on the soft smooth skin on the inside of her thigh.

She said, 'Thank you, Rolf. For what you are about to do, thank you. I've dreamt of your tongue loving me, there, for more nights than you'd believe.'

Rolf had no words to describe the flood of emotion that her words inspired. His lips touched her sex. His tongue tested the slit between her pussy's lips.

Penny threw the bedclothes aside. 'I want to watch, please?'

He nodded.

'Thank you, Lover.'

Hearing her call him what Trixie often did almost put him off but Penny was seeping and he could taste her and that was more powerful than any pangs of guilt. His tongue wormed into her. Penny gasped and made little encouraging wordless sounds. Rolf savoured her lemony-salt juices for a while but he knew that what a woman

177

wants more than anything, when a tongue is on her sex, is to have her clitoris licked. He parted her gently with his little finger and his thumb. His tongue ran up and found the sensitive nub it sought. Rolf started by wagging from side to side, keeping alert for her reactions. Even with his limited experience, he'd learned that different clits enjoy different caresses. When he worked his tongue's tip between the left side of Penny's clit and her sex's lip, and palpitated, her thighs twitched and her knees drew up in a spasm.

Sure that he'd found the magic spot, he persisted with that stroke and began to slide a finger into her. She was slippery but incredibly tight. Would he be able to get his cock into her without hurting her? He'd find out, soon, very soon.

Penny's head thrashed from side to side. She gasped, 'Yes, yes, yes.'

Rolf felt up behind her pubic bone and found her g-spot. Manipulating it was the key to making her wet, and she'd need to be very wet when he put his cock into her.

She said, 'I want you, Rolf. I want you so much. I'm ready, please, Rolf?'

He pulled himself up the bed and looked down into her eyes. 'Are you sure you want this?'

'Yes, please, yes.'

'And you want it right now?'

'Oh God, Rolf, do me! Put it in me. I'm begging you.'

'It might hurt.'

'I don't care! Make me take it!'

He decided it'd be cruel to tease her any more. His fingers took hold of his cock and guided it until its head felt the heat and the wetness. He rose up on two straight arms and pushed his hips slowly forward.

She screamed, 'Fuck!' and clawed down his chest with eight sharp talons.

Spurred by the sudden pain, he rammed into her. She screamed again but her legs wrapped his hips and her heels drummed on the backs of his thighs. That thrust had only taken him halfway into the strangling tightness. He jerked, three more short hard jerks, feeling as if he was violating her and that was part of the fierce pleasure.

Rolf's wiry pubic hair ground on Penny's soft bald mound.

She gave him an incongruously shy look. 'I came when you entered me,' she whispered. 'Did you feel it?'

'No. Sorry I missed it.'

'I can come again. I come easy and often. Fuck me hard, Lover, and maybe you'll feel the next one, or the one after that, or . . .'

Penny proved her boast by climaxing three more times before Rolf's orgasm flooded into her and triggered her fifth.

'I think I've had enough for tonight, Lover,' she breathed against his heaving chest. 'Of course, if *you* want to go on?'

'I'll let you rest,' he told her.

Twenty-five

Rolf woke lying along the edge of the bed with guilt rising in his throat like bile. His eyes opened. There, directly in front of his face, Penny stood beside the bed. Her thighs rose slender but shapely from sheer black hose with lacy tops. Looking higher, he was confronted by her naked sex. Its outer lips were smooth but swollen, as if his ravishing had bruised them, which perhaps it had. They were divided by a very neat vertical slit that was bifurcated by the ridge of her clitoris. He hadn't had the chance to inspect it closely, not visually, the previous night but now he saw that it was longer and thicker than her mother's was, or than his Rachel's had been.

His guilt was forgotten, rinsed away on a tide of lust.

'Do I like my pussy?' she asked.

'Very much. You're beautiful there – and everywhere.'

'I'm yours, there, "and everywhere". Whatever you want to do to me, or have me do for you, I'm ready. Last night was incredible, Rolf, and so romantic, but now I'd like us to be *bad*. I want us to do things normal people don't do. Things they *want* to do but don't dare.'

'I'm not sure I know what those things would be,' he confessed.

'Of course you do. Men have a natural instinct.' She cocked her head to one side. 'Rolf, you have six leather belts in your closet.'

'Do I?'

'Yes. Would you mind if I borrowed one or two?'

180

'No, I don't mind, but they're much too long for your tiny waist, Penny.'

'I could get a leather punch. Would it be OK if I made some more holes?'

'Sure, but are you going to cut the extra lengths off? Wouldn't it be easier for me to just buy you some new belts?'

'They wouldn't be *your* belts. That's the point. They have *you* on them. And I won't cut them short, I promise. You'll still be able to wear them.'

Vaguely flattered, Rolf told her, 'Do what you like with them, Penny.' He reached out to stroke her flank.

She shivered under his touch. 'I *love* leather, Rolf. Don't you? The feel of it; the smell of it; the taste of it?'

'I don't know that I've ever tasted leather.'

'*I* have. I stole one of your belts, about two weeks ago. I've kept it under my pillow since then. At night, I've sucked on it and I've rubbed myself on it, you know . . .' She touched her fingers to her sex in case he didn't understand.

'You've been masturbating with one of my belts?'

'Yes. Am I bad?'

'Well, that's certainly naughty, perhaps a bit kinky but not actually "bad".'

'I told you that I was a kinky little bitch, Rolf, remember?'

'Who likes to talk dirty.'

'Do you mind?'

'No.'

'In which case, your nasty little whore had better go fix you some breakfast before you take one of those belts to her bottom, hadn't she? Something light? A toasted prune Danish, maybe?'

'That'd be fine.'

'Twenty-five minutes?'

'OK.'

It took him that long to shave and shower. She'd laid clean pyjama pants and a fresh robe out for him. Rolf considered marching downstairs stark naked, just to show

181

her that he was as uninhibited as she was. He decided that he wasn't ready for that, not quite yet. Maybe he'd learn to be. He couldn't have a better teacher.

Penny set his Danish down in front of Rolf and stayed standing beside him, her naked thigh touching his shoulder.

'Aren't you going to have one?' he asked.

'I've eaten, thanks.'

'You aren't going to sit down?'

'I'm standing here in case you wanted to fondle me while you eat.'

'Oh.' He ran the fingers of his left hand from behind her right knee, up the length of her thigh, to cup the right cheek of her bottom and give it a loving squeeze.

'Do you like my bum, Rolf?'

'It's lovely.'

'Would you like to play with it?'

'Play?'

'You can do what you like to me, provided you force me, remember? Do I have to prove that I'm depraved?'

'Perhaps you do.'

'Then I will, this once.' She took his left hand in both of her and folded three of its fingers into his palm. 'Like this.' Penny pushed his extended finger into the butter on the table. Her right hand guided his fist. Her left tugged her left cheek away from her right one. She leaned forward a little and put his buttery finger to the pucker of her anus.

'You want me to . . .?' he asked.

'Please.'

He expected more resistance but her sphincter yielded easily to his gentle pressure. Inside, though, she was incredibly tight and burning hot.

'Like that?' he asked.

'Deeper, please?'

'It doesn't hurt?'

'No. It will when you force me to bend for you and you fuck me in there, I think, but I can take your finger easily enough.'

Was she going to keep the promise Trixie had reneged on? Rolf wasn't going to rely on that. He'd savour the

182

forbidden pleasures as they came and not bank on what was promised, he decided.

The butter only lubricated her rectum deeply enough that his finger's second knuckle was inside her. From there, his skin dragged on hers. She winced.

'Enough?'

'I want it all, Rolf. Force it, please? Force *me*! How many times must I tell you that's what I want?'

He wriggled and rotated his finger, persuading her tight channel to open up for him, and applied pressure.

'Oh fuck, Rolf, Lover, that feels so *good*!'

'You really like it?'

'Love it. Can you – you know – push it in and out?'

He abandoned his Danish, half-eaten, and wrapped his right arm around Penny's thighs to brace her. His left fist pushed and pulled. Rolf tried to imagine the sensations his finger was enjoying, transferred to his cock. As he pushed in, it was almost like penetrating a soft and yielding solid. As he pulled, her flesh clung to him as if reluctant to let him retreat.

Penny bent over more and clawed at the table. 'It's even better than I thought it'd be,' she gasped. 'Please, may I . . .?'

'May you what?'

'*This!*' She thrust two fingers into the butter and put them between her thighs. Her position wouldn't let Rolf watch but it was obvious she was masturbating with furious intensity. He pushed harder, striving for further depth. She doubled over. Her projecting elbow sawed the air. He wondered exactly what she was trying to do, and then he knew. Where his finger was, deep inside her, he felt fresh pressure, pushing up. She was feeling where his finger was going, from inside her pussy!

'You're a depraved little bitch,' he told her.

'Yes, I am. Finger-fuck my bum-hole, hard, please, Rolf. I think I'm going to be able to . . . Oh yes! Oh, Rolf, you are the most amazing man and what you are doing to me, it's so . . .'

She convulsed and fell to her knees, dragging herself out

of his arm and off his finger. Rolf pulled her face into his lap, cuddled her shoulders and rocked her. 'There, there.'

'Rolf,' she said in a very tiny voice, 'I'm going to be the best bitch-whore-slut-slave you ever fucked or dreamt of fucking, I promise.'

'You already are the best,' he said.

Penny looked up at him with gleaming eyes. 'But we've only just begun, right Rolf?'

'Right.'

'Finish your breakfast, then, and we'll play some more games, where you make me do very bad things, even if I scream, OK?' She rose and fetched him coffee before sitting opposite him. 'What do you want to force me do next?'

'What would you like – to be "forced" to do?'

'There are so many things that I've imagined you doing to me, Rolf.'

'For an innocent little virgin, you seem to know a great deal about sex – the kinky kind of sex.'

She grinned. 'I told you I've been sneaking my Mom's toys, to play with? Well, I also found her secret stash of naughty books.'

'Your mother reads porn?'

' "Erotica", she'd call it. Didn't you know? Look in the case in her walk-in closet, on the top shelf, behind all those hat boxes. She's got all sorts of good stuff. You'll be surprised. That's where I've educated myself from.'

'She didn't tell me.'

'She wouldn't, would she. You should have guessed, though. If she liked to cook, you'd expect her to read cookbooks, right? She likes sex, so she reads sex books.'

'Why does she keep it a secret from me?'

'In case you didn't understand, I guess. Like, if she had a cookbook and it had a recipe for stewed octopus, you might think she liked them and might serve them to her, even though she hates them. In her sex books, there'll be things she'd like to try and things she wouldn't. She wouldn't want you to get them confused. Me neither. There are things in those books that even I wouldn't dare try.'

'What sort of books are they then, apart from being about sex?'

'Oh, lots of different types. One of *my* favourites is called *The Story of O*. Reading it makes me horny but I wouldn't *really* want have my poor bum branded with a red-hot iron.'

'Ouch!'

'I think about it though, sometimes. Would you like to brand my bottom with your initials, Rolf?'

'Of course not. What's your second favourite book?'

'It's illustrated, like a comic book. It's by a man named John Willie. It's about a slender blonde, looks a bit like me, except she's got bigger tits than I have. Her name's Gwendolyn and she wears tight corsets and belts and hobble skirts and incredibly high heels. She's always getting captured by bad people and tied up in uncomfortable positions, bent and stretched and twisted – all sorts of positions. There's not a lot of actual sex, no real fucking, in the book. It's mainly about bondage.'

'Which is something *you* like.'

'I think I would. I've never had the chance to try it. There's been no one I could trust to tie me up, till now. Are you going to tie me up, Rolf? I'd be so helpless!'

'And you'd *love* that.'

'I wouldn't be able to resist, no matter what terrible things you did to me, Rolf.'

'You're really serious about this "being forced" thing, aren't you.'

'Oh yes! It's what I dream of. And you, you're so big, and powerful . . .'

Rolf finally got his mind around the concept of Penny's desire to be dominated and degraded. He'd always considered himself a kind and gentle man but now he realised that only a sadist is equipped to be kind to a devout masochist. He had that in him, it seemed. Under his civilised veneer, dark cruelty lurked, waiting to be invited out, or to escape.

Penny had issued a clear invitation. The sophisticated beast in him responded.

'I'm going to use you,' he said. 'You are going to amuse me.'

Understanding blossomed on her face. 'Yes, Rolf. Of course. No matter how much I protest?'

'No matter how much,' he confirmed.

She looked at the floor. 'Thank you, Rolf.'

He rose. Rolf was taller than Penny by almost a foot but this time, when he stood up, he towered over her as if he was a giant and she a child. She shivered. Her eyes were big and liquid, looking up at him. He took her by her ponytail and strode off, giving her no choice but to trot beside him. Up the stairs he marched, with her stumbling but unable to fall because his grip in her hair kept her upright. By the time he got her to his bedroom there were tears in her eyes. Rolf cupped Penny's pussy. That too was weeping.

By the one hand in her hair and the other between her legs, he tossed her onto the bed, onto her back. His hands took her ankles and yanked them into the air, dragging her bottom to the bed's edge. Rolf's grip transferred to just above and behind her knees. He forced her thighs apart and up into her armpits, curling her bottom up and presenting him her seeping pussy.

Penny whimpered, 'No! No!' but he knew to ignore any plea for mercy that didn't include 'Red Light'.

He knelt, still holding her in place. His mouth came down on her sex, not reverently, as it had before, but greedily. His cheeks moved from side to side, opening her. His lips and tongue slurped and sucked and lapped, gobbling up her juices. Her flavour had changed. Before, she'd tasted quite tart, with a tang of something like lemon. Today, her juices were more like those of a very ripe cantaloupe, sweet without cloying. Perhaps it had to do with her hormones. She'd been a virgin when first he'd tasted her. Now, he, his stiff hard cock, had made a woman of her. *That* might have changed the nature of her essences.

The thought made him feel immensely powerful, almost magical.

The shaft of Penny's clit, being so much longer and thicker than her mother's, was easy to grip between his lips to force its sheath back. His tongue's tip circled the nub's naked head.

Penny writhed and moaned, 'No,' again and again, encouraging him to tongue-lash her into a convulsive climax.

He rose triumphantly from his conquest. His robe fell. He commanded her, 'Take my pants off.'

She sat up on the edge of his bed and tugged at the cord of his pyjama pants with quivering fingers. They fell, to be kicked aside. Naked and powerful, he told her, 'Open your mouth.'

She begged, 'Please don't make me take your cock in my mouth.'

He took a fresh grip of her hair with one hand. His other forced her jaws to open. Rolf's hips pushed forward. His cock's head passed between Penny's gaping lips and slid over her tongue.

For a moment, he hesitated. Trixie had been adept at taking his cock deep into her mouth, even into her throat. It had likely taken her years to learn how to do that without choking. This had to be the first time Penny'd had a cock in her mouth. Could she, unpractised, do what her mother did?

Well, she claimed that she wanted to be used and abused. It was time for her to learn what that really meant. Rolf dragged Penny's head towards him and impaled her mouth on the rigid shaft of his throbbing cock.

She looked up at him with a strange expression in her eyes, part distress, part glee.

Rolf asked her, 'Red Light?'

Her head shook a little, as much as she could manage in his iron grip.

Rolf drew back, dragging the head of his cock across the flat of her tongue and out from between her lips. Penny struggled to get her mouth back to it. His hips swayed, smacking her cheeks with his shaft. She tried to twist, to get her lips to his cock's head, and whined like a puppy when she failed.

Rolf relented. He drove slowly into her mouth, giving her tongue the chance to work around his cock's head but not stopping until it butted against the back of her throat. Her breath was loud, rasping though her nose, but she wasn't choking so he pushed harder and felt her throat open for him. Keeping careful control, Rolf rocked, half an inch in, half an inch back. In his head, his own voice was bellowing, 'You're fucking Penny's throat, Rolf, and she *loves* it!'

Penny's mouth was filling with saliva. It was drooling out around Rolf's shaft and running down to saturate his balls.

Once more he asked, 'Red Light?', and once again she shook her head. Rolf felt he should do something *more*, something even more obscene, to the sweet young girl who had declared herself his willing slave. He certainly needed more sensation than a half-inch thrust could deliver if he was going to climax. He pulled his cock all the way out and twisted Penny's ponytail to turn her face up.

'Tongue out, flat,' he commanded.

His right fist pumped his shaft furiously. As he felt his cream boil up, he aimed the eye of his cock at Penny's tongue. His orgasm flooded from him, splashing her tongue and into her gaping mouth and splattering her cheeks and throat. Rolf let his second and third jets flop on her shoulders and between her breasts.

Drained, he staggered back. Penny smiled. Her forefinger scooped his drooling jism from her golden skin and took it to her mouth.

She said, 'Delicious, Rolf. Thank you.'

Twenty-six

Penny was dressed in a demure white cotton shirt with a striped tie, a flirty little grey flannel skirt, ankle socks and penny loafers. Her ponytail had been converted into a pair of ribbon-tied bunches.

Rolf looked her up and down. He raised an eyebrow. 'Are you going for the "schoolgirl" look?'

She gazed up at him from under her long lashes. 'It's the "naughty schoolgirl" look I'm trying for. I'm not wearing any panties under this skirt. Don't naughty little girls who go out with no undies on get punished, on their bare bottoms?'

'You're going *out* like that?'

'We need milk and bread, and some other stuff,' she explained. 'I have to go to the store.'

'I'd better drive you, to keep you safe from those big bad schoolboys. I'd hate to see you get your bunches dipped into inkwells.'

'Thank you.'

He made a mental note. She kept on hinting about corporal punishment but since that spanking he'd given her, the one that had triggered their perverse affair, he hadn't laid a hand on her, at least, not in *that* way. Rolf had mixed feelings on the subject. He was so much bigger and stronger than she was, he'd have to be very careful not to harm her. And then there was the problem of how much he might like it. He'd fallen into the role of a dominating master easily enough. What if he was also, deep down, a sadist? Could he live with himself if he discovered that he took real pleasure in hurting women?

But if corporal punishment was what they wanted, then . . .? He decided not to pursue that line of reasoning. It led to places he wasn't ready to explore.

No sooner had he turned onto the blacktop than Penny pulled her skirt up and produced her compact's mirror, which she held at an angle between her thighs.

'What on earth are you doing?' Rolf asked.

'Just checking. I was wondering, maybe, now I'm not a virgin any more, if it showed.'

'And does it?'

'Could be. I think I look riper, juicier, down there.'

'You do?'

'See for yourself.'

'Later. I have to keep my eyes on the road.'

'But you can drive with one hand, so you can *feel* if there's a difference.' She took hold of his right wrist and guided his fingers to her sex.

He palpitated her pussy's lips. 'You're wet, but then you're always wet.'

'Not always. Just when I'm with you.'

Rolf retrieved his hand.

'Please don't stop what you were doing,' she asked. 'I was enjoying it.'

'Mm, me too.' He put his hand back and slid a finger between her lips.

Penny slumped and spread her feet. 'It's about half an hour to the store, isn't it? There's no traffic. Want me to . . .?' Her fingers walked across the front of his slacks.

'Not while I'm driving, Penny.' Remembering the dominant/submissive roles they were playing, he added a firm, 'When I want you to give me a hand-job, I'll tell you.'

'I was thinking more of a blow-job.'

'That too.'

'So if I grope you without being told to, do I get punished?'

There she went again, hinting for what she obviously craved. In a stern voice, he told her, 'You'll get punished

190

when and how I decide. You might find it more painful than you expect.'

'Yes please!'

It was difficult to put on an act of being annoyed when his fingers were dabbling in the dew of her pussy, so Rolf said no more.

She came out of the supermarket with a half-full cart. When she got into the car, Rolf asked her, 'Just bread and milk?'

'Lots of frozen bread, some cold cuts and some bags of milk that we can freeze. I don't want to waste any more of our precious days together by going out shopping, Rolf.'

'So you've got everything?'

'Almost. Tack shop, please?

En route to the tack shop, they had to pass Sag Harbor Cinema. 'Look, Rolf!' Penny squealed. 'It's a double bill, *Rififi* and *Clochemerle*. Can we, Rolf? Can we please?'

'In French, right? I'm not much for movies with subtitles.'

'Then you'll *love Rififi*. For the first half hour, there's no dialogue and no music. It's a classic, Rolf.' She gave him an imploring look and suddenly he saw her as the little girl she'd dressed up as. 'I never got to make out in the back row of a cinema, back when I was a teeny, Rolf. Please?'

The theatre was empty except for one other couple, an androgynous pair, both wearing berets, sitting near the front. Rolf set his giant tub of extra-butter popcorn and his super-sized cola on the seat next to his, in the back row, as Penny had requested. To his surprise, the opening sequence of *Rififi* was riveting. He almost forgot that Penny had other things in mind than watching the screen.

An hour into the movie, Penny nudged him. She whispered, 'We *are* going to make out, aren't we?'

'If anyone was to see a man my age kissing a girl who looks as young as you do right now, they'd call a cop.'

'That's half the fun. Please?'

Rolf glanced around to make sure they weren't being observed before putting his arm around her shoulders. She turned to him with her mouth wet and voracious. After a long and breathless kiss, she asked, 'Touch me, please? Between my legs? And pass me the popcorn?'

In his youth, Rolf had made out with girls in theatres, but it had never been like this. Back then, if he'd managed to grope a breast through a sweater, he'd counted himself lucky. He handed the popcorn over and slid his hand up Penny's leg. She spread her thighs to accommodate him. 'Would you take your cock out for me, please, Rolf?'

'Penny!'

'Then I'll do it.'

Constrained by being in a public place, even though no one could see them, Rolf allowed Penny to unzip him and pull his shaft out through his fly. He had to admit, the risk *did* make it more thrilling. Penny dipped her hand into the tub of buttery popcorn.

'Nice and slippery,' she told him, and ran her greasy fingers up his shaft. 'So slick, stiff and slick. I *love* hot buttered cock. Remember when I buttered your finger and you pushed it up my bum? That felt *so* good, Lover.'

'Careful! You'll make me . . .'

'I know. I intend to. Back then, other girls used to brag about the boys they'd jerked off at the movies. I got *so* jealous! Now it's *my* turn, but with a *man*, not just a boy.' She began to masturbate him in earnest.

'But if I climax . . . The – mess?'

'I've thought of that.' With her free hand, she set the popcorn down on the floor between his feet. 'We've still got lots to do today,' she told him, 'so I won't make this last too long.' Her hand pumped fast and hard. Rolf bit his lip. His legs stiffened. On the screen, shots were fired, by who and at whom, he didn't know or care. His scrotum tightened and he climaxed, mainly splattering into the tub.

The closing titles rolled down the screen.

'That was nice,' Penny said. 'Can we go now?'

'It's a double feature.'

'I've got a different sort of double feature in mind, starring you and me, Lover. It'll be better, and naughtier, than *Clochemerle*, I promise.'

Back in the car, Penny hugged Rolf's arm. 'Thank you! You made my fantasy come true. I'll never forget that. You're going to make *all* my sexy fantasies come true, aren't you?'

'If I can, and if they aren't too . . .'

'Crazy? Don't worry, Lover. I know my limits. I don't want us to do anything that isn't safe, relatively speaking.'

Rolf cleared his throat. 'Relatively speaking?'

'Just teasing.' She pecked his cheek. 'Tack shop? I want to buy a treat for you, Lover, for being so good to me. You'll have to come in and help me pick it out.'

'For me, from the tack shop?'

'You'll see.'

Penny had obviously been browsing. She knew exactly where the items she wanted were. The leather punches were in plastic packages, hooked onto a board near the front. She took one and marched straight to the back of the store, sucking in deep loud open-mouthed breaths. 'I just *love* the smell of leather, don't you?'

'And you like the taste, you tell me,' he whispered into her ear.

'And the texture,' she added.

The bin she went to was marked $7.50–$15 so Rolf didn't have to worry about her spending all her allowance on him. Penny selected a two-and-a-half-foot-long black leather riding crop and swished it through the air. 'What do you think?' she asked. 'Whippy enough to deliver a good sting?'

'The stables provides crops when we go riding,' he said, suspecting that his observation wasn't relevant. His stomach tightened as he waited for her to confirm his suspicions.

'It's not for a *horse*, silly,' she said with a giggle. 'You *know* why I want to buy you a crop, or maybe two.'

Very softly, he said, 'A beating from one of those would feel a lot different than a spanking, Penny.'

She beamed. 'I know! Try this one, Rolf. See how it feels in your hand.'

He had no choice but to take a couple of cuts at the air. Penny turned and went on tip-toe to bend over and reach down into the bottom of the bin. Her position lifted her short skirt dangerously high up the backs of her thighs. Rolf was *very* aware that her bottom was bare under her skirt, and within inches of being exposed.

From the depths, he heard her say, 'You could give that crop a practical test, right now, if you liked, Rolf.' Her hips wiggled at him.

'I'll wait, thanks.'

'Not for too long, I hope.' She heaved herself up with another crop, about six inches shorter and twice as thick, in her hand. 'We'll take these two, if you like them. Or would you like three, or four?'

'Two will be plenty, thanks.' He grinned and added, 'When I've worn these two out, I can always buy some more.'

Penny laughed out loud. 'You're priceless, Rolf.'

Rolf wondered if the store clerk was surprised that a mature man would blush when a pretty schoolgirl, presumably his daughter, bought him a pair of riding crops.

All the way home, Penny caressed and licked her purchases. 'Which one do you like best?' she asked.

'It's more a matter of which one *you* like best, isn't it?'

'I won't know that until I've felt them, will I.'

'You're serious.'

'Yes, very serious.'

'You expect me to drive you home and then whip your bottom with one of those crops?'

'Not necessarily. We don't have to do it today if you aren't ready for it yet. It's up to you when you do it. I just wanted to have them handy for when the urge takes you.' She giggled. 'It'd spoil the mood if we had to stop in the middle of whatever we were doing and run out to buy the toys we needed, wouldn't it?'

'You're a regular Girl Scout.'

'I could dress up as one if it turned you on, Rolf.'

He grunted. Whatever he said, she was likely to turn it into a *double entendre*. His cock had already recovered from what she'd done to him in the theatre. It didn't need any more encouragement.

Hell! He'd climaxed just an hour ago and his cock was stiff again already? What was Penny doing to him? Turning him into some sort of sex-maniac?

Twenty-seven

Penny had said that she had something she wanted to do. Rolf had volunteered to build submarine sandwiches for their early evening meal. They'd missed lunch, except for a handful of popcorn each. Anyway, he needed a few moments alone, to sort his thoughts out. When she was with him he was so obsessed by her lithe young body and her eagerness to indulge in depravity that lust fogged his mind.

He considered his situation. It didn't take him long to come to a conclusion. Penny had seduced him into spanking her and fucking her and oral sex, both ways, and she still wanted more, more, more. It wasn't all her fault. He'd lusted after her. That'd most likely shown. Now, he decided, there was no way back. She couldn't regain her virginity, nor he his relative innocence. When there is no way to retreat, a man must go forward. If it all came out, somehow; if their perverted relationship were discovered, he'd already done more than enough to condemn himself in society's eyes. He might as well go all the way, wherever that was. Penny obviously knew exactly what she wanted. He'd discover his own dark desires as he went along.

Well, *that* was a relief! No more wrestling with his conscience! He was evil, by most people's standards. So be it. He couldn't escape his depravity so he might as well enjoy it while he could.

As he mentally abandoned the last shreds of his inhibitions, one more thought occurred to him. In everything he and Penny had done, so far, she'd led the way. From the time she'd explored his cock while he slept to the incident at the theatre and to the purchase of those vicious crops, everything had been her idea, her initiative. He owed it to his masculinity to change that. From here on, he vowed, Rolf was going to be in charge. He was going to turn Penny into no more than what she professed she wanted to be; his abject sex-slave.

When she came into the kitchen, she'd abandoned her schoolgirl outfit and with it, her look of youthful innocence. She was a brand new Penny, one that better reflected her true character. The ankle-strap sandals she was wearing might have been Trixie's because their heels were spikes that were all of five inches tall. Her stockings were certainly Trixie-style, black and glossy, with lace tops, that reached halfway up her lovely thighs.

Otherwise, she was naked except for one of Rolf's belts, that she'd punched extra holes in. She'd been able to cinch her waist so tightly that her skin was folded and creased. It must have restricted her breathing, Rolf thought. Her hair had lost its schoolgirl bunches. Her platinum locks fell smoothly to below her shoulders, adding years of sophistication to her looks. Penny had made her face up like a Vegas showgirl's, with heavy blue mascara and shadow, sequins at the corners of her eyes and with her lips painted glossy crimson. She'd looked younger than her years, that morning. Now she looked older. Both effects betrayed her depravity.

Penny turned to show him that the extra length of his belt hung behind her, dangling from her waist down to the tops of her thighs.

'Do I look like a bad girl?' she asked, her voice husky.

'Very bad.'

'Good, 'cause I am. I want one of Mom's martinis, please?'

'You may have a white wine spritzer.'

She pouted prettily, turning herself back into a naughty teen.

Rolf smiled. It was time he acted on his resolution to

197

take charge of their games. 'Penny, you know where your Mom keeps her toys, right?'

'Of course.'

'Fetch me the lubricant, and that cream that makes a clit more sensitive, and a vibrator, your choice which one. Bring them to my den.'

Her eyes widened. 'Lubricant? Does that mean . . .?'

'You'll find out what it means, in due course. Go!'

'Yes, Rolf. Rolf? You're different now, much more masterful. I like it.'

His eyes narrowed. 'Penny, you have your instructions.'

'Sorry! I'm gone!' She turned on her heels, flexed her bum's cheeks at him, and scurried away.

Rolf set the sandwiches on a little table next to his big leather chair, poured Penny's drink for her, and moved his footstool to beside his chair. Penny brought the things he'd ordered, plus the crops, and laid them out on the sideboard.

'We'll eat a little later,' he decided out loud. 'Come here, Penny.'

She trotted to him, expectantly. He turned her round and unbuckled the belt from around her waist.

'You don't like it?'

'I like it fine. Cross your forearms behind you.' She obeyed. He ran the belt back around her waist, but now also over her arms, and pulled it strangling tight.

'Oh!' she said. 'What are you doing, Rolf? You aren't going to hurt me, are you?'

'Yes, I am.'

She licked her lips. 'Please, no, Rolf? Please don't hurt me? Are you going to use those wicked crops on my poor little bottom?'

'Not tonight.' He unbuckled the belt he was wearing and pulled it from its loops.

'No, not that!' she squealed. 'Anything but the *belt*.'

Rolf put the self-covered buckle into his right palm and wrapped the belt around his fist twice, leaving eighteen inches of supple leather dangling.

'Lover, that'll hurt bad!'

'Yes, it will. You remember "Red Light"?'

'I remember.'

'You'll need to.' He tossed a cushion to the floor, in front of the footstool. 'Kneel on the stool.' His left fist took a handful of her hair to help steady her as she knelt, awkward without the use of her arms. 'Head down, face resting on the cushion.' Again, his grip in her hair helped lower her. Rolf walked around his eager victim, inspecting her. With her kneeling up on the stool, with her head down to the floor, her body was inclined at a steep angle. Her slender flanks were uppermost, with her bottom silhouetted, its divide looking very much like the cleft in the top of a Valentine's heart.

She was helpless and vulnerable. An unfamiliar emotion flooded through Rolf, somehow enlarging him. He was Penny's absolute *master*. Her joy and her pain were his to dispense or withhold, at his whim. It was incredibly exhilarating.

'Don't move,' he told her, totally unnecessarily. He quickly stripped naked, using just his left hand. The belt had become a part of his right one. He had no need of clothes. He was clad in his own masculine *power*.

Rolf circled Penny, inspecting his eager victim. His strap touched her bottom. 'You know what I am going to do to you, don't you.'

'Please don't. I couldn't stand it, not the belt.'

'Red Light?'

She shook her head and bit her lip.

'I'm only going to give you twenty, this time,' he told her. It was important that he set a limit before he started. If he didn't it might prove irresistibly tempting to just keep on, and on, and on.

'Not twenty,' she begged.

'Twenty.' His hand drew back. The first slap of leather on tender skin landed halfway up her thighs, delivered at less than half the force he was capable of.

Penny gasped and winced.

'One.' The next landed at the juncture of her thighs with her bottom, harder but not full force. 'Two.'

'Please, Rolf, no! I'll do anything you want but don't do this.'

'Red Light?'

She gave an impatient shake of her head, telling him that her pleading was to be ignored. So be it. He wouldn't ask her again. The belt rose and fell, each blow counted in a calm and even voice, though his excitement was rising. Penny sobbed and made gurgling noises and babbled incoherently but she didn't invoke 'Red Light'.

By the time Rolf reached 'twenty' there were broad scarlet lines criss-crossing her thighs, with white diamonds of skin between them, but her bottom's cheeks were completely deep crimson, mottled with purple.

Rolf twirled his belt from around his fist and set it aside. Where his belt had punished Penny, his hands stroked. Rolf's caresses weren't for Penny's pleasure. They were for his. His fingers savoured the ridges he'd raised on her flesh. His palms absorbed the fever-heat that glowed from her skin. The sounds she made were half whimpers, half purrs. Rolf cupped his hand between her thighs. She was slick there, as if she'd already climaxed. One of his fingertips trailed up through the valley between her bottom's cheeks. It lingered at the pucker of her anus.

Penny shivered. 'You aren't going to . . .?'

'Yes, I am.' He applied a slight pressure.

'Please, no. I've never . . .'

'You are, now.'

He fetched the lubricant and squeezed a jet onto her tailbone. Rolf's self-control was so strong that he was able to squat behind Penny without touching her and simply watch as the thick clear fluid slowly trickled down her bottom's crease, pooled in the slight dimple of its tiny aperture, then spilled to flow over her perineum and on to coat her sex's bulging lips.

'You're too big,' Penny protested. 'Your cock'll never fit in me there.'

'I'll make it fit. I'll force it.'

'Beast!'

'True.'

Coming out of character, Penny dryly observed, 'You're a fast learner, Rolf.'

'You know what Oscar Wilde said – "Be careful what you wish for. You might get it." '

'On my own head, or up my own bum, be it.'

Rolf laughed.

Penny switched back into her 'maiden in distress' role, overdoing it, with 'Oh you monster, to treat a poor young girl so cruelly!'

'Funny, is it? We'll see how well you laugh in a few minutes.' Rolf squeezed more lubricant over his cock and took his stance, close behind her, his legs slightly bent to lower himself into position. His left fist gripped the belt that ran around Penny's waist. The thumb and two fingers of his right hand steered his cock.

Perhaps it *was* impossible. Her anus was a pin-hole. By comparison, his cock looked like a glistening cudgel. He nudged her, just below her bum's opening, then let his cock's head rise to obscure it. Rolf applied pressure. All he felt was resistance. He pushed harder, and harder. Rigid as it was, his cock began to bend. Determined, Rolf wrapped his fist around his shaft to stiffen it and leant into Penny, bearing down. For a long moment, nothing happened. Rolf bunched his left biceps. He *pulled* on the belt.

And the head of his cock disappeared into her. He could feel the tightness of her sphincter, squeezing his shaft just behind its head.

Penny whimpered.

'Funny?' he asked.

'God no! Rolf, you're destroying me!'

'Red Light?'

Her head shook.

'Very well.' His right hand released his shaft. His left arm lifted Penny by the belt, raising her body to horizontal and then a little higher. 'Head up,' he said.

His right arm reached over her. His fingers burrowed into her hair, massaging her scalp. He made a fist. The pain of having her hair pulled made Penny suck air. Her head was strained back, arching her throat. Both of Rolf's grips

201

were cruel and secure, in her hair and on her belt. Using those, he drew her back, slowly and inexorably impaling her rectum on his cock. He kept pulling until his pubic hair pressed hard against her tailbone. Her sheath compressed his cock as if to expel it but it was too powerful for her to fight against.

God, but it felt good!

Penny hissed. 'It's too big, Rolf. Please, Rolf? Can we stop now? Can I do something else for you? I can't stand this, please?'

He pushed her, and pulled her. She babbled, 'No, no, no,' and, 'Oh my God!'

Rolf kept his hips still and pumped her on his cock, using her bottom's clinging sheath to masturbate with, reducing a lovely young girl to nothing more than an obscene sex-toy. Now he understood why she needed to be forced, or pretend to be. It was like the tango, a rite of male domination, initial female resistance and eventually, total surrender. How could a woman submit unless her man forced her?

His rhythm accelerated. Rolf began to grunt. At last, his hips could keep still no longer. Still pushing and pulling Penny bodily, he thrust and thrust and thrust . . . . . . and released, sending his boiling cream to flood Penny's insides.

Two more short hard jerks emptied him. With tender care, he lowered Penny's tear-streaked face back to the cushion, pulling her off his softening cock.

'Rolf,' she gasped. 'That was incredible.'

He unbuckled the belt that trapped her arms. 'All you expected?'

'And more.'

'Did you climax?'

Her 'Yes' held reservations.

'You want more?'

'I – I can usually come three or four times.'

'That's why I had you bring the clit lotion and the vibrator. Take care of yourself.'

'Here? In front of you?'

'Yes.'

'You want to watch?'

'Yes, but I'm starved. I want my sandwich. You can amuse me by diddling yourself while I eat.'

'You really know how to humiliate a girl, Rolf.'

'I'm learning.'

He sat back in his chair, proudly naked, legs splayed, cock wet and limp on his thigh. Penny fetched the cream and a nine-inch gnarled imitation cock. She pulled the footstool to where he'd be able to see her sitting on it but when she touched her bottom to its leather, she winced and stood back up.

'You really did a number on my bum, Rolf.'

Not wanting to comment, he grunted something unintelligible around a mouthful of submarine sandwich.

Gingerly, Penny knelt in front of the stool, facing him, knees spread far apart, and leaned way back to rest the small of her back on it. Looking obliquely down on her, Rolf had a perfect view of her pussy and her belly. Her breasts were puffy-peaked in silhouette. Her head and face had dropped back, invisible.

Penny squeezed a small round globule of cream onto the tip of her right index finger. Two fingers of her left hand eased her clit's sheath back. The pad of her index finger smoothed cream onto her clit's exposed head with tiny circular movements. Her left hand reached for the vibrator. She turned its base one-handed, as if she'd used it often before. She likely had. Penny'd told him she'd been in the habit of secretly borrowing her mother's toys.

She held the buzzing vibrator partly pressed against her clit's shaft and partly against her fingertip. Both finger and vibrator moved subtly, the finger rotating and the vibrator pressing rhythmically. Her body tensed. It was obvious that Penny's entire being was focused on a part of herself that was no bigger than a split pea.

Rolf brushed crumbs off his fingers and sat forward for a closer look. After a while, a muscle in Penny's right thigh twitched. Her belly knotted, relaxed, and knotted again. She moaned, 'Oh damn!'

'Problem?'

'I was almost there, and then I lost it.'

'Need a hand?'

'I'll get there.'

She took a deep breath and started over. Once more, she twitched and then tightened and held the tension, quivering with the strain.

'Hell!' She writhed up and forward onto her knees, with both hands still clamped between her thighs. Penny toppled towards Rolf, landing with her face on his thigh, and slid her cheek up his leg to get her mouth to his limp cock. Her lips worked, mumbling his shaft into her mouth. Her eyes looked up into his, imploring. By instinct, he took her head in his hands and pushed his hips at her, filling her mouth with his cock. It had been sated. Rolf would have sworn he couldn't have achieved another erection for an hour, or at the very least a half-hour, but he could feel it engorge and begin to stiffen.

Penny's face screwed up. She let out a barking cough around Rolf's cock and convulsed into a climax.

Her head lifted, letting his semi-stiff shaft fall. 'Thanks. I needed that. It's a different sort of climax, Lover, when my mouth is full of your cock. I liked it.' She looked at his lolling member. 'Want me to take care of that for you?'

'I can wait.'

'Good, because my favourite programme is coming on. Mind if I turn the TV on?'

'Your favourite? I didn't know you had one.'

'*CSI*. It's about forensic detection. It's very authentic, I hear. Very educational.'

'Are you thinking of taking up a life of crime?'

She grinned. 'Maybe someday, but I'm too busy enjoying a life of debauchery right now.'

Twenty-eight

It was a Thursday, one of the days the cleaning women came. Rolf and Penny packed a cooler of drinks and a basket of snacks and went out to the pool for the day. Partly, Rolf wanted to be out of the cleaners' way. Partly, he felt that the erotic vibrations between him and Penny were so powerful that anyone who came near them would suspect they were having an *affaire*.

He swam two dozen lengths and then sprawled on his side on a lounger that he'd adjusted to lie flat. The hot sun dried him in moments. Through slitted eyes, he watched Penny swim, smoothly and effortlessly, an erotic mermaid in a minute thong and minuscule bra. After a while, he picked up a book, not to read but to conceal his erection. The cleaners might be looking down from upstairs.

Penny climbed out. 'Anything interesting in your book?' she asked, slyly.

'Depends on what interests you.'

'I think you know.' She threw herself into the lounger beside him, on her tummy. 'Check my bum, Rolf.'

He sat up and looked. 'Very nice.'

'What I meant was, it's all healed.'

'That's good.'

'It is, but it's prettier when it's been marked, by you.'

'Are you hinting?'

'Of course.'

'We'll see.'

She rolled over. 'I'm *so* horny, Rolf.'

'That's a change.'

'Tease. Seriously, Lover, I want you and I want you bad.' Her fingers pushed down into the front of her thong.

'Penny, there are eyes around.'

'Not in the sauna, there aren't.'

'True.'

'Please?'

Feigning a reluctant sigh, Rolf stood up.

'Bring the cooler,' Penny said as she ran to the cedar shack.

She was naked by the time he got inside. As he set the cooler on a bench, she dragged his trunks down to his ankles.

'You're in a rush,' he observed.

'Love your cock! Up on the top bench, please?'

'Is that any way for a good little sex-slave to talk to her master?'

'Sorry. Up on the top bench, on your back, pretty please with sugar and sprinkles on. Is that better?'

'You have something special in mind?'

'Sort of. Rolf, if I'm really good, can we play with your crops tonight?'

'If that's what you want, I'd better not do anything too strenuous until then. You know how beating your bottom takes it out of me.'

'For what *I* have in mind, right now, all you have to do is lie back and enjoy.'

'*That* I can manage.' He stepped up to the top slatted shelf and stretched out, his hands linked behind his neck.

'I'm turning the heat up,' Penny announced.

'Isn't it hot enough in here?'

'I want us to sweat, *really* sweat.'

Rolf closed his eyes. Penny never ceased to amaze him. At nineteen, and a virgin until just over a week ago, she was full of creative ways to make love. It had to be those sex books of Trixie's. Perhaps he should open up that secret case and read a few of them for himself. Maybe not. It might be better to just wait and see what perversions Penny came up with. As she'd warned him, a woman might read about a sex act, but that didn't mean she craved it or was even ready to try it.

A fingertip caressed his hipbone. His cock twitched in response.

Penny said, 'Good cock!'

Rolf felt her loom up beside him and slitted his eyes to see what she was up to. Penny was kneeling up on the lower bench. Her tender young breasts, already beaded with sweat, were no more than a foot from his mouth. He licked his lips.

'Thirsty?'

'Some.' He expected a lascivious wet kiss or perhaps some of the cooler's wine, from her mouth to his, which was one of Trixie's favourite tricks. The mother and daughter had so much in common in the ways they made love.

Penny took her right breast in both hands, thumb touching thumb, index finger touching index finger, making a ring around her delicate flesh. She squeezed, working her hands towards her nipple. Perspiration ran ahead of her hands, gathering. She reared up and leaned over him. 'Mouth open, please?'

Rolf's lips parted. Penny's perspiration dripped from the tip of her nipple, into his mouth.

'Mm!' he said. 'Tasty.'

She lowered until her nipple touched his lips. He pursed them around her swollen peak and drew it into his mouth.

'Next one,' she announced, and squeezed the sweat off her left breast for him to suckle and savour. 'My turn.' She climbed up, astride him, and lay flat on his torso. 'Such a nice big firm bed,' she said. 'Lots of room for a little girl.' She wriggled and by then they were both coated with sweat, so that her writhing slid her skin on his. 'I love how massive your chest is, Rolf.'

His cock was trapped between her belly and his. Each movement of her body tormented his shaft.

'There's a lump,' she said, pressing down.

'I'm sorry if it makes you uncomfortable.'

'That's OK. I know how to accommodate it, but first . . .' She arched over him and dipped her head. The flat of her tongue ran up the middle of his chest and to the hollow of his throat where she made deliberately exaggerated slurping sounds as she sucked at the sweat that had pooled there. 'Yummy!' Her face darted from his throat to an earlobe and down to nip a nipple and back to slathering her tongue across the width of his broad chest.

'I could eat you all up,' she told him.

'I wouldn't object.'

'You like to have your cock in my mouth, don't you.'

'Very much.'

'Me too. I like the feel of it, Rolf, the shape and the texture. I like the taste of it, the precum and the come. You know what else I like about having your cock in my mouth?'

'No?'

'When it really fills my mouth, in so deep it makes it difficult for me to breathe, and then – when I come – it's *fantastic!* It's like my climax is trapped inside me and has to fight to get out, so I ride that magic wave for a long long time before it breaks.'

'I wouldn't want to choke you.'

'Oh, you won't. It's up to me, isn't it? I can always pull back if I have to. If I couldn't, because you were holding me by my hair for instance – which I *love* – well, I trust you. You never lose control, Rolf, so I know I'm safe in your hands, no matter what.'

'You trust me that much?'

'Absolutely. With my life.' She reached out to either side of him and gripped the bench's slats. 'Enough talk!' Feet lifted, her full weight on him, Penny pushed and pulled, slithering to and fro, forward and back. His cock popped up between her thighs. She clamped on it, locking her ankles to squeeze her legs together on it, and writhed harder. 'I bet I could get you off like this,' she claimed. 'Ever had a "thigh-job" before?'

'Not that I recall, and I would remember, if I had.'

'Another time,' she said. 'It's time for my exercises.'

'Exercises?'

'Sit ups. Must keep trim.'

'You're trim.'

With one lithe contortion, Penny swung herself round to sit up on Rolf's belly, facing his feet. Her fingers guided his cock. She hitched forward, impaling herself. Her feet hooked behind his calves. A wriggle made sure he was embedded deeply. Her fingers stretched up towards the ceiling. She swung forward and touched her toes.

The movement did incredible things to Rolf's cock. It was stiff and engorged but her weight forced it to bend to the horizontal. The action pressed his cock's head hard against the slippery inside of her sheath and slide on it at the same time. Before he had time to even grunt, she'd swung up again, all the way back to whip his face with her wet ponytail, and forward again. Penny's entire young body had become an instrument of masturbation, working his cock in the most extreme manner he could imagine.

Down she went, and up, and down, an erotic pendulum, and he wanted to move, to grab her hips and just *fuck* into her, but the torment was so exquisite that his will was paralysed. He lay and endured, and endured, and just when he felt his climax begin to seethe – she stopped, sitting upright on him.

'Nice?' she asked.

'Very.'

Penny cupped his balls. 'You were close, weren't you.'

'Yes, I was.'

'You could have just taken over.'

'I know. I can wait.'

'You're incredible.'

'You too.' He reached up and put a hand to either side of Penny's ribcage. The space between his hands was so narrow, it seemed incredible that it contained a heart and two lungs and muscles and veins and arteries. Her ribs felt so delicate that it seemed to Rolf that if he simply pressed his hands together, she'd be crushed between them.

'Lift me,' she said.

His hands dropped to her waist, his arms braced and he heaved her up, bodily.

'Now down,' she asked.

He lowered her, impaling her on his shaft once more.

'May I come?'

'Of course.'

'You later, OK?'

'OK.'

'Hold my ponytail?'

Rolf wrapped the length of sodden hair around his fist. Penny leaned back, letting his grip on her hair support her. Her legs swung apart. Her hands went between her thighs and began to play. 'It's nice when I do myself with your cock inside me. Is it nice for you, too?'

'Very nice.'

'How? What do you like about it?'

'I like it that you are enjoying yourself. I like the way you twitch, inside. My cock loves that.'

'Can you feel this?' She slapped at her clit with two fingers. 'I'm not hurting you?'

'I can feel it but it isn't hurting.'

'Good.' Her fingers beat faster, and faster. 'And later, the crops? Please?'

'You shall have your cropping, Penny.'

'I'll be bound?'

'Yes, you'll be bound.'

'Oh, fuck! Just thinking of it . . .' Her fingers beat an accelerating tattoo. Penny's entire body tensed. She threw her head back and let out an ululating wail that got louder and louder and higher and higher until Rolf feared the cleaning women would hear it from the house. He reached up and clamped his palm over her mouth. Penny's free hand dragged his wrist down until his hand was over her throat and then she strained against it, strangling her wail down to a thin scream of wracking delight. Between straining to pull against Rolf's iron grip on her hair and striving to push her throat against the palm of his powerful hand, Penny's body vibrated like a bow-string.

She shuddered. Her hips ground down. Despite the heat of the sauna, Rolf felt a warm flood of fluids gush from around his cock and soak into his balls.

Penny collapsed back onto him. 'Oh fuck! Oh, Rolf, that was the best, the very best, *ever*! Will you do that again for me?'

'Do what again?'

Penny rolled over to look into his eyes. 'Hold my throat when I'm coming.'

'I don't know that that's such a good idea.'

'We can do it safely. If you just put your hand there and I press against it, what could go wrong? If I passed out, I'd drop back. I'd be in control. Please, Rolf? It really does give me fantastic orgasms, like none I ever had before.'

'I'll think about it.'

'Oh, thank you, Rolf.' She showered his face and chest with kisses. 'I'll do *anything*, Rolf. After you make me come like that, there's *nothing* I won't do for you.'

He grinned. 'There's nothing you won't do for me, anyway.'

'True. So, what shall I do for you, right now?'

'Right now? Get me a glass of wine. I'm parched. As for sex, I think I'll save this erection for later, after I've given you your treats.'

'Treats?'

'Bondage and the crop.'

She threw her arms around his neck. 'Rolf Carmichael, you are the very best stepdaddy a girl could ever have.'

His cock drooped. It was nice to hear her sing his praises but he really wished she'd chosen her words with a little more care. Despite his plunge into depravity, his conscience wasn't *quite* dead.

They dressed again and swam some more, until the sound of the cleaners' van told them the house was theirs again.

'Can we eat early and have a nice long sexy evening?' Penny asked.

Rolf smiled. 'I'm hungry and I still have an erection,' he told her, 'so "yes" to both.'

211

He watched her lithe young body dip and sway as she did things at the stove. Rolf couldn't help but feel proud of himself. Before Penny, and Trixie, of course, he hadn't known any women he'd rate as 'wild'. It hadn't taken him long to learn about the more exotic sex games. He fancied he'd become quite adept at inflicting erotic corporal punishment, though using a crop would be something new and – he admitted – exciting. And he'd mastered the art of buggery. And this new thing – controlling how a woman breathed – he'd have to be very careful but in light of how incredibly it intensified Penny's orgasms – how could he not explore it? Sanely, of course.

Penny said, 'It'll be almost an hour.'

'So, what shall we do to amuse ourselves till then?'

She pouted and looked at him though her eyelashes, sure signals that she was going to ask a favour. 'Rolf, Lover, I don't know what it is about me today . . . Perhaps it's because you've promised we'll try the crops, but I'm *so* horny. What you did to me in the sauna was incredible, but today, it seems, no sooner do I come than I'm hot again.'

'Poor baby.'

'Rolf, would you mind if I masturbated again? I'll still be good and horny for you later, I promise.'

'Go ahead.'

'Will you watch me?'

'I wouldn't miss it.'

'Thank you, Lover.' She ran from the kitchen, calling over her shoulder, 'I'll be right back.'

In seconds, she returned with one of his belts that she'd punched extra holes in. She handed it to him. 'Would you put this around my waist, *very* tightly, please?'

He reached the belt around her and threaded the end through the buckle. Penny sucked in. Rolf drew the belt tight.

'Tighter?' she asked.

He pulled until the flesh around her waist creased and folded. The leather sank into her.

'Tighter?' Her voice was a gasp.

212

Rolf gave one more strong tug before pushing the buckle's tang through a hole – a hole that had never been used before, he noted.

Breathlessly, she asked him, 'Sit in the captain's chair, please? And take your swim trunks off? I like to see your cock.'

Rolf sat. Penny climbed up past him to sit on the edge of the kitchen table, facing him, her feet resting on the arms of his chair. Her sweet, innocent-looking but deeply depraved pussy was no further than the length of her slender thighs from his face.

'Do you like to look at my cunt?' she asked.

'Very much.'

'Do you like to watch girls play with themselves?'

'I like to watch *you* do it.'

'I bet you've never seen anyone do it the way I'm going to show you, right now.'

'I haven't?'

'Just watch.' Her feet turned outwards. Her knees spread wider. She hitched forward on the table to present her sex for his inspection.

Rolf swallowed. His hand almost reached out to touch Penny's pussy but drew back. This was *her* show. She'd obviously planned a special performance, like a toddler might practise a dance to show off to her family. He shouldn't spoil her act.

She took the long dangling end of the belt with two fingers flat and lengthwise on it, so that she could direct it with accuracy. Her hand lifted. She slapped down, gently, striking the tender bulge of her pussy.

So this was her show? He already knew that she liked to beat her clit with two fingers. This wasn't so very different.

She slapped again, harder, and a third and fourth time before she paused and inspected herself. '*Now* I'm hot and wet, and extra sensitive,' she announced. 'So now . . .' The thumb and fingers of her left hand spread the lips of her pussy wide. Her right hand fed the end of the belt into herself, pushing more and more of the leather into her soft depths.

213

Rolf watched wide-eyed as four, five, six, perhaps eight inches of his belt were worked into Penny's intimate sheath. When there was no more slack, when the belt ran taut from its buckle, over her clit, to where it entered her, Penny closed her eyes and leaned back a fraction.

'Watch me,' she breathed.

One finger of her left hand followed the strap inside her, holding it in place. Two fingers of her right hand pressed down on the leather, exactly where it ran across her clit. She pulled back an inch, then pressed down an inch. 'I love the feel of leather moving inside me.' Penny pushed harder, and faster, rubbing the coarse side of the calf hide on the sensitive head of her clitoris.

She bit her lower lip. Rolf's hand dropped to his throbbing cock. He was determined not to jerk off but his straining member was desperate for some sort of contact. He stroked himself, but with a gentle, restrained touch.

Penny was rubbing furiously. Her juices frothed on the lips of her pussy. Her knees strained wide apart. She was panting, either from the belt's restriction or from the throes of lust. Penny's face contorted. With a wild yelp, she snatched the belt from inside her, slipped her feet from the arms of Rolf's chair and slithered down into his lap, impaling herself on his cock.

He sat, half in shock, as her sheath convulsed on his shaft, pumping out her essences. As he recovered his senses, he wrapped his arms around her and began to thrust upwards.

A bell on the oven chimed.

'Supper's ready,' Penny told him. She untangled her limbs from his and climbed off his lap.

Rolf didn't know whether to just take her, or to protest, or . . . He decided to do nothing. He was the *man*. He was in charge, of himself as much as of her. Rolf Carmichael could make himself wait. When he *did* fuck her, it'd be the fuck of her life, and of his, he promised himself.

Twenty-nine

Penny's mitted hands took a casserole from the oven and set it down in front of Rolf. 'Just a minute. Don't touch it yet. It's too hot.'

She disappeared and reappeared shortly after, with two more belts and a plump cushion. The cushion went on the floor, beside Rolf's chair. She handed him one strap and put the other one around her own neck. When she'd buckled it, she put two fingers between the leather and her throat. 'It isn't tight, you see? It can't get tight, because it's buckled. It's safe, I promise.' Penny worked the belt around so that its loose end dangled down her back.

Rolf nodded, reassured. He didn't mind playing her kinky games, just so they didn't get too serious or too dangerous.

Penny turned her back to him with her wrists crossed over her tailbone. Rolf understood but the belt she'd given him had no extra holes. How was he supposed to restrain her wrists with it? Of course! He found the middle of the belt and put that behind her wrists, then crossed it in front, and went behind again, working criss-cross up her arms. By the time he got to her elbows there wasn't quite enough slack to buckle.

'Tighter?' Penny suggested.

He pulled, drawing her elbows closer and closer until they touched, and he had just enough leather to buckle the belt up.

Penny turned to face him. Her arms were drawn so far back that they'd disappeared. The same strain lifted and

215

presented her breasts. She was transformed into some sort of mythical erotic sylph, a naiad, perhaps, a wooden one, carved to serve as the figurehead on the prow of a galleon.

'How are you going to eat like that?' Rolf asked.

'I won't be able to, unless your fingers feed me. I couldn't be much more helpless, could I?'

'With your legs strapped together, you would be.'

She smiled. 'Maybe next time. The paella will be cool enough by now.' She sank gracefully onto her knees, on the cushion beside Rolf's chair.

He took the lid off the casserole. A cloud of saffron-flavoured steam rose. He waved it away and selected a choice piece of lobster from the rice bed. Like a fledgling chick, Penny looked up and parted her lips. He fed her the morsel and took a shrimp for himself. As they both chewed, he toyed with her nipple. She arched and almost purred.

'This is a pleasant way to eat a meal,' he commented.

'Thank you. We can eat this way more often, if you wish.'

'I wish.' He found her a tender nugget of pork.

Before long, his fingers were greasy and grains of rice adhered to them. Penny dutifully licked and sucked them clean, then feigned fellatio on two. Rolf's cock responded. Well, he had total control over her, so he could indulge his member. Holding her by her improvised collar, he drew Penny's face down into his lap. While she sucked his cock, he sorted through the rice for slivers of chicken. When his cock became demanding, he pulled Penny's mouth off it and rewarded her efforts with another piece of lobster, which he knew was her favourite.

Being a fair man, as she chewed, he dropped a hand to fondle her sex. Two fingers slid into her so easily that she had to be wet and ready.

'That's so good,' she told him. 'Your fingers drive me crazy, Rolf. So does your tongue.' She paused and eyed his shaft. 'And your cock, of course.'

Rolf ate faster and fed Penny faster.

When the dish was about half gone, she looked up at him and purred, 'Lover, I can't eat any more. All I can

216

think about is what you are going to do to me this evening. I've never needed sex so badly as I do right now. If you don't do the things you said you'd do to me, right now, I think I'll scream.'

He looked at her as sternly as he could. 'You need me to crop your poor little bottom until you beg for mercy and then fuck you hard and long, do you?'

'Please?'

He pushed back from the table and stood up. She crooked her neck, offering the belt around her throat. 'My leash?'

He lifted her by the belt and by her hair. She marched ahead of him and he followed her lead, assuming that she'd 'set the scene' somewhere. The 'somewhere' proved to be his den. Both crops were on the side table, beside his chair. The leather footstool was in front of it, with a cushion on the floor as it had been the first time he'd buggered her. Without prompting, she knelt on the cushion and leaned forward, forcing Rolf to support her weight by the belt around her throat.

'Are you OK? You can breathe all right?'

Her voice was a bit strained when she replied, 'I'm fine, honest.'

He picked up the longer crop. 'Penny, are you absolutely sure that this is what you want?'

Her voice still thin, she replied, 'Absolutely. More than you could imagine, Rolf. It's like – like my entire future depends on it.'

'You remember "Red Light".'

'Of course. If it's more than I can bear or even if I just find I don't enjoy it, I won't hesitate to use that, but Rolf?'

'Yes?'

'You remember to ignore anything else but "Red Light"? If I scream or curse you or beg, you'll take no notice?'

'I remember. I'll ignore anything but "Red Light". Penny, I'm going to give you twenty.'

'Thank you. I'm ready, Rolf. I've longed for this, for years. Please don't make me wait any longer.'

'Very well.' He brought the crop down hard across the backs of her thighs.

Penny squealed and writhed, twisting and swaying, for she was suspended in mid-air, supported only by her knees and by the belt around her throat. Rolf paused for long enough that she could evoke "Red Light" if she wished but although her breath rasped, she didn't use those words.

He slashed again, and again, trying not to let the vivid lines his crop drew cross. When a blow landed too far over for the loop of the crop to strike her bottom, it 'cracked' around like a whip and left an instant mulberry stain on her hip. That one made her wail but she still didn't use her words.

She *did* begin to curse him, calling him, 'Fucking sadist' and 'Monster'. At about the tenth stroke, she switched to begging, telling him, 'Enough, please. I can't stand it. You're killing me!' After the fifteenth, she babbled incoherently, like someone on a drug-induced trip to an erotic paradise. 'I love you, Rolf. You are my God! Oh, fuck, but I'm flying and there is *nothing* but the pleasure and the pain and I am *nothing* but you are *everything* and . . .' And the rest of her words were totally incoherent.

At twenty he threw his crop aside. Unlike the results of the beating he'd given her with his belt, the livid lines were quite distinct, raised and white but edged with purple. Even as he watched, the white lines were suffused with pink and then crimson. What he'd inflicted on this girl – it was horrifying. It was thrilling.

Maintaining his role as sadist, Rolf pulled Penny upright by her hair and her leash. He held her close, as her comforter. His hand dropped to her tortured bottom and squeezed each cheek viciously, in turn, as her tormentor again.

She sobbed against his chest, murmuring, 'I love you, Rolf. I love the sweet pain that you've given me. Let me please you, please? Anything, anything at all.'

The sadistic role was too intoxicating for him to abandon. Rolf dropped into his big chair, dragging Penny after him by her belt-leash. She toppled, helpless, but managed to fall with her cheek on his thigh. Taking her by her hair and the belt, he heaved her up to get her mouth to his cock.

She gasped, 'Thank you,' before taking his cock's bulbous crown into her mouth.

Rolf shifted an inch on his seat, lining his shaft up with Penny's restrained throat. When it was aligned, without warning, he thrust. His cock slithered through her mouth and lodged in the opening to her throat. She looked up at him with both tears and gratitude in her eyes.

He asked, 'Red Light?'

She shook her head, almost imperceptibly. He pushed back with her hair and the belt, then slammed her face forward, burying his cock all the way into her throat once more. For the next few minutes Rolf fucked Penny's face, showing no mercy, just *doing* it! His cock had been ready since that morning, since he'd watched her swim. Much as he tried to prolong his furious glee, his cock couldn't wait. His final thrust was deep and hard but it ended with an incredible boiling explosion that filled Penny's throat and mouth and finally spilled from her lips to drool down her chin.

With his climax complete, remorse flooded though Rolf. 'Are you OK?' he asked, cradling her head.

'I've never felt better,' she told him, her words bubbling through white froth.

Thirty

Penny, dressed in just an old thin shirt and a pair of uncharacteristically modest white cotton panties, went into the kitchen. She took a plate of pig's liver from the fridge and set it on the counter. Her hooked fingers ripped the breast pocket of her shirt half off. She shucked out of the shirt and tore at the seam of one sleeve until it hung by threads. Her panties came off and were ripped. She dipped their crotch into blood from the liver and arranged them carefully on the floor, making sure that the blood didn't touch the tile. The liver went into the garburator. She washed the plate thoroughly and then added it to the other clean plates in the dishwasher.

Satisfied that the scene was properly set, she went upstairs to fuck her stepfather for the very last time.

Rolf was snoring softly, a tribute to the pair of Trixie's sleeping pills that Penny had ground up and added to his late-night after-sex snack. There was a tall chest of drawers just inside the door. Penny eased the top drawer open. Inside, under some of Trixie's underthings, was a draw-string chamois bag that contained Rolf's .38 calibre Ruger revolver. She set the bag on top of the chest and carefully manipulated the weapon through the thin leather – moving the safety to 'off' and cocking the hammer. Very gently, she tilted the bag and let the gun slide out, close to the bronze statuette of *David*. With leather covering her fingertip, she nudged the revolver until its grip was handily angled towards the doorway. She sniffed at the leather, noted a slight oil stain, smiled, and returned the bag to the drawer.

There were two belts hanging behind the bedroom door. One was the one she'd punched extra holes in. The other was the one Rolf had used to secure her arms. Penny took them both down and to Rolf's bed with her.

Rolf was lying on his right side. Penny slid under the covers, facing him, and rolled onto her back, thighs spread. Taking great care not to wake Rolf, she lifted his left hand and guided it to rest on her sex. Two of her fingers curled behind two of Rolf's and eased them up between her pussy's lips. Holding his hand in place with her right hand, she reached over with her left and took a gentle grip on the shaft of his cock.

By the bedside clock, it was eleven-fourteen. Penny waited until eleven-twenty before tightening her hold on Rolf's cock and working it lightly. Rolf blinked awake and grinned at her.

Penny moaned, 'I'm *so* horny, Lover. *Please* do me?'

His fingers moved inside her. 'Were you? Were you using my fingers to diddle yourself?'

She nodded sheepishly. 'I thought maybe I could get off without waking you but then your lovely cock was *so* close . . . I couldn't resist touching it, Rolf, I love it so. Do you forgive me?' Her stroking fingers made her plea irresistible.

Rolf groaned. He drew his right arm up from under the bedclothes and set his hand on the top of Penny's head. 'If you love my cock that much, *show* me.' He pressed down.

Penny's mobile lips parted to take the head of his cock into the wet heat of her mouth. She paused with it resting on the flat of her tongue, waiting for his need to drive him. It took six seconds. His hand forced her head halfway down the length of his shaft. Rolf's fist knotted in Penny's hair. He dragged her face up, *almost* off, before pushing slowly down again. She gave him credit. He didn't lose control. It seemed that Rolf had learned to savour his pleasures and not to rush them. Where another man might have let loose and simply fucked between her lips until he climaxed, Rolf moved her mouth on his cock slowly and deliberately, obviously enjoying the process without allowing the intensity of his pleasure to overcome his willpower.

The muscles of his thighs tensed under her palms. Perhaps she'd misjudged him? There was no way she was going to let him climax so soon. That'd spoil *everything*. She'd just cupped her hand around his balls, meaning to handle them too roughly, 'by accident', when he justified her faith in him by pulling her up the bed for a long deep kiss.

'Rolf?' she wheedled, 'it's been three long days since you've buggered me. Have you grown bored with my bum-hole? Don't you like it any more?'

He hugged her close. 'I adore your bottom, Penny. It's the loveliest little bum in the whole wide world.'

'Does it feel good for you when you fuck it?'

'It feels incredible.'

'Tight enough?'

'Perfect.'

'Not too tight?'

With the tiniest edge creeping into his voice, he said, 'Penny, I told you, your bum is absolutely perfect.'

'Then?'

'Penny, I'm going to make wild love to your bottom, right now.'

She snuggled closer and whispered into his chest. 'When I was playing just now, your fingers, my pussy? I was thinking about you taking me against my will, raping my poor bottom, and I was screaming for mercy and struggling but I couldn't do much because you had my arms strapped the way I like and I had my leash on.'

'Is that what you'd like, right now?'

'Mm – well – after.'

'After what?'

For an answer, she squirmed out from under the bedclothes and knelt with her arms and legs spread and her bottom presented to his face. *That* he had to understand.

He did. His palms parted her cheeks. His face burrowed into her bottom's valley. Penny felt that delicious wet squirmy sensation of his tongue trying to work its way into her bottom-hole. Rolf was really getting quite good at it. It wasn't the best anilingus she'd ever enjoyed but it ran a close second.

She let herself pant a little, to encourage him, and then asked, 'Fingers, please? Open me up, Rolf. Stretch my hole so it can take that monstrous great cock of yours.'

She felt one finger press and relaxed her sphincter to welcome it. Rolf probed deeply and moved his finger around, pressing to either side and up and down. The finger withdrew and returned, joined by another.

'I can take three fingers,' she encouraged.

Three thick fingers really did things for her. The distended feeling started her pussy weeping. It almost distracted her but she remembered to glance at the clock and it was eleven forty-two.

'I can't wait any more,' she said. Penny took up the belt with the extra holes and buckled it around her throat. As soon as it was in place, she passed the other belt back to Rolf and joined her wrists behind her. Now that he'd had practice, his fingers were swift and deft as he restrained her arms from her wrists to her elbows.

'Keep me horizontal, please, Rolf. I like that best. Just hold onto the belt and let me strain against it, OK?'

She felt him take the slack. Now that he was adept, he only needed one hand to present his cock's head to her partly-open wet pucker. Penny concentrated on letting her ring relax. There was pressure. She took a deep breath and pushed back.

He was in!

She writhed a little, making it good for both of them but especially for Rolf. That was only fair. Penny let her full weight press against the strap around her throat. Her face began to feel hot and swollen. She moaned, 'Noooo!' That was simple and Rolf was used to it. Sometimes, if she cried out something he hadn't heard from her before, he stopped and asked her if she wanted 'Red Light'. It'd never do for him to pause now. His cock pistoned into her bum. Under his breath, he panted, 'Slut, bitch, whore,' just as she had taught him to do.

There was a sound on the stairs. Penny gurgled out another long ululating cry.

The door crashed open. Andrew stood there, stunned. Rolf's thighs vibrated against the backs of hers. Mentally, Penny screamed, 'The gun, Andrew! It's right there!'

He picked it up in a trembling hand.

She silently screamed again, 'The trigger!'

The way she'd adjusted it, an ounce of pressure would fire it. As if she was watching through a telescope, Penny saw Andrew's finger hook around the trigger, and ...

Thirty-one

Andrew paid the cab off a hundred yards from the new home he'd only ever seen in photographs. His coming home for the mid-term break was to be a surprise. That'd been Trixie's idea. She might be a ditz and a bit of a drinker, but she was *so* sweet. No sooner had the three of them moved into the Sag Harbor house than she'd mailed him a door key. 'You should have a key to your own home, even if you can't use it for a while.'

When he'd been worried that the letters Penny sent him were a bit impersonal, it'd been Trixie who'd explained that her daughter was so fervently in love with him that she had to keep a lid on her emotions or break down. When he got there, face-to-face, he'd soon discover just how strong Penny's passion for him was.

The silly woman had even mailed him travelling money, in cash no less! As if he didn't have money of his own, and credit cards. Crazy, huh? Crazy-nice.

He crunched up the circular white-gravel path and paused to admire his Dad's and Trixie's home, that he'd be sharing with them from after university until he and Penny married and got their own place. It was certainly big enough for four adults to live in. Andrew approved of there being so many trees, especially an enormous weeping willow that would provide ample shade even on the hottest day. A man and a girl would be invisible, under there. It was a tree that had grown specifically for romantic interludes.

The key fitted perfectly. He eased the door open, slipped in and set his carry-all down in the hall, making sure that his camera, its case's strap looped into the handle of his bag, didn't make a clunk on the random-pine floor.

It was getting close to noon. Chances were, there'd be someone in the kitchen and that someone would most likely be his Penny. Trixie'd bragged to him about how Penny did most of the cooking. Where would the kitchen be? His nose told him which direction the aromas of bacon and coffee were coming from. A late breakfast, it being Sunday? Andrew eased his feet out of his sneakers and tip-toed to the kitchen door.

Penny wasn't in there. Nobody was. What *was* in there was a shirt of Penny's, that he recognised from a picture she'd sent him, and the shirt was torn. On the floor there was a pair of panties, also ripped, with dark blood staining the crotch.

Women bled down there, and accidents could happen, but Penny'd never dump her soiled underwear on the kitchen floor. Something bad was up!

There was a strangled cry from somewhere upstairs. It sounded like a stretched-out, 'Nooooo!' The distorted voice could be Penny's. Andrew rushed back into the hall and bounded up the stairs. There was a door partly open, opposite him, when he got to the landing. Penny's anguished moans were coming from behind it. He barged through the door and stopped, stunned. His brain froze as it frantically tried to process what his eyes were showing him.

His Dad was naked and kneeling up on the bed. His loins were thrusting at Andrew's beloved Penny, who was on her knees before him. Her arms were bound behind her by straps, rendering her completely helpless. There was another strap in his Dad's fist, a strap that was tight around Penny's throat. It looked as if her bulging eyes were trying to tell him something.

His father was either fucking or buggering his fiancée and at the same time he was strangling her!

Whatever it meant, he had to stop this nightmare! There, almost at his eye-level, on top of a chest of drawers, was a revolver with its grip towards him. A revolver makes people do things, or stop doing them. Andrew snatched the gun up and pointed it at his Dad's shock-blanked face. His finger curled onto the trigger, though he hadn't decided whether he was going to shoot or not, or *what* he was going to do.

The revolver went off. His father was thrown against the wall behind the bed by his shoulder. Andrew dropped the gun and blurted, 'Dad?'

Thirty-two

Naked except for elbow-length latex gloves, Trixie followed Andrew up the stairs. By the time she got into the bedroom Andrew had fired the revolver and dropped it. He was standing frozen in shock. Rolf was slumped against the wall behind the bed, also in shock, clutching his shoulder. Penny was rolling off the other side of the bed, away from any blood that might splatter.

Trixie took the bronze *David* from on top of the chest of drawers and brought it down on the back of Andrew's head, hard. He fell. She set the statuette aside and bent to pick up the revolver. There was a desperate question on Rolf's stunned face. Trixie held the gun a foot higher than was natural for her and fired twice, rapidly, one round hitting high on Rolf's gut, the second higher again, into his chest, between his ribs. She paused and took a more careful aim. Her third shot, the fourth to hit Rolf, went through the fleshy part of the arm of the hand Rolf had clamped over his first wound, and into his heart.

Trixie tugged the top drawer of the chest open, took the chamois bag and tucked it into Andrew's jacket pocket. She set the revolver back on the floor, peeled the glove from her right arm and hand, took another firm grip on *David*'s bronze legs to leave fingerprints and set him down on his side. Penny turned her back towards her mother. Trixie released the belt that confined her daughter's arms and took it, plus the one from around her throat, and swiftly went downstairs.

Penny ran to her bedroom and took a four-minute hot shower. She couldn't see where any blood had got on her but it wouldn't have to be visible to be detectable to a forensic scientist. A quart of bleach followed the draining water. She dried off and dressed in a soiled top, shorts and sneakers that she'd worn out running the day before. There was a burr stuck to the back of her top. Both her shorts and her sneakers had grass stains.

By the time Penny got down to the kitchen her mother had already fed her bloody panties, torn shirt and both of Rolf's belts to the garburator. While Penny wiped the floor with a bleach-soaked rag, 'just in case', her Mom put her latex gloves into the garburator and followed them with a quart of bleach. So that the mechanism wouldn't seem too clean, Trixie took a plastic bag with coffee grounds, potato peels and the bones from three T-bone steaks from under the sink and put those down the garburator.

The women nodded to each other. Penny took off out the back door to sprint into the forest and run on the spot there, to work up a good sweat. Trixie went into the hall and opened the case to Andrew's camera. She changed its lens, took out its memory card and put another one in. There were some photos of Penny hidden in the hall closet, along with a gun-cleaning kit and oil, wrapped in a rag. All of those went into Andrew's bag, under his underwear.

Satisfied, Trixie went back into the kitchen, picked up the phone and dialled 911. When the operator answered, Trixie's breathless voice babbled, 'He's gone mad! He's shot my husband! Help me!'

The operator said, 'Please calm down and take your time. First, tell me where you are calling from.'

Forty minutes later, a paramedic slammed the door of the first ambulance. It pulled away. Penny came running out of the trees, dripping sweat, and demanded, 'What's going on?'

Two more paramedics came out of the front door of the house, pushing a covered gurney towards the second ambulance. Before she could be stopped, Penny rushed to it and uncovered Rolf's head.

229

She clutched at her mouth, gasped, 'Oh my God!' and fell to her knees.

Two uniformed policemen helped Andrew, dazed and in handcuffs, from the house and towards a police cruiser.

Thirty-three

The defence attorney, Arthur Rimbold Porteaux, was short and stocky and in his sixties. He wore black three-piece suits with subtle pinstripes. A heavy silver fob chain decorated his paunch but no one had ever seen him consult any watch but the Rolex Oyster he wore on his plump left wrist. His mellifluous voice suggested that he finished each meal with a wedge of crumbly Stilton, a bottle of crusted port and a Churchillian cigar. In fact, he'd never smoked and he hadn't touched alcohol in eleven years and four months. He was charging Trixie Carmichael eight hundred and fifty dollars an hour, plus expenses.

No one was ever going to be able to claim that Andrew Carmichael hadn't received an adequate defence.

Despite Arthur Porteaux's best efforts and his use of every peremptory challenge the law allowed, four of the jurors were male, over forty-five, and had probably quarrelled at least once with their own sons.

The prosecuting attorney, Denis Flaherty, was of medium height, thin, forty, and moved incessantly, as if his batteries had been overcharged and he needed to expend energy before he exploded. He wore tan slacks and oatmeal jackets. When he paced – and if he was on his feet, he was pacing – his eyes were fixed on a point on the floor some ten feet ahead, as if the gravity of his thoughts weighed his head down. Even so, from time to time he threw quick glances at individual members of the jury. Those looks were so meaningful, so intimate, that their recipients felt

231

that they and they alone defended the legal system of the State of New York, if not that of the entire country.

Denis Flaherty summed up. 'Ladies and gentlemen of the jury, the accused, Andrew James Carmichael, has freely confessed to the heinous crime of shooting his own father to death. However, he offers a smorgasbord of mitigating defences for us to choose from, none of which are remotely viable.

'He shot his father by accident. There just happened to be a revolver in his hand and it just went off, all by itself.

'A revolver, as I'm sure you all know from the movies and television, has a safety catch. It also has to be cocked before it will fire. This particular weapon, Andrew Carmichael would have us believe, took its own safety off, cocked itself, and fired, all through some mysterious agency that *wasn't* Andrew Carmichael. Further, that unlikely series of events occurred not once, not twice, not three times, but four times, in succession.'

Denis Flaherty paused and looked up to pierce the eyes of juror number four, an attractive Filipino woman in her late twenties, with a confiding look that suggested that she was far too intelligent to be taken in by Andrew's bizarre story.

Denis's eyes dropped. He resumed pacing and continued, 'But then he assures us that while the revolver was in his hand, it only fired once.' Denis pointed his forefinger and crooked his thumb above it, to demonstrate one shot being fired.

'I remind you, ladies and gentlemen, that at the time of the murder there were only three people in the house – the victim, who certainly didn't put four .38 calibre bullets into his own body from ten feet away – the victim's wife, who heard the first shot and rushed to the scene too late to save her husband, and who felled Andrew Carmichael from behind – and Andrew Carmichael, who admits firing one shot but *in one of his various defences*, denies firing the other three.'

Denis spun on his heel and spread his arms in the direction of Trixie and Penny. Both of them had eyes that sparkled with unshed tears.

'As a matter of routine, the police forensic laboratory tested Andrew Carmichael, Trixie Carmichael and Penelope Sanders for G.S.R.' He turned back to the jury with an apologetic smile. 'That's Gun Shot Residue. When people fire guns, burnt powder gets on their hands. Penelope Sanders tested negative for G.S.R. Trixie Carmichael tested negative for G.S.R. Andrew Carmichael, however, tested *positive*. He *had* fired a gun on that fateful day.'

Denis spread his hands on the ledge of the jury box and gave juror eleven, a plumber who wanted all this over with so that he could get back to work, a look that spoke of his sympathy for all the time that was being wasted.

'Now we must consider the matter of premeditation. Was the murder an act of impulse or was it coldly and carefully planned? If the former, then the accused is guilty of murder in the second degree. If the latter, then he is guilty of murder in the first degree. That boils down to two questions. Did Andrew Carmichael just happen to stumble across a firearm at the very moment that he was engaged in a bitter quarrel with his father? Or, did he take that revolver to his father's home with the intent of slaying him? In other words, we must ask, how did the revolver get into Rolf Carmichael's bedroom?

'The last previously known location of the revolver in question, Rolf Carmichael's own weapon, was in a locked drawer in Rolf Carmichael's Manhattan office. *Andrew* Carmichael was a frequent visitor to that office and doubtless knew where to find the revolver he planned to kill his father with. Neither Trixie Carmichael nor Penelope Sanders had ever entered that office. No one, not even the accused, has tried to say that they had.

'It might seem superfluous, considering all the other evidence, but there is another link to the chain that carries the fatal revolver from a locked drawer in Manhattan to a bedroom in Sag Harbor. That is the simple chamois pouch that the police found concealed on Andrew Carmichael's person. That pouch was stained with gun oil, ladies and gentlemen. That oil was identical in composition to the oil that had been recently used to clean that revolver. A can of that very same oil was found in the accused's bag, along with a gun-cleaning kit, all wrapped up in a rag that has been scientifically identified as a part of one of his own shirts. It had his DNA on it.

'He stole his father's revolver. He cleaned and oiled it. He put it in a chamois bag. He carried it to his father's home with the express purpose of committing *parricide*.

'There is *no doubt* that that leather bag is the very one that Andrew Carmichael used to carry the revolver in.' Denis gave the jury a sad smile. 'I'm sure that the accused used the bag to protect the pockets of the extremely expensive cashmere jacket his doting father had bought for him.

'The murder was premeditated, ladies and gentlemen. It couldn't be anything else.

'In a yet further defence, the accused asks you, "Acquit me of the charge of murder, because the first shot, the one I freely *admit* I fired, but by 'accident', wouldn't have been fatal on its own."

'Ladies and gentlemen, the medical evidence fully agrees with the accused. The first shot that he fired wouldn't have been a fatal one if the victim had received immediate medical treatment, *which was why* Andrew Carmichael calmly and deliberately followed that first shot with three more, carefully aimed, deadly shots.

'Which brings me to yet another of Andrew Carmichael's assorted defences: "diminished responsibility, or temporary insanity".

'He says, "I discovered my father in the acts of raping and murdering my beloved fiancée. Perhaps, while I was out of my mind with justifiable rage, I took up the revolver and, not knowing what I was doing, fired and fired and fired."'

Denis mimed a crazed gunman, firing rapidly and repeatedly. He ended with a shrug. 'It happens. People *do* go crazy with anger and commit acts that they'd never perform when in their right minds. Such people, in these circumstances, might fire *one* shot, and then be shocked back into their senses. Alternatively, they might point the gun and fire and fire and fire until it was empty, and *then* slowly come to their senses. Would such a person, in such a frame of mind, fire four times but not six? You have heard the psychiatric evidence. People just don't *do* that.

'We know that Andrew Carmichael spaced his shots, showing perfect self control, because his father had time to clutch at the first wound, the one that shattered his right shoulder, before the other three shots killed him. We know that, because there was blood on the palm of his left hand and because one of those subsequent three shots carved a bloody path through the flesh of his forearm before it pierced his heart, the heart of a man who loved his son, who had nurtured him and raised him on his own since his wife's death – a son whose education he had spent a considerable sum of money on.'

Denis's face crumpled, as if he were about to shed the tears the widow and her daughter were so bravely holding back, but he seemed to recover his self control before he embarrassed himself.

'And this was Rolf Carmichael's reward for his generosity, to be mercilessly gunned down, in his own bed, by the most ungrateful son any father has ever sired.

'In a similar alternative defence, Andrew Carmichael claims that he killed his father to save the life of his beloved fiancée, Penelope Anne Sanders. The young lady herself has testified that she wasn't even in the house, let alone in bed with, being brutally raped and murdered by, her stepfather. Her evidence is corroborated by a witness who saw her return from a long run in the woods around the house, approximately an hour after the time of the murder.

'Andrew Carmichael has stated that Penelope Sanders was his beloved fiancée. Let us examine his claim that Miss Sanders was his betrothed.'

Denis counted on his fingers. 'There was no ring. A rich young man became engaged to a rich young woman, and yet he didn't give her an engagement ring?

'No one, not a single soul, knew of this fantasy engagement, not even Miss Sanders herself. In further witness of this, let us consider her letters to Andrew Carmichael. There were about a score of them, written to him at university and saved by him. In them, she gives him – weather reports. She talks about the horses she has ridden. She discusses her mother's new obsession with collecting scrimshaw.'

Denis's expression spoke of the banality of Penny's letters. 'Penelope Sanders wrote to her stepfather's son, who she addressed as if he was a dear brother, on a dozen topics, *none* of them love, or passion, or wedding plans.

'Penelope is a nice girl, as you all saw when she was in the witness box. She treated her new "brother" with great kindness. She did *not* at any time encourage any romantic feelings he might have had for her.

'It is *not* a defence, but it is obvious that Andrew Carmichael developed an unhealthy, perverted even, obsession with Miss Penelope Sanders. He stalked her. We have heard that at first, Penelope Sanders didn't know who was following her, and she filed a report with the local police. We have heard her testimony, and that of her mother, that when they discovered it was Andrew who was the stalker, the two of them confronted him. He promised to cease and desist, and so they went to the police and withdrew their official complaint against "person or persons unknown".

'Andrew Carmichael has testified that Miss Sanders had told him about her stalker and had named him as a certain "Billie Blair" from Ridge River, who had been charged and convicted of attempted rape against Miss Sanders when she was much younger.

'Ladies and gentlemen, there is no "Billie Blair" of Ridge River. There never was. Further, neither Mrs Carmichael nor her daughter, Penelope Sanders, has ever resided in that city. They hail from Seattle, Washington.

'And then there are the photographs. I remind you that seven eight-by-ten photographic prints were found in Andrew Carmichael's possession, concealed in his carry-all bag, and a further twenty-two were recorded on the memory card in his electronic camera. All of those pictures were taken by his camera, which he'd taken to university with him, so no one else could have used it. We know they were taken by that camera because there is a mark on the lens and that mark shows as a tiny flaw in each and every one of those twenty-nine pictures.

'A young man, it might be argued, could well take twenty-nine pictures of the girl he loved. So he could. However, in none, not a single one, of those photographs, is Miss Sanders looking at the camera. They are all what photographers call, "candid" shots – pictures taken when the subject wasn't posing, wasn't even aware that a camera was pointed at her.'

Denis's face showed his distaste for the topic he was forced to bring up next. 'And the nature of those photographs? Suffice that I remind you of three in particular. Two of those three were secretly taken through partly open doors. A *bedroom* door. A *bathroom* door. Miss Sanders's privacy was violated, in rooms where she fully expected privacy and was performing the most *private* and intimate acts.

'The third of the photographs that deserve special mention was taken under a table, with the lens pointed up Miss Sanders's skirt.'

He paused for a long moment to let the obscenity of that sink in. 'Can you imagine? What sick mind would do such a thing – to the girl he claims he "loves"?

'Andrew Carmichael tells us that he couldn't have stalked Miss Sanders because he was away at university and had, in fact, never been to Long Island in his entire life, before that fatal day. Interesting. He'd never been anywhere near Sag Harbor, but there were banknotes in his possession, five new twenty-dollar bills, with consecutive serial numbers, bills that had been issued by a bank in Sag Harbor.

'He has "explained" how those notes came into his possession. He tells us that Trixie Carmichael, his stepmother, mailed them to him, along with other bills totalling five hundred dollars, to pay his air-fare home. Think about that. Andrew Carmichael, the son of an extremely wealthy man, a millionaire in his own right, a man with over twenty-four thousand dollars in his current bank account and the bearer of four major credit cards, needed his stepmother to mail him a few dollars, *in cash*, to pay for his fare home. Not even in the form of a cheque, but in *cash*. Does that seem reasonable? Would *you*, ladies and gentlemen, tuck five hundred dollars in crisp new bills into an envelope and entrust it to the mails? Would you then, as Andrew Carmichael maintains Trixie Carmichael must have, forget that you had done so?

'Further . . .'

Thirty-four

Trixie helped Penny out of her coat and hung it in the hall closet before taking her own off and putting it away. Both women were in mourning black – pumps, hose, skirts, blouses and hats. Trixie's heels were half an inch higher than Penny's. Her skirt was three inches longer. Trixie's felt hat had a broad brim and a high crown and was decorated by a silk grosgrain ribbon that dangled down her back to below her waist. Her daughter's hat was a simple cloche with a half-veil. Trixie reached up and plucked the long pin from Penny's hat, took her cloche and set it on the hallstand, ready to be taken upstairs and returned to the box it had been kept in from the day after her father's funeral to the day before Rolf's death.

Trixie asked, 'Is it time for drinks?'

'Not yet, Mother. Later, perhaps.'

They strolled into the dining room. Trixie said, 'Well, that went very well, I thought, though the judge's summing up and directions to the jury seemed a little harsh on poor Andrew, don't you think? He didn't give them much choice but to find the boy guilty of murder in the first degree.' She sat at the table.

Penny, standing behind her, said, 'Judges don't like rich white boys to commit parricide. Many of them have sons of their own, so it hits them where they're vulnerable.' Penny undid the bow around the crown of her mother's hat and, holding the ribbon, took the hat off Trixie's bubbly curls.

'What will the sentence be, do you think?'

'It *might* be death, though he'd never actually be executed. I'd guess twenty-five to life.'

'Not more?'

'He's only been convicted of one murder, even it was of his Dad.' Penny paused. 'Hands, Mother?'

Trixie put her arms behind her, around the back of the chair, with her wrists crossed. 'If that's your guess, that's good enough for me, Penny. You're so clever when it comes to legal matters – cleverer than Rolf's dead wife ever was. One might even say that it was she who made Andrew kill Rolf – by creating the situation.'

Penny wrapped silk ribbon around her mother's arms and wrists, and tied a double knot. 'Be fair, Mother. Rachel tied all the money up as securely as was legally possible.' Penny's nimble fingers undid Trixie's blouse and spread it wide, baring her lush breasts.

'What Rachel couldn't do, and no one can, is to get around the legal principle that no one may benefit from a crime they commit.' Penny's fingers found her mother's nipples and pinched them with crushing force. 'That's even more true,' she continued, 'when a son murders his father. So, with Andrew not able to inherit, that leaves just one possible heir to the Carmichael millions, *you*, Mother.'

Trixie winced at the torment her daughter was inflicting on her. Through the pain, she gasped, 'You're so clever, Penny.'

Penny released one of Trixie's breasts to put her hand under her mother's chin and tilt her parted lips up to meet her own. 'Now shut up and kiss me.'

nexus

The leading publisher of fetish and adult fiction

TELL US WHAT YOU THINK!

Readers' ideas and opinions matter to us so please take a few minutes to fill in the questionnaire below.

1. Sex: Are you male ☐   female ☐   a couple ☐?

2. Age: Under 21 ☐   21–30 ☐   31–40 ☐   41–50 ☐   51–60 ☐   over 60 ☐

3. Where do you buy your Nexus books from?
☐ A chain book shop. If so, which one(s)?
_____

☐ An independent book shop. If so, which one(s)?
_____

☐ A used book shop/charity shop
☐ Online book store. If so, which one(s)?
_____

4. How did you find out about Nexus books?
☐ Browsing in a book shop
☐ A review in a magazine
☐ Online
☐ Recommendation
☐ Other _____

5. In terms of settings, which do you prefer? (Tick as many as you like.)
☐ Down to earth and as realistic as possible
☐ Historical settings. If so, which period do you prefer?
_____

☐ Fantasy settings – barbarian worlds

- ☐ Completely escapist/surreal fantasy
- ☐ Institutional or secret academy
- ☐ Futuristic/sci fi
- ☐ Escapist but still believable
- ☐ Any settings you dislike?

_____

- ☐ Where would you like to see an adult novel set?

_____

6. In terms of storylines, would you prefer:

- ☐ Simple stories that concentrate on adult interests?
- ☐ More plot and character-driven stories with less explicit adult activity?
- ☐ We value your ideas, so give us your opinion of this book:

_____

_____

_____

7. In terms of your adult interests, what do you like to read about? (Tick as many as you like.)

- ☐ Traditional corporal punishment (CP)
- ☐ Modern corporal punishment
- ☐ Spanking
- ☐ Restraint/bondage
- ☐ Rope bondage
- ☐ Latex/rubber
- ☐ Leather
- ☐ Female domination and male submission
- ☐ Female domination and female submission
- ☐ Male domination and female submission
- ☐ Willing captivity
- ☐ Uniforms
- ☐ Lingerie/underwear/hosiery/footwear (boots and high heels)
- ☐ Sex rituals
- ☐ Vanilla sex
- ☐ Swinging

☐ Cross-dressing/TV
☐ Enforced feminisation
☐ Others – tell us what you don't see enough of in adult fiction:

_____

_____

_____

8. Would you prefer books with a more specialised approach to your interests, i.e. a novel specifically about uniforms? If so, which subject(s) would you like to read a Nexus novel about?

_____

_____

_____

9. Would you like to read true stories in Nexus books? For instance, the true story of a submissive woman, or a male slave? Tell us which true revelations you would most like to read about:

_____

_____

_____

10. What do you like best about Nexus books?

_____

_____

11. What do you like least about Nexus books?

_____

_____

12. Which are your favourite titles?

_____

_____

13. Who are your favourite authors?

_____

_____

14. **Which covers do you prefer? Those featuring:**
    (Tick as many as you like.)
- ☐ Fetish outfits
- ☐ More nudity
- ☐ Two models
- ☐ Unusual models or settings
- ☐ Classic erotic photography
- ☐ More contemporary images and poses
- ☐ A blank/non-erotic cover
- ☐ What would your ideal cover look like?

    _____

15. **Describe your ideal Nexus novel in the space provided:**

    _____

    _____

    _____

16. **Which celebrity would feature in one of your Nexus-style fantasies?**
    We'll post the best suggestions on our website – anonymously!

    _____

THANKS FOR YOUR TIME

Now simply write the title of this book in the space below and cut out the
questionnaire pages. Post to: Nexus, Marketing Dept., Thames Wharf Studios,
Rainville Rd, London W6 9HA

Book title: _____

NEXUS NEW BOOKS

To be published in September 2007

LONGING FOR TOYS
Virginia Crowley

Robert and James are upstanding members of the community. They are young professionals with bigoted, conservative upper middle class girlfriends. When Michele – a gorgeous stripper at the notorious club Hot Summer's – sees Robert's shiny red new roadster, she is overcome by a desire to possess it. Manipulating his friends and neighbours with offerings of ever more sordid sexual delights, she engineers Robert's descent into a tangled world of erotic temptation. As his character degrades from that of an altruistic medical researcher into a drooling plaything around the manicured fingers of his keeper, Robert's fiancée and best friend try to help him; unfortunately, their involvement also subjects them to the irresistible lure of pretty toys.

£6.99   ISBN 978 0 352 34138 9

BEING A GIRL
Chloë Thurlow

Late for a vital interview on a sweltering day, casting agent Jean-Luc Cartier pours Milly some water and holds the glass to her lips. When the water soaks her blouse he instructs her to take it off. Milly is embarrassed but curious. As Milly strips off her clothes, more than her shapely body, it is her deepest nature that is slowly uncovered.

Jean-Luc puts her over his knee. He spanks her bottom and her virgin orgasm awakens her to the mysteries of discipline. Milly at 18 is at the beginning of an erotic journey from convent school to a black magic coven in the heart of Cambridge academia, to the secret world of fetishism and bondage on the dark side of the movie camera.

£6.99   ISBN 978 0 352 34139 6

If you would like more information about Nexus titles, please visit our website at www.nexus-books.com, or send a large stamped addressed envelope to:
   Nexus, Thames Wharf Studios,
   Rainville Road, London W6 9HA

NEXUS BOOKLIST

Information is correct at time of printing. To avoid disappointment, check availability before ordering. Go to www.nexus-books.com.

All books are priced at £6.99 unless another price is given.

NEXUS

☐ ABANDONED ALICE	Adriana Arden	ISBN 978 0 352 33969 0
☐ ALICE IN CHAINS	Adriana Arden	ISBN 978 0 352 33908 9
☐ AQUA DOMINATION	William Doughty	ISBN 978 0 352 34020 7
☐ THE ART OF CORRECTION	Tara Black	ISBN 978 0 352 33895 2
☐ THE ART OF SURRENDER	Madeline Bastinado	ISBN 978 0 352 34013 9
☐ BEASTLY BEHAVIOUR	Aishling Morgan	ISBN 978 0 352 34095 5
☐ BEHIND THE CURTAIN	Primula Bond	ISBN 978 0 352 34111 2
☐ BEING A GIRL	Chloë Thurlow	ISBN 978 0 352 34139 6
☐ BELINDA BARES UP	Yolanda Celbridge	ISBN 978 0 352 33926 3
☐ BENCH-MARKS	Tara Black	ISBN 978 0 352 33797 9
☐ BIDDING TO SIN	Rosita Varón	ISBN 978 0 352 34063 4
☐ BINDING PROMISES	G.C. Scott	ISBN 978 0 352 34014 6
☐ THE BOOK OF PUNISHMENT	Cat Scarlett	ISBN 978 0 352 33975 1
☐ BRUSH STROKES	Penny Birch	ISBN 978 0 352 34072 6
☐ BUTTER WOULDN'T MELT	Penny Birch	ISBN 978 0 352 34120 4
☐ CALLED TO THE WILD	Angel Blake	ISBN 978 0 352 34067 2
☐ CAPTIVES OF CHEYNER CLOSE	Adriana Arden	ISBN 978 0 352 34028 3
☐ CARNAL POSSESSION	Yvonne Strickland	ISBN 978 0 352 34062 7
☐ CITY MAID	Amelia Evangeline	ISBN 978 0 352 34096 2
☐ COLLEGE GIRLS	Cat Scarlett	ISBN 978 0 352 33942 3
☐ CONCEIT AND CONSEQUENCE	Aishling Morgan	ISBN 978 0 352 33965 2

- - - - - - ✂ -

Please send me the books I have ticked above.

Name ....

Address ....

....

....

.... Post code ....

Send to: **Virgin Books Cash Sales, Thames Wharf Studios, Rainville Road, London W6 9HA**

US customers: for prices and details of how to order books for delivery by mail, call 888-330-8477.

Please enclose a cheque or postal order, made payable to **Nexus Books Ltd**, to the value of the books you have ordered plus postage and packing costs as follows:

UK and BFPO – £1.00 for the first book, 50p for each subsequent book.

Overseas (including Republic of Ireland) – £2.00 for the first book, £1.00 for each subsequent book.

If you would prefer to pay by VISA, ACCESS/MASTERCARD, AMEX, DINERS CLUB or SWITCH, please write your card number and expiry date here:

....

Please allow up to 28 days for delivery.

Signature ....

Our privacy policy

We will not disclose information you supply us to any other parties. We will not disclose any information which identifies you personally to any person without your express consent.

From time to time we may send out information about Nexus books and special offers. Please tick here if you do *not* wish to receive Nexus information. ☐

- - - - - - ✂ -